ALSO BY CRAIG LANCASTER

600 Hours of Edward
The Summer Son
The Art of Departure
Edward Adrift
The Fallow Season of Hugo Hunter
This Is What I Want

EDWARD UNSPOOLED

EDWARD UNSPOOLED

CRAIG LANCASTER

MISSOURI BREAKS PRESS

Text copyright © 2016 by Craig Lancaster
All rights reserved.
Cover design by Brian Zimmerman (http://cre843.com/)

Printed in the United States of America.

Published by Missouri Breaks Press, Billings, Montana

ISBN-10: 0-9827822-8-4
ISBN-13: 978-0-9827822-8-6

For Edward's friends and fans everywhere.

*And for the #teamedward crew at THE Book Club—
Charlotte, Tracy, Donna Y., Emma, Deborah, Janet, Kat, Ellen,
Audrey, Collette, Alexina, Lynda, Susie, Loo, Gisella, Michelle,
Donna M., Sarah, Joel, John, Helen C., Ros, Kathy, Philippa,
Karen F. and Karen G.—and most of all for their inimitable
leader, the wonderful Helen Boyce. Thank you for loving him
with your whole hearts.*

And for Elisa, who brings the beauty to every day, in every way.

JANUARY

HELLO, POPPYSEED

I don't know what to call you.

That may seem like a major issue. It is a major issue, as you'll find out in approximately thirty-three to thirty-eight weeks when you're born and begin to realize that using names is how we get along in this world. You'll also learn that I don't like the word "approximately." It has no discrete (I do like the word "discrete") meaning. Sometimes, circumstances force you to use an unsatisfying word, and I suppose you'll find that out soon enough, too. I hope, for your sake, that it doesn't bother you as much as it bothers me. I don't like hope. I prefer facts. I'd rather know for certain that it won't bother you, but that is impossible right now.

I'm your father, by the way. My name is Edward Stanton Jr. We—and when I say "we," I mean your mother and I—don't know what to call you yet. Your mother, whose name is Sheila Renfro Stanton, has a girl's name. I have a boy's name. We don't know if you're a boy or a girl, so we can't name you yet. And I don't even want to get into unisex names.

Between the eighteenth and twenty-sixth weeks of pregnancy, a test called an ultrasound could be done to determine whether you're a boy or a girl, but your mother doesn't want that. She says she wants to be surprised when she gives birth to you, which will happen sometime between the thirty-seventh and forty-second week of pregnancy if all goes according to plan. (I don't want to scare you, but a lot can go wrong in pregnancy, and I'm sure I'll be telling you more about this later.)

If you could read this, I could imagine what you might be thinking: That is a five-week span—thirty-five days. Here we are, in 2014, and medical science has not allowed us to achieve more precision in the timing of childbirth. It's damnable (I love the word "damnable").

As it is, Dr. Arlene Haworth at St. Vincent Healthcare here in Billings, Montana, believes that you've been inside your mother's womb for four weeks. Dr. Haworth said that means you're only a cluster of cells about the size of a poppyseed, which isn't large at all. You are, technically, an embryo, which is a word I like very much. I suggested to your mother that we ought to call you something even when we don't know whether you're a boy or a girl, but she says "the baby" is just fine. I have tried to accept this, even though you aren't even a baby yet and I'm agitated by such imprecision. You're an embryo. When I pointed this out, your mother got cross with me and said, "We are not calling the baby 'the embryo.'" When I said that we could call you "Cellular Stanton," which has a pleasing poetic ring, she told me to get in my car and leave the house for at least two hours.

Dr. Haworth gave us the news about you two days ago. I like lists, so I will tell you, in list form, what I've been doing since we found out:

1. Wigging out (which has nothing to do with wigs; I wish we could give you a language that makes sense, but that's probably not possible in the short time between now and your appearance, if all goes according to plan).

2. Reading everything about pregnancy and childbirth that I can find on the Internet.

3. Trying to pin down when, exactly, you were conceived so I

can make a better estimate of when you might arrive, even with the five-week variable at the end of the pregnancy.

4. Shit.

I'm sorry about that last one. I don't like odd-numbered lists.

It's January 15th now, so if I back up thirty days on the calendar (four weeks, plus two extra days to account for the time since we talked to Dr. Arlene Haworth) I arrive at December 16th, 2013, nine days before Christmas. (You're going to love Christmas.) The problem is that your mother and I did not engage in sexual congress that day. I love the phrase "sexual congress." It has dignity to it, unlike many of the phrases my friend Scott Shamwell uses to describe intercourse, like fucking, screwing, getting it on, the beast with two backs, boning, bopping, humping, bumping uglies, and the old in-and-out. Also, unlike the actual Congress, something is accomplished when sexual congress is in session. That's a joke, by the way. I'm pretty funny sometimes. You'll find this out, too.

We did engage in sexual congress on December 15th, December 17th, December 18th and December 19th, so you can see now why pinning down the date of your conception may be difficult. I'm sorry I cannot give you, or us, more clarity than that. My daily notebooks contain the times and dates for every instance of sexual congress your mother and I have had, but the dates before and since are immaterial. Nonetheless, if you're someday interested in this information, I will be happy to share it with you. If it's important to you to at least know where you were conceived, I'm afraid I have more bad news. Your mother and I engaged in sexual congress in our bed on the 15th, 17th and 18th, but it happened on the living-room couch on the 19th, on account of the fact that I tried rum and egg nog for the first time, had too much of it, and became what your mother calls "randy" in the latter part of the evening.

I should probably now address the "wigging out." This is a slang phrase that means becoming panicky or nervous. It has fallen into disfavor with young people, I'm made to understand, but I still like it.

Here's the thing, C.S. (I have to call you something, so we'll go with this): We did not come lightly to the decision to have a child. It's alarming that I have to say that, but I've learned not to expect much from other people. There's a word for my outlook, and that word is "cynical." You will be born into this world with innocence, but I can say with near certainty that cynicism will come to you eventually. Neither of these things, innocence or cynicism, is a logical approach, and that bothers me as well. You might as well get used to it now: I'm often bothered, by many different things. (An example: Your mother's unwillingness to have an ultrasound. I'd rather we knew whether you were a boy or a girl as soon as possible.) My overall point is that some people decide to have a child the same way they decide what to have for breakfast. Your mother and I exercised more rigor (I love the word "rigor") over our decision-making.

Let's move on.

Your mother and I have been married for six hundred and sixty-nine days. You've probably already done the math and know that we were married on March 17th, 2012. That's also St. Patrick's Day, and we both had bad memories from childhood of being pinched by other kids for not wearing green on that day. St. Patrick's Day is an illogical holiday. We decided to co-opt (I love the word "co-opt") the holiday for our marriage, and I'm pleased to report that the color green and pinching no longer mean anything to us on March 17th. We're pretty smart sometimes.

We spent the first year of our marriage, plus a couple of early months when we were just living together, focused on our business, which was a motel in the eastern Colorado town of Cheyenne Wells. The motel was built by your grandfather and grandmother on your mother's side. I'm sorry you won't get to meet them. They have been dead since August 7th, 1997. You also won't get to meet my father, your other grandfather. He has been dead since October 30th, 2008.

All of this is a long-winded—wind doesn't actually have physical dimension; this is just a figure of speech—way of saying that the six hundred and sixty-nine days of our marriage have been full of challenges, so the prospect of adding you to our situation sometimes worries me. OK, it worries me all the time, but I want to be clear that this is not your fault. I'm sure you're a perfectly friendly embryo, but that friendliness doesn't mitigate (another good word) against my anxiety.

Your mother, knowing I am worried, suggested that I write this note to you, and I think she was wise to make the suggestion. I feel a little better, even now, when we haven't resolved anything. If it's all the same to you, I would like to keep writing to you. As I think about it now, I realize that I have much to impart to you, much that I think you ought to know if you're going to have my name. I have been alive for many years—a lot longer than you have, and that means you will probably have to deal with losing me someday, just as I've dealt with losing my father and your mother has lost both of her parents. Before I go, I would like to tell you some things. I promise to stick around as long as I can, to the extent that I have any control over it.

The first thing is that your mother loves you very much. We've been living in Billings, Montana, where I'm from, since May 18th of last year, and she hasn't been as happy here as I'd hoped. But C.S., you have to know this: I've never seen her as happy as she was when we found out about you.

You're probably wondering if I love you, too. I'll be honest: I do not know. I don't know you yet. Despite what I said about you being a friendly embryo, I don't know that for certain. I guess that's just my optimism coming through. I don't know if embryos are capable of friendliness or asshole-ishness. (A slight digression: "Asshole," used to describe a person, is highly imprecise. "Asshole," to describe the hole in your ass, although probably not in yours yet, is perfectly precise.)

What I'm saying is, you're just a cluster of cells. I think I'm supposed to love you, so the best I can give you right now is that I'll try.

But your mother, she loves you. It's unqualified. You have the best mother an embryo could ask for.

I don't know what to make of this, Edward.

OK, look, I'm glad you're writing to our child. Not an embryo. Not a cluster of cells. A child. Perhaps if you thought of him or her as a child, rather than in the strict clinical definition of this stage of development, you'd find it easier to express love. You're a particular man, and I love you for that, but you better come to love this child or we're going to have major problems around here.

Also, I don't think it's appropriate—AT ALL—to talk about how and when this child was conceived. That's nobody's business but ours, and I REALLY can't believe you told the child that we had sex on the couch. Also, and I told you this at the time I realized you were doing it, it's strange that you write down every time we have sex.

But, like I said before, you're a particular man, and your ways don't always make sense to me, but I love you, and yes, I love our child. (AND YOU BETTER LOVE OUR CHILD, TOO. I'M NOT KIDDING.) So if this is what you need to do, go ahead.

And another thing: I have reasons for not wanting an ultrasound, and I explained them to you before. I want our child to tell us who he or she is. I don't want to start imposing things on the child before we've even met.

I am glad you're talking about my unhappiness with our child. Maybe, eventually, you'll be ready to talk about it with me.

I love you.

Sheila

HELLO, AGAIN

I realized in looking over my entry yesterday that I didn't follow through on telling you how your mother and I came to the decision to have a baby (that is, you). Usually, I have little trouble organizing my thoughts, but you've messed that up for me. When I think about what I want to say to you, so much comes to mind that I end up talking about a lot of different things, including those that caused your mother to scold me. I will try to do better from now on, although I make no promises. Promises don't really mean much anyway without concrete action to back them up.

Telling you about this decision requires a bit of what's called backstory, a word that means supplemental information designed to give fuller context to current events. In other words, for you to understand why we decided to have a baby while living here in Billings, Montana, you need to understand how we ended up here.

I will try to keep the backstory brief, as many people abuse it. I know my father did. Sometimes, when I would ask him about something, he would say, "Teddy, let me tell you a story." And then, in addition to calling me by a name I didn't like, he would tell me about something not even remotely related to my inquiry. I think he thought he was using metaphors or telling me fables to illustrate a larger point, but most of the time he was just indulging his own bloviations (a wonderful word). I will try hard not to be that kind of father to you.

When your mother and I married on March 17th, 2012, we were preoccupied with making the motel she owned, which her mother and father left to her when they died, more profitable. This was a challenging venture, because the motel is in a small, agrarian (good word) town in eastern Colorado. I thought the motel was rundown and behind the times, so we spent a lot of the money I brought to the marriage (more on this some other time) to upgrade it: new television sets in every room, the best available cable service, a new paint job, new curtains and new linens, a better computer system, new paving in the parking lot. All told, we spent $1.235 million. You would think that kind of investment would change things, but it didn't, and when the railroad came to your mother later that year and offered $325,000 for the land her motel sat upon, she said she was tired and that we ought to just give up. She cried herself to sleep many nights over that, and she kept apologizing to me for all the money we'd spent. I didn't care about the money. Don't get me wrong, C.S.: $1.235 million is a lot of money, but I have a lot more than that because my father was a rich man and left it to me. Scott Shamwell, whom I'll tell you about another time, says I'm still fucking loaded, and he is correct.

After we sold the motel, we had the problem of deciding where to live. We talked about staying in Cheyenne Wells, but your mother said she couldn't face seeing her motel knocked down and the judgment of the townspeople that she was a failure. (I don't think anyone thought she was a failure, but this is how your mother felt, so I tried to "validate" that feeling, in the words of Dr. Bryan Thomsen. I'll tell you more about him later, too.) I told her that I had a perfectly good house right here in Billings, Montana. My father bought it for me in 2000, after he could no longer deal with me living at home with him and my mother, and I kept ownership of the house even after I moved to Colorado to be with your mother. It's a complicated story, but I'll get to it all eventually, I think. It would be better to know this definitively, but such a thing is unknowable, and to be honest, you still cause my thoughts to scatter a little bit. It's not your fault.

Living in Billings, Montana, has been a big change for your mother, and it hasn't been easy for her. To illustrate for you just how big this change has been, consider the following differences between Billings, where I've lived most of my life, and Cheyenne Wells, Colorado, where your mother lived for most of hers:

	BILLINGS	CHEYENNE WELLS
Population	106,954	846
Density*	2,399.7	846
ZIP codes	17	1
Square miles	43.52	1.0

*—per square mile

I got these figures from Wikipedia, which isn't the most unimpeachable (excellent word) source, but for purposes of this note I will set that aside and posit (another fine word) that the numbers, while not necessarily precise, show just how different Billings is from Cheyenne Wells.

In practical terms, it means that your mother has encountered too many people, too many roads, and too many buildings for her to be as comfortable as she was in Cheyenne Wells, among people she had known her entire life (except for those born after her, whom she had known for only part of her life—trust me, as much as you'll want to keep tabs on things like this, it gets exhausting).

Your mother found a job soon after we arrived here on June 19th, 2013. She works at a yarn store on the West End of town called Purl Jam, running the cash register and helping to keep the shelves stocked with the proper varieties of yarn. She says she likes the job, mostly, and goodness knows (that's an idiom—you won't want to think about such phrases too deeply or they'll just frustrate you) there are enough varieties of yarn in the world to keep her busy. But she has frustrations, too. She doesn't get along with some of her coworkers, and she doesn't like working as much now that she's no longer the boss. I'm her only friend, and she tells me that while she loves me she thinks it's unfair to ask me to be everything to her. She says she hopes she doesn't hurt my feelings when she says that.

Now we're getting to what I wanted to tell you: Your mother came home from work on October 18th, 2013, a Friday, and said she needed to talk to me. We sat down in the living room, she on the couch and I on the adjacent love seat, and she told me she wanted a child. I will concede that this was not entirely unexpected; the night before we got married, your mother looked at me and got serious and said, "Edward, I'm probably going to want a kid someday." And I said, "OK."

On October 18th, 2013, I found out she was serious, and I said "OK" again.

Your mother went on to say that raising a child would be a natural progression for us, that it would give depth and meaning to our lives as a married couple, and I'm sure it will, assuming you don't emerge from the womb as an asshole and make our lives miserable. She also looked at me and said, "Edward, time is drawing short. You're forty-five years old and I'm no spring chicken, either, and we need to do this while we still can." (Don't even ask about the "spring chicken" thing.)

Her prescription for this was simple: She wanted us to engage in sexual congress. Lots and lots of sexual congress. Sexual congress nearly every day. I didn't mind, at least not in the beginning. I never had sexual congress before I met your mother, but I've become pretty good at it, and I like it very much. The only real complication we've had is that I have Type II diabetes, which inhibits the flow of blood to my tallywhacker and makes it harder for me to get it up (another idiom). Luckily for us, medical science has conquered this problem, and I'm able to take something called Viagra when I need it. That opens up the bloodflow to my tallywhacker and makes it easier for me to get it up and engage in sexual congress with your mother.

(I'll make a brief detour here and tell you something funny that Scott Shamwell said. He calls Viagra "dick pills," and told me once that he's "been living on dick pills and diet soda for years." That seems impossible to me, but I'm not in the habit of contradicting Scott Shamwell. You'll probably like him. I say "probably" because your mother hasn't decided whether she'll let you meet Scott Shamwell.)

Your mother and I engaged in sexual congress forty-nine times between October 19th and December 19th, the most recent possible date of your conception. She won't like that I've told you this, but it's a matter of record in my notebooks, so it seems silly to hide this information from you. You won't have a point of reference on this, so just take it from me that this is an unusual amount of sexual congress for anyone not in the pornography industry (more on the pornography industry in a later note). As much fun as sexual congress is, it becomes wearying when you're awakened in the middle of the night because "conditions are optimum" or you're jumped on when your wife walks in the door after work because she feels like "a horny beast." As wigged out as I was when we found out your mother was pregnant, I was also relieved because our frequent flings at fornication (this is alliteration) are now likely to abate (this is a good word). I need a rest.

Two things, Edward:

1. I found this while you were sleeping. I haven't slept well in days, which you'd have no way of knowing, because you fall asleep promptly at 10 p.m. and don't wake up again for nine hours. I watch you sometimes, because you're so peaceful, and I wish I had that kind of peace. Tonight, though, I went looking for your notebook because I specifically asked you to leave it out so I could read what you're saying to our child, and you hid it from me. So here's a little hint for you: Don't hide things from me. What's the point, anyway? If the best you can do is put it in your sock drawer, it's not going to be hard for me to find. But don't hide things from me.

2. Enough with telling the kid about all the sex we've been having. I'm so upset with you right now, I may never have sex with you again, which will solve this particular problem. Also, no talking with our child about pornography.

OK, I'm sorry. I'm not really upset with you, Edward. I'm pretty peeved about the way you hid the notebook. Don't do that anymore. As far as what you're writing, I don't get why you say some of the things you do, but the fact is that I suggested you write these notes to help with your "wigging out" over the child, and so I have to trust that you're saying things that make you more comfortable. I can't be mad at you for that. I do want you to know that I see through this whole "C.S." thing. That stands for Cellular Stanton. You think you're being clever. It's OK.

I think you kind of glossed over how difficult things have been for me here in Billings. It's deeper than just being away from the place I lived most of my life. It's not Cheyenne Wells, as a fixed location on the earth. It's that my mom and dad kept the motel alive until they died and went in the ground, and I couldn't keep it going. It's that I had friends there, or people who knew me, and I don't have any friends here. WE don't have any friends here. You have a couple of friends. But they're not ours.

And I know you like Scott Shamwell, but I don't. That's my right. I was mostly kidding when I said I didn't want him to meet our baby. Mostly.

Here's the thing: I'm lonely. I'm sad. I'm scared. I probably don't talk about these things enough with you, because I want to be strong, and because you think I'm strong.

You just turned over in your sleep, and now you have put your right hand on my thigh. I like that. I like that very much. I want to be wherever you are, Edward. We're in Billings now. I've just got to make it work.

Love,
Sheila

MEA CULPA*

*—this is Latin; just wait till you see what a mess
English makes of Latin

I'm sorry I let three days go by without writing to you, C.S., but things got busy around here. It makes me think of a singer named John Lennon, who was in the Beatles (a famous rock 'n' roll group you'll no doubt hear about), and one of his songs talked about life being something that occurs when you're busy preparing for other things to happen. I don't know. It seemed like a trite phrase the first time I heard it, but it makes some sense to me now.

Your mother and I have been preparing for your arrival. We've chosen the day she will quit work (February 10th, 2014), we've talked about how we'll renovate our second bedroom for all the things you'll need, and we're signing up for childbirth classes.

Your mother never had to work. Let's be clear on that. She wanted to, because it gave her something to do. We don't need the twelve dollars an hour she makes. As I told you in a previous note, I'm fucking loaded. I have nearly six million dollars, and the stock market keeps going up, so I literally make money faster than we could ever spend it now that we're not renovating a motel anymore.

I haven't been working since we came to Billings, Montana, but once your mom stops working and prepares for your arrival I might just take a job that my lawyer and your grandmother's husband, Jay L. Lamb, offered me a long time ago. I don't know. Your mother and I will have to talk about it. As for Jay L. Lamb, I'm sure I'll talk more about him in a future note to you. That's a complicated story.

Here's an interesting coincidence: I've been telling you about Scott Shamwell, my friend whom your mother doesn't like, and last night he came to the house. Some people would lazily call that ironic, but it's not irony. It's just a coincidence. Life will go easier on you if you know what words actually mean.

Scott Shamwell didn't call before coming over, and that annoyed your mother, but I was glad to see him. He lives in a town north of here called Roundup, so I don't see him often. We used to work together at the *Billings Herald-Gleaner*, but neither of us works there now.

Scott Shamwell brought beer. His were Pabst Blue Ribbon—"the only decent beer for a goddamn true-blooded American," he said—and he brought me a non-alcoholic beer on account of my Type II diabetes. He said, "Near Beer—when you don't want to get drunk but still want to piss a lot." I'm not sure what that means. I already pee a lot, because I have to take a diuretic for my Type II diabetes.

Your mother was annoyed at Scott Shamwell. She told him, "We've already eaten," and he said, "Not to worry, little missy. I'm drinking my dinner." He smiled at her, so I think he was being nice, but she said, "My name is Sheila. I'm going in the bedroom to watch TV." Scott Shamwell and I sat at the kitchen table and drank our beverages. We would have sat outside, but it's January and cold in Montana. That would have been uncomfortable.

Scott Shamwell is going through a difficult time. He got involuntarily separated from the *Billings Herald-Gleaner* two days before Thanksgiving. "Involuntarily separated" is a fancy way of saying "fired." After you're born and as you grow up, C.S., you'll find that some people are preternaturally (excellent word) unable to say things simply and directly. Instead, they'll say things like "involuntarily separated." It must make them feel better or more important. That's what Dr. Bryan Thomsen says. Such people are not to be trusted.

Also, Scott Shamwell's father, Studd, and older brother, Studd Jr., are under federal indictment on charges of methamphetamine production. It was a big news story around here when it happened, back in September. Apparently, Studd and Studd Jr. had converted a barn on the family farm into a meth lab and were making a lot of money selling drugs. Scott Shamwell doesn't deny this—"It's hard to say they were making cotton candy," he says, and I'm not sure what cotton candy has to do with it—but he contends that the federal agents are trying to lump him in with his father and brother, even though he lives in his own house in town, had a job at the newspaper, and hasn't spent much time at the farm since he was a kid.

"The feds have got my balls in a vise grip," he told me.

That seemed like an unusual interrogation technique. "Isn't that illegal?" I asked.

Scott Shamwell just laughed, and that's when your mother came out of the bedroom and said, "Edward, can I see you in here for a minute?"

I excused myself, with Scott Shamwell waving me off with his beer bottle. I put my non-alcoholic-beer can in the trash, and went to the bedroom.

Your mother stood just inside the door.

"Your friend is a drug dealer," she said.

"No, he's not. His father and brother are."

"Oh, big difference."

Your mother does this funny thing when she gets mad. When I say "funny," in this case, I mean it in the sense of being remarkable, not in the sense that it makes me laugh. If I laughed when your mother got mad, I'd be in a lot of trouble.

What your mother does is she crinkles up her nose, where there are little lines running across it, and she shortens her words. If she's not angry, her words come out normally, with distinct breaks between them so you can understand what she's saying. When she's angry, the spaces between the words disappear and everything runs together. Thus, what she said next had this run-together quality:

"Heneedstogohomenow."

I started to argue with your mother, but then she stamped her foot on the hardwood floor of our bedroom, and that was my signal to abandon my argument.

I went back into the main part of the house, and Scott Shamwell already had his coat on.

"Don't mean to cause trouble, Ed buddy."

I didn't want Scott Shamwell to feel bad about what your mother said, so I tried to come up with an excuse. "It's just... we're about to go to bed." It was just after seven o'clock in the evening. That was a dumb thing for me to say.

Scott Shamwell came over to me and chucked me on the shoulder. "OK, dude."

He opened the door and stepped outside, and I said "goodbye." After I closed the door, I heard him from the sidewalk, his sing-song voice penetrating the walls of our house: "Goooood niiiiggghhhht, Missusssss Stantooooon."

Scott Shamwell is pretty funny sometimes, but I knew your mother was not going to like that, and she didn't. When I came back inside, she was in the living room, still mad, and she said, "Youneedtotellhimtocallnexttime."

I told her I would tell Scott Shamwell that. All other responses were fraught (I love that word) with peril.

I hope I don't have to choose sides between your mother and Scott Shamwell. First of all, that's not a choice at all. I will always choose your mother over everyone. That very thing is what makes Scott Shamwell significant in our lives. He's the one who made me understand that I loved your mother.

I hadn't intended to get into this with you at this early date. The things I originally planned to tell you about in these notes are intricate enough without bringing an explanation of love into it. No one can explain love, anyway, C.S. It's inexplicable (good word) and irrational, and that's what makes love what it is. I have a fact-loving brain, and thus concepts that defy logic and quantifiable data challenge me. Nothing is less logical and less quantifiable than love.

After I grew close to your mother, I left her in Colorado and came back here and tried to adhere to others' ideas about where and how I should live. When I say "others," I really mean my mother. Your grandmother. I'll have much to say about her later, but I'll say this now: You're going to enjoy your grandmother. And, if you're anything like me, you're going to be flummoxed (I love that word) by her a lot.

Scott Shamwell told me then that if I loved your mother, everybody else should leave me alone and let me enjoy love while I had it in my life. We were sitting in my Cadillac when he said this, and he got a faraway look in his eyes, as if he was thinking about something beyond the car we were in. He seemed subdued and sad afterward. It confused me. I probably should have asked him what was wrong, but I was thinking about your mother and what I would have to do to get her back into my life. The next morning, I started driving to Colorado.

I don't know that I would have done that had Scott Shamwell not talked to me the way he did. I can't say for certain, and I don't like to rely on conjecture. But Scott Shamwell had a clear way of looking at the situation, and that helped me figure out what I wanted to do. I'll always be glad we hung out that night. It occurs to me now that I never told your mother about this. I should have.

I don't want to lose him as a friend. I hope I don't have to.

CLOSING THOUGHT

I have an idea, C.S. Because I continue to have trouble focusing my thoughts in these notes—and I still blame you, even though it's not really your fault because you have no idea you're causing this confusion in me—I think I should close them with small bit of what I consider the wisdom I've accumulated in my life. This,

I'm told, is what fathers do. This way, even if my thoughts are otherwise scattered, you'll at least have one lesson to take away when you read this.

Today, I'm going to go back to something I said at the beginning of this note. I made reference to John Lennon, who was in the rock 'n' roll group the Beatles. I can't say I'm a big Beatles fan and when I say "big," I'm referring to my enthusiasm, not to my girth. Among Beatles fans, however, there is often a dispute as to which member, John Lennon or Paul McCartney, was the better singer and songwriter.

This is a silly argument, as all measurable data points to Paul McCartney as the superior singer and songwriter.

Here are the facts:

	LENNON	MCCARTNEY
No. 1 songs*	22	29
Albums recorded**	125	142

*—with the Beatles and as a solo act (or, in McCartney's case, as a member of Wings)
**—includes all original albums, compilations and live albums with the Beatles and afterward.

A lot of people look at these numbers and say that it's unfair to John Lennon, because he was murdered in 1980. I don't see how you can fault Paul McCartney for that, but some people do.

In any case, the numbers don't lie, C.S. If you learn to trust quantifiable data, like I have, you can avoid many silly arguments. I highly recommend this course of action.

Edward...I don't know what to say.

I wish you'd told me about what Scott said to you.

I was so sad when you left Colorado with your mother. I'd grown attached to you, and I thought I'd never see you again, and then suddenly, one morning, you called me and said you were on your way. I don't want to say that was the happiest day of my life—who can really say that about any day?—but it was one of them, for sure. I wish I'd known this about Scott. It changes things, I think. He still drives me a little crazy, because he's so loud and obnoxious, and I'm still worried that he really is a drug dealer, but he's your friend and he delivered you to me. I can't dislike him.

The fact that I didn't know about this brings up something I've been thinking about lately. Sometimes, I think we talk plenty. We talk in the morning, and we talk at night when I come home from work. I tell you how my day was at Purl Jam. You tell me about your day of keeping weather data and reading the newspaper and looking up interesting things on the Internet.

But I think we need to talk even more, about more meaningful things. In that sense, I'm glad you're writing these notes to our child. I do wish you would stop putting the notebook in your sock drawer, though. Cut it out.

I love you.

P.S. Have you considered that George Harrison might have been the best Beatle? My daddy thought so, and I think so, too.

TUESDAYS

I have to tell you something. I've alluded to it previously, but now is the time for me to just come out and say it. I don't like it when other people aren't direct with me, so it would be hypocritical of me to not be direct with you.

I have something called Asperger's Syndrome. What this is, exactly, gets debated from time to time—in fact, right now, it's not even considered a diagnostic category anymore; it's now called Social Communication Disorder. That's all doctor talk anyway. It frustrates me.

Whatever it's called, I have it, and it means that I have trouble with social situations. This isn't something I realized about myself. I was made to understand this through extensive work with my counselors, first Dr. Ruth Buckley and then Dr. Bryan Thomsen. I still have trouble with social situations, because that difficulty is part of me and there's little I can do to change it. But just knowing helps.

This disorder exists on a spectrum. Some people aren't functional at all, or even verbal. Some people, like me, are highly functional in the right circumstances. My disorder comes with what Dr. Buckley called "a strong streak of obsessive-compulsive behaviors." What this means, in the common lexicon (a good word), is I have trouble letting things go. The parenthetical phrase I just used is a good example of this. I possess an impressive vocabulary, and I like to show it off, and when I use a word I really like, I tend to point it out. I used to always say "I love the word (whatever the word was)," and your mother pointed out to me that some people found that grating. (I think your mother was one of those people.) She suggested that I change it up by saying "a good word" or "excellent word" or "I really like that word" or "interesting word." I've been trying to do that. I don't always succeed.

Other ways my disorder manifests itself: I record the daily high and low temperatures, the precipitation levels and other data. I kiss your mother eight times on the lips before she leaves for work in the morning, and eight times on the lips when she comes home in the evening. The number eight is significant for us. That's the number of times we kissed on the first day we ever kissed. I think it's important to honor that number.

I used to write daily letters of complaint that I never sent (Dr. Buckley's idea, because sending them tended to get me in trouble—just wait till you hear about the Garth Brooks incident!). I don't do that anymore. If someone legitimately makes me angry, I try to deal with it at the time, and if that means writing a letter, then I go ahead and send it. I understand what Dr. Buckley was trying to do; she wanted to channel my behaviors in a direction that wouldn't hurt me. But the daily letters of complaint also made me focus on things I was unhappy about. At the time, I lived alone, I was having difficulty with my father, and I didn't have any friends. I find now that I'd rather focus on the good things about my life. I'm married. I don't have a lot of friends, but I have some. And you're on your way. I'm still a little wigged out about that, C.S., but I'm trying to get comfortable with it.

If you could read this now, you might wonder if you, too, will have Asperger's Syndrome, or whatever it's being called once you're born. I hope you would wonder that, as it would be a sign of an intelligent mind. The answer is murky. I don't know if you will have Asperger's Syndrome. Some experts think there is a strong genetic link, but much remains unknown about why some people have it and some do not. It's also more prevalent in boys. We don't know if you're a boy or a girl. I'm sorry I can't offer more information than this.

What I can tell you is that by the time you're old enough to read this, we'll know one way or another, and if you do have Asperger's Syndrome, we will be dealing with it in the proper way. My father didn't handle it well, and that caused problems I do not want to repeat with you.

Twice a month, every other Tuesday, I drive ten blocks from our house on Clark Avenue to Dr. Bryan Thomsen's office on Lewis Avenue. Dr. Bryan Thomsen and I sit for an hour and talk about things—mostly my frustrations and challenges, but we also sometimes just chat amiably (like that word) about the weird winter weather we've been having or the prospects for the Billings Mustangs baseball team or anything else that is on my mind. I meet with Dr. Bryan Thomsen at 10 a.m., and he has to block out his 9 a.m. appointment, too, because he was regularly going over his allotted time with that patient and making me late for my own appointment. I finally had to put my foot down (idiom—again, try not to think about the literal sense of these words too much or you'll just get angry) and tell him that I could not put up with his tardiness any longer. He agreed to keep his 9 a.m. appointment open on my Tuesdays, and he uses that time to catch up on paperwork. It has been a good compromise.

It turned out that Dr. Bryan Thomsen was the first person I told about your impending arrival. I haven't even told my mother, because I know once I do shit's going to start getting real up in here, as Scott Shamwell is wont to say.

"Congratulations, Edward," Dr. Bryan Thomsen said. "That's exciting news."

"Yes."

"You are excited, aren't you?"

I proceeded to tell Dr. Bryan Thomsen that the second definition of "excited" in my *Second College Edition of The*

American Heritage Dictionary is "at an energy level higher than the ground state." This relates to physics, not human emotion, but it's more accurate reflection of how I feel about you so far, C.S.

"So you're not happy?" he asked.

"I am neither happy nor unhappy. I am, to use a slang phrase, wigging out."

"Over what?"

Dr. Bryan Thomsen often asks me such open-ended questions even when he has a good idea about the answer. It's part of his job. I've learned to live with this and just answer him.

"It will be a strange person we have to take care of. What if he or she is mean? What if he or she has health problems? What if he or she doesn't like us? And I haven't even gotten into the hundreds of things that can go wrong in pregnancy and childbirth, things that could put C.S.—"

"C.S.?"

"Cellular Stanton. That's what I call the baby, which isn't even a baby. It's a mass of cells right now." I was annoyed. I don't like being interrupted.

Dr. Bryan Thomsen laughed. "OK. Go on."

"These things could put C.S. or Sheila, or both of them, in grave danger."

"But you planned this pregnancy, correct? I know you pretty well, Edward. I have to think you knew about the risks, no matter how remote, beforehand."

"Yes," I said. Like Dr. Buckley before him, Dr. Bryan Thomsen is usually correct about things.

"Does it just seem more real now?" he asked. "Is that why you're not excited?"

"I'm worried."

"About?"

I looked down at my left hand, at the platinum band on my third finger.

"Sheila is not excited. Not like I thought she'd be."

Dr. Bryan Thomsen leaned forward in his chair. "Let's talk about that."

If you need me to explain this when you finally read it, C.S., just tell me so. Some of the things Dr. Bryan Thomsen and I talk about are private, so I've devised a code for this next part.

(17) (28)(23)(20)(12) (12)(26). (10)(26)(33)9(22) (28)(16)(23) (21)(27)(13)(22) (28)(16)9(28) (17) (28)(16)(17)(22)(19) (33) (23)(29)(26) (21)(23)(28)(16)(13)(26) (16)9(27) (10)(13)(13)(22) (15)(23)(17)(22)(15) (12)(23)(31)(22)(27)(28)9(17)(26)(27) (28) (23) (11)(26)(33), (31)(16)(17)(11)(16) (14)(20)(29)(21)(21)(23) (32)(13)(27) (21)(13) (10)(13)(11)9(29)(27)(13) (28)(16)(13)(26) (13)'(27) (22)(23)(28)(16)(17)(22)(15) (12)(23)(31)(22) (28)(16) (13)(26)(13) (13)(32)(11)(13)(24)(28) (28)(23)(23)(20)(27) 9(22) (12) (17) (12)(23)(22)'(28) (19)(22)(23)(31) (31)(16)(33) (27)(16) (13)'(27) (11)(26)(33)(17)(22)(15). (17) (11)9(22)'(28) (13)(30) (13)(22) (27)9(33) (14)(23)(26) (11)(13)(26)(28)9(17)(22) (28) (16)9(28) (27)(16)(13) (17)(27), (10)(13)(11)9(29)(27)(13) (17) (16)9(30)(13)(22)'(28) (27)(13)(13)(22) (16)(13)(26) (11)(26)(33) (17)(22)(15), (10)(29)(28) (31)(16)(13)(22) (27)(16)(13) (11)(23) (21)(13)(27) (29)(24)(27)(28)9(17)(26)(27) (16)(13)(26) (13)(33) (13)(27) 9(22)(12) (14)9(11)(13) 9(26)(13) (26)(13)(12), 9(22) (12) (27)(16)(13) (12)(23)(13)(27)'(22)(28) (14)(13)(13)(20) (20) (17)(19)(13) (28)9(20)(19)(17)(22)(15) (28)(23) (21)(13).

After I said this, Dr. Bryan Thomsen praised me for being observant and told me to not be afraid to ask your mother if she's OK if I'm concerned about her. He said we'll continue to talk about this as needed. That made me feel better, both to get it off my chest (idiom again) and to know that Dr. Bryan Thomsen is ready to talk to me if I need to. We've come a long way, he and I.

CLOSING THOUGHT

I've mentioned before that I have a fact-loving brain, so you can expect most of my offerings here to be concrete, fact-based information—the kind of information that leaves no room for interpretation (like my earlier contention about Paul McCartney's musical superiority to John Lennon—there is no way that anyone, given the facts, can contend otherwise, and quite frankly your mother's suggestion that George Harrison is the best Beatle is laughable in the extreme, because of the actual data and because the sample size of George Harrison's solo work is so small. And now, of course, he is dead, just like John Lennon).

Occasionally, however, I will offer you some advice that is more in the vein of what experience, rather than incontrovertible (learn this word) facts, tells me. This is one of those occasions.

My advice to you is this: When something doesn't work at first, don't give up on it. Give it some time.

I've been thinking about that tonight as I reflect on today's meeting with Dr. Bryan Thomsen. You might not know it from the way I talk about how much I respect him, but Dr. Bryan Thomsen and I did not get along at all when we started working together. When Dr. Buckley told me she was retiring and that Dr. Bryan Thomsen was taking over her practice, I was crestfallen. I didn't want to work with him, not after all the years Dr. Buckley and I had put in together. When I started working with her on July 18th, 2000, I'd been kicked out of my parents' house and was about to be put into the house on Clark Avenue that I now live in with your mother, I'd been fired from my job in the county clerk's office, and Garth Brooks was pursuing litigation against me for harassing him. I was in bad shape.

Dr. Buckley helped me turn that around. She put me on a drug regimen—eighty milligrams of fluoxetine daily—that helped ease some of my compulsions. She made suggestions about how to do the things I wanted to do without getting in trouble. And she gave me a weekly appointment so I could open up about the things that irritate me. (I'll say right now that I hope your list of irritants is not nearly as long as mine. Life will go better for you the less you're bothered by people and their dumb habits.)

Dr. Bryan Thomsen didn't have much chance of comparing well with Dr. Buckley. At least, that's what I thought. He still falls short in some ways. I mentioned his tendency to impinge (nice word) on my appointment time. He also doesn't ask questions as well as Dr. Buckley did. This is a difficult thing to quantify, but it's true.

I will say this on his behalf, however: He read every single note Dr. Buckley ever wrote about me, and that showed a commitment to understanding me and my condition. And Dr. Bryan Thomsen has been helpful in my dealings with my mother, who is a good but controlling woman. If Dr. Buckley were to announce that she wanted to resume her practice, I would, of course, be more than happy to work with her again. But that's not a likely occurrence; the last I heard, Dr. Buckley is traveling the world since the death of her husband last year. Since I'm not likely to be treated by her again, I'm perfectly happy to continue with Dr. Bryan Thomsen. We've even had a bit of a breakthrough in the past couple of years. Where once I met weekly with Dr. Buckley, I need to see Dr. Bryan Thomsen only every other week. When I lived in Colorado, he and I would talk on Skype, a computer program, every two weeks.

I've been fortunate, with Dr. Buckley and now with Dr. Bryan Thomsen. If I had been less patient, however, I might not have discovered how well Dr. Bryan Thomsen and I work together. That's conjecture, which I don't generally like, but in this case I'm engaging in informed conjecture. That's not unassailable, like a fact, but it will have to do.

	DR. BUCKLEY	DR. THOMSEN
Years as my therapist	2000-11	2011-present
Number of sessions	534	92 (so far)

I'm so mad at you right now.

After you fell asleep, I read your note to our baby. BABY, EDWARD! When you say our baby is just a mass of cells, you diminish what this child is and will be. Yeah, yeah, you'll say you're just being factual, but what you're being is HURTFUL. And I don't like it and I want you to stop.

But what I'm really MAD about is your coded message. HOW STUPID DO YOU THINK I AM??? Did you think I wouldn't figure it out? Or are you just messing with me? DON'T MESS WITH ME, EDWARD!!!! You assigned each letter a number value and increased it by eight. You know how I knew this? BECAUSE THE ONLY LETTER THAT WOULDN'T BE A DOUBLE DIGIT NUMBER IS THE LETTER 'A.' Once I figured out that A was 9, how hard do you think it was to figure out the rest of your stupid code? NOT HARD. AT ALL.

It makes me so mad that you did this. I came into the bedroom and was going to yell at you, and you were sleeping. You were sleeping, and I could have just smashed your head. I could have done it. I wanted to do it. I still might. You should be glad I didn't.

Also, it makes me UNBELIEVABLY angry that you told Dr. Thomsen about the pregnancy without telling me you were going to do that. I do not want to tell anyone until after the first-trimester screen, and I TOLD you this. I didn't say not to tell anyone but that it was OK to tell Dr. Thomsen. I said don't tell ANYONE. And you did. And I'm so mad at you. Are you going to ignore everything I say? You better not. I'll leave. I'm not kidding.

I'm not sleeping with you tonight. I'm sleeping on the couch.

You're stupid and I'm really mad at you.

I'm sleeping on the couch and hoping I'm not so mad in the morning.

You better hope so, too.

UH, OH

Your mother was no less angry today. I found her note to me first thing after I woke up at 7:38 a.m. It was stapled to my T shirt. I read it quickly, and then I spent the next four minutes and thirty-seven seconds checking my head for damage. It had none, and for that I am thankful.

I found your mother at the dining-room table, eating a bowl of oatmeal.

"Sheila," I said, and she raised her right hand and jutted it toward me, palm up. That's a signal to shut up. She wouldn't even look at me.

I sat across from her. She kept her head down.

"Sheila," I said. She shook her head slowly. I didn't say anything else.

When your mother finished eating, she stood up, took her bowl into the kitchen, placed it in the sink and ran some water into it. My job is to wash the dishes, and I appreciate that she doesn't allow food to harden on them before I get to it.

She went from there to the living room, and I followed her. "Sheila," I said, and at this your mother turned and stared at me. Her eyes were red and watery and hard. That seems like a weird description, but it's what I saw. They were the hardest eyes I've ever seen, and I could not look back at her. She extended the index finger of her right hand and jabbed it at me, but she didn't say anything. I'm six feet, four inches tall, an entire foot taller than your mother, and I felt so tiny compared with her.

She turned away, snagged her purse off the couch, and walked out the front door. I went to the front window and pulled the curtain aside just enough to watch her start our Cadillac DTS, back it out of the driveway onto Clark Avenue, and make a dangerous left turn. Ordinarily, I would talk to her about that and reiterate (good word) my desire that she make right turns whenever possible, but I think I should keep my mouth shut today.

Your mother didn't kiss me before she left. It's the first time that's ever happened, and we are now in an eight-kiss deficit. I hope she isn't as angry at me when she gets home this evening. I would like to kiss her when she gets back, at least eight times but maybe sixteen. In any event, I don't want to fall further behind.

We've fought before. C.S., you're going to read this someday and maybe you will think, "My parents never got along," and I want you to know that's not true. I love your mother, and she loves me. One of the things I've struggled with in my life is knowing that I'm loved, because where's the proof? Someone can tell you that you are loved, but nobody can prove it with empirical data. This football player at Notre Dame claimed that he was loved by a girl who died, and in the end it turned out there wasn't a girl at all. People lie about love all the time. My father loved me—I also know this definitively without empirical proof—but he also did mean things to me. My mother loves me (also true) but doesn't always act in my best interest. And your mother loves me, even though she left me today without kissing me eight times. She knows that will bother me. She might have denied me the kisses precisely because she knows it will bother me. That's not a loving thing to do.

And still: Your mother loves me, and I love her.

We do fight, however. We fought on the same day we first practiced kissing, because I told my mother in a phone call what we'd been doing. Your mother slapped my bitchin' iPhone out of my hands and hurt my ear, and I cussed at her, and she started crying. Telling my mother about our kissing was a bad idea. That prompted her to come to Colorado and make me go back home to Montana. I didn't stay here; I soon figured out that I loved your mother, and I returned to Colorado to be with her.

We've fought about other things, too. One of the strangest things we fought about was the decision to move to Billings, Montana, where your mother now seems to be so unhappy. I didn't want to sell the motel in Cheyenne Wells. We had put a lot of money into it, and I was willing to put in a lot more. Your mother, however, lost her will to fight to keep it going. We had a big grand re-opening of the renovated motel and advertised in the Denver newspaper and offered deals on rooms, and we still had only four guests that first night. Your mother was inconsolable, and though we tried for the next three months to get more business, we never did. She said, "I don't want to do this anymore," and I said, "OK."

It was your mother's idea to come to Billings, Montana, not mine. I won't lie: Now that we're here, I'm comfortable being in the town where I grew up. Your mother seemed happy here, too, at least at first, but it didn't last. I thought that the news we were having a baby would cheer her up, but it hasn't. She gets angry with me because I'm not ready to say I love you—and I'm not, C.S., and it's nothing personal—but she doesn't seem to be enthused, either. This is a bigger problem than I know how to fix.

It's 11:03 a.m. I won't see you mother for another six and a half hours. I wish this day would hurry up. I don't like wishing my hours away, because after all, you don't get many of them even in a long lifetime. But I want these six and a half hours gone. I want to see your mother. I miss her.

CLOSING THOUGHT

I violated your mother's wishes by telling Dr. Bryan Thomsen that we were expecting you. Your mother's wish is that we don't talk about you to other people until the end of the first trimester; when she spoke of this, she said that's the point where she should begin to show signs of pregnancy, so people will know anyway.

Your mother is very smart. I wish I'd honored her wishes.

At this point, we're a little more than four weeks into your mother's pregnancy. The blastocyst (an awesome word) has split, forming the placenta and the embryo, and your body is beginning to develop. Here's what lies ahead:

WEEK	DATES	WHAT IS HAPPENING
Week 5	Jan. 22-29	Circulation system growing
Week 6	Jan. 30-Feb. 6	Face begins to form
Week 7	Feb. 7-14	Your mom's boobs get big
Week 8	Feb. 15-22	You'll start moving
Week 9	Feb. 23-March 2	You'll be muscling up
Week 10	March 3-10	Bone and cartilage forming
Week 11	March 11-18	You'll look like a person
Week 12	March 19-26	You'll be gaining weight
Week 13	March 27-April 2	You'll be big as a peach

April 2 seems a long way off, but I know it really isn't. It's impressive to think that you'll soon no longer be a mass of cells but a little gestational (good word) human the size of a piece of fruit.

I don't like peaches. But I'm starting to like you.

I'm writing this at 4:13 a.m. because I'm still having trouble sleeping. But my heart is at peace, Edward, even if my head isn't, and I want to thank you for that.

I'm sorry I woke you up by laughing. It's just that when I came into the bedroom and saw you asleep in your Dallas Cowboys helmet that was signed by Tony Romo, I couldn't help myself. I wondered if you were joking about my threat to throw things at your head. Then you woke up, and it was clear that you weren't joking, that you were really afraid of me, and that really upset me. I feel so out of control right now, but I would never hurt you, my love. Thank you for letting me hold you and stroke that beautiful, undamaged head and stay with you until you fell asleep.

Thank you, too, for the summary of the first trimester. I threw up for the first time yesterday, and I guess there will be more of that. I am looking forward to getting bigger boobs. I've never had big boobs, so this will be fun.

Something needs to change, Edward. I'm not sure what yet (I'm thinking about it). I think it needs to change with me, not you. But I'm not going to threaten you anymore. That was wrong. And that wasn't something I've ever done before, so I hope you know I'm being truthful when I say I'm sorry.

I love you.

Sheila

YOU WON'T BELIEVE THIS

Anyway, facts are better than belief, and I have facts.

With that in mind, I have some things to tell you:

1. I'm going to stop calling you C.S. Your mother doesn't like it, and that's the best reason. But I also realized something: According to the chart I outlined yesterday, every day you're becoming more than a collection of cells. Soon, you're going to be an actual baby, which means you won't be Cellular Stanton (C.S.). You'll be Baby Stanton (B.S.)

I'm sure you can see the problem. B.S. is not a good name.

2. Your mother and I erased the kiss deficit this morning. I kissed her sixteen times before she left for her job at Purl Jam, even though she warned me that she had "throw-up mouth" on account of the fact that you're causing her to vomit. You better be worth all this trouble, kid. (I'm going to start calling you "kid.")

3. I think I have a brother.

4. Nothing. I just don't like odd-numbered lists.

It's weird to say this, because I've been alive for forty-five years and sixteen days, and I didn't know until a few hours ago that I might have a brother. That's strange.

I'll tell you how it happened.

I had just finished washing the breakfast dishes when the doorbell rang. I actually jumped, because it's unusual for us to have visitors here at the house, and it's unprecedented (learn this word) at 9:11 a.m. since your mother and I moved here.

I went to the front door and opened it, and a man I know was standing on the front step. He started to speak, but I cut him off.

"You're *Billings Herald-Gleaner* sportswriter Mark Westerly," I said.

"You remember me?"

"Yes." What a silly question that was. I used to work with him at the *Billings Herald-Gleaner*. I liked him, because he never did stupid things that broke his computer.

"Do you mind if I come in?" he asked.

"Please." I motioned him into the living room. He sat down in the love seat, and I said, "That's my spot." He moved to the couch. That was a close one.

Mark Westerly ground his hands together. "It's been a while since I've seen you," he said.

"I got involuntarily separated from the *Billings Herald-Gleaner* on November 16th, 2011," I said.

"I don't work there anymore, either."

"You were involuntarily separated, too?"

"No," he said. "I separated voluntarily." He chuckled, and I smiled at him. I always did like sportswriter Mark Westerly.

"Why are you here?" I asked.

Mark Westerly clapped his hands together. "You're a get-down-to-business guy," he said. "I like that about you. Here's the deal, Edward: I represent someone who wants to meet you. Now, this isn't something bad, and you're not in any trouble. I know it's kind of weird to have me just show up like this."

It was a little weird, but I was also intrigued.

"I want you to come with me and meet this person," he continued. "You'll probably know who he is when you meet him, and he'll explain everything. He asked me to come see you first, since you and I know each other."

He looked at me. I looked at him.

"What do you think?" he asked.

"Why did you voluntarily separate yourself from the *Billings Herald-Gleaner*?"

Mark Westerly threw back his head and laughed. I laughed, too, because I didn't want him to feel ill at ease. I didn't know what was funny.

"Believe it or not, it has something to do with why I'm here. I'll tell you about it after you meet my friend, if you still care. What do you say?"

"Do I need to bring a lunch?" I asked.

"No. It's right here in town."

"Well, OK."

We drove through downtown Billings and over to the South Side in Mark Westerly's Chevrolet Nova. It was a good, sturdy little car, but I couldn't help but think that my father, if he were alive, would have made fun of it. My father—your grandfather—believed that Cadillacs were the finest cars made. He left me one when he died, and I would still have it if not for the fact that I drove it into the back of a snowplow and totaled it. (Strange word, "totaled." It means that a car has been totally destroyed, but the past-participle construction confuses me. It seems that a more accurate word would be "de-totaled," as in, "This car was once total, but it isn't anymore." Language frustrates me sometimes.) Now, I drive a newer Cadillac DTS. My father would be proud of me, I think. I don't like to rely on conjecture, but my father— your grandfather—is dead, so conjecture is all I have.

We pulled up in front of a house on a corner, directly across from South Park. My father—your grandfather—was always complaining about the South Side, saying it was dirty and that the people who lived there didn't have any initiative. I don't know if that was true or not—my father had a lot of particular ideas that didn't always stand up to scrutiny—but this house was nice. It was old and needed a good paint job, but the front yard was well-groomed. I liked it.

"What is this?" I asked Mark Westerly.

"The man who wants to meet you lives here."

We got out of the car and walked up the sidewalk to the front door. Before we could reach it, a man opened the door and stepped onto the front porch. He had a pot belly, like mine, and he wore nice blue jeans and a T-shirt that said EVERLAST across it.

"Thank you for coming," he said. He seemed to be looking me up and down, as if searching for something in particular, and as I drew closer to him, I saw faint pink lines all over his face, like little pieces of thread. That's when I figured out who he was.

"You're Hugo Hunter," I said.

He extended his hand, and I shook it. "You know me?" he asked.

"Yes. I mean, I don't know you, but I know who you are." Hugo Hunter is famous in Billings, Montana, and he used to be famous in a lot of other places, too. He was a boxer. He won a silver medal at the 1992 Olympics that should have been gold. I watched it on TV that summer, and he was disqualified for knocking someone out after the buzzer. But that was an incorrect ruling. TV replays clearly showed the knockout punch coming just before the buzzer. I remember my father watching with me and saying, "That's the biggest horseshit call I've ever seen." My father knew about horseshit.

Hugo Hunter patted me on the shoulder like we were old friends. "That's a start, I guess. Come on in, and let's talk."

"I'll wait out here," Mark Westerly said. That was strange.

Hugo Hunter opened the door and ushered me inside.

Hugo Hunter's house smells like old people. I don't know what all old people smell like—to accumulate that knowledge would require a lot of a time and a strong constitution—but I know what my Grandpa Sid and Grandma Mabel's house in Dallas smelled like, and that's the scent in Hugo Hunter's house, too. That's odd.

Hugo Hunter and I sat in his living room and talked. He hasn't been famous for a while, and I tried to remember the last time I'd seen him on TV. I couldn't recall. The pink lines on his face weren't there before. Neither was the gray that sprinkled through his hair. On the wall across from me was a picture of him from his younger days. He had on his boxing trunks and held up a gloved fist in a menacing manner.

I pointed at the picture. "I'm talking to Hugo Hunter. Wow!"

Hugo Hunter sat opposite me. He clasped his hands together. "It's not as exciting as it seems, believe me," he said.

"Why wouldn't I believe you?"

Hugo Hunter kind of scrunched his nose up at that question, and then he didn't answer it.

"Edward—is it all right if I call you Edward?"

"It would be incorrect to call me anything else."

Hugo Hunter laughed. "OK. Edward. There's no easy way to do this, so I'm just going to be direct."

Hugo Hunter could say that, but I wasn't going to believe it until I had proof. In my experience, most people aren't straight talkers. I've told you this before.

"I would appreciate that," I said.

He leaned into the space between us and looked directly at my eyes, unblinking. "I'm pretty sure I'm your brother."

I won't lie: That was direct.

"I don't have a brother," I said.

Hugo Hunter leaned back, but his eyes stayed locked on mine. "Up until a few months ago, I didn't think I did, either. But I do have a brother, and you're him."

"He."

"Huh?"

"Grammatically, it should be 'he.'"

"Really?"

"Yes. I'm very good at grammar."

"It sounds kind of strange."

"Good grammar often does."

Hugo Hunter smiled at me. He had a nice smile. I looked at his face, at his white teeth, at the little lines that I now recognized as healed-up cuts. I looked at his eyes, and the skin around them crinkled in a way that reminded me of someone. The color of the eyes was familiar, too.

"You're a pretty interesting guy," he said. "Mark said you would be."

I blurted it out. "My father is your father, isn't he?"

His voice turned soft. "Yes."

"You were born in 1975, weren't you?"

"Yes."

"I know who your mother is."

"Was. She died."

"So did my father."

"I know."

My chest felt like it was caving in on itself. "I don't know who your mother was," I corrected. "I know about her. I know what happened."

Hugo Hunter stood up and moved toward me. "Do you need some water or something?" he asked. "You don't look good."

I didn't pass out. That's the good news, kid. I did have to lie down for a few minutes on Hugo Hunter's couch. He didn't seem to mind, but I was a little bit embarrassed. Finding out you have a brother when you're forty-five years and sixteen days old takes a lot out of you.

When I felt good enough to sit up again, Hugo Hunter brought in Mark Westerly, and the three of us put everything together.

I told Hugo Hunter about how my mom found out that my father was having an affair, and how she left us for a short time. I told him that my mother referred to his mother as a whore, and he got mad at me and said, "My mother was a saint." He looked like he wanted to punch me, and then, as if he hadn't gotten angry at all, he said, "I'm sorry. Go on." I told him how my father and I had flown to Denver, picked up an International Harvester truck and taken it to Odessa, Texas, to be outfitted with a drilling rig. (My father—also maybe Hugo Hunter's father and your grandfather—was in the oil business before he became a politician.) I told how after we had come home from Texas, my mother met us at the airport in Billings, Montana, and she and my father got back together.

Hugo Hunter told me how he had been raised by his mother and his grandmother, how his mother died at age thirty-two because of pancreatic cancer (cancer sucks), and how his grandmother died many years later, soon after one of his losses as a professional boxer.

And Mark Westerly told me how he found out about my father and Hugo Hunter's mother right after the Olympics in 1992, on the very same day I first saw Hugo Hunter in Billings, Montana. He flew home that day to a big celebration downtown. My father sat up on the dais with Hugo Hunter, and I watched from the crowd below as my father introduced him. Later that night, after Hugo Hunter and his grandmother and everyone else had gone home, the grandmother told Mark Westerly about my father— apparently Hugo Hunter's father, too.

"And I kept it a secret for a long, long time, because Aurelia asked me to," Mark Westerly said to me. "But several months ago, I couldn't see keeping the secret anymore. Hugo's grandmother is gone. So's your dad." He looked at Hugo Hunter. "Shit, I've got to get used to saying he's Hugo's dad, too, I guess. Anyway, you two guys are the only ones left. You should know."

Hugo Hunter smiled at me. Aside from the gray, he has black hair. He's way shorter than I am, and thinner, too. Nobody would think we were brothers, but we apparently are.

"We should know, shouldn't we?" he said.

It was a curious question. I thought about it for a few seconds, and I realized he was correct. "Yes," I said. "I think so.

Hugo Hunter wrote a book. That's why Mark Westerly came to get me, and why Hugo Hunter wanted to talk to me today. With Mark Westerly's help, he wrote a book called *Hugo Hunter: My Good Life and Bad Times*, and it will be coming out in less than a week. He's going to be traveling a lot and appearing on national TV, and he wanted to meet me before any of that happened.

"I'm not going to talk about you, or subject you to anything," Hugo Hunter said. He voice lowered to a grave tone. "I mention in the book that I've recently learned who my father is, but I name no names. I'm not after anything here, and I don't want to bring any attention you don't want. But it's only fair to let you know, because it's possible that other people who know about your dad and my mom could start talking. So I wanted to make sure you heard it from me."

Mark Westerly nodded.

I looked at them both. "I thought you wanted to know me."

"Oh, Jesus," Hugo Hunter said. "God, yes, of course I do. I'm leaving pretty soon, but I'll be back. Absolutely, yes. I want to know you. I hope you want to know me."

I thought of how I clipped out the stories about Hugo Hunter when he was in the Olympics, and how my father—his father, perhaps—and I watched some of his professional fights on pay-per-view. "I feel like I already do."

Hugo Hunter laughed again. "I might surprise you."

We exchanged e-mail addresses and phone numbers. I pointed out to Hugo Hunter that I have a bitchin' iPhone and he could send me messages there. He said, "I'm not too big into texting and stuff like that," but he promised to send something from his travels. He said, "I'll be back in a few weeks, and we can get together then." That sounded good to me.

"Do you want to get a blood test?" he asked me.

"Why? I'm already married."

"No, I mean to make sure we're actually related."

I was surprised that he thought of it first. I'm usually the one who most fervently seeks data.

"It would be nice to know," I said.

"Cool," Hugo Hunter said. "We'll do that when I get back."

Hugo Hunter also told me I have a nephew. That's exactly how he put it: "Oh, you have a nephew." Hugo Hunter's son is named Raj, and he's grown up now. I wanted to say something about you, kid, but your mother would be unhappy if I did, plus I don't know if you're a boy or a girl, so it would have been difficult to give Hugo Hunter any specifics. I'll have to tell him another time, when I have more to say and your mother won't be upset.

That was it. We shook hands again, and Hugo Hunter said, "I'm really glad we met," and I said, "So am I," but I have to be honest: I don't know if I'm glad or I'm bewildered. Maybe it's a little bit of both.

My father has been dead since October 30th, 2008, which is a long time, and still he keeps surprising me.

CLOSING THOUGHT

You apparently have an uncle, kid. If you've read to this point, you might be saying, "No shit." You shouldn't say that. "Shit" is a bad word.

Hugo Hunter, your uncle, is also famous. He might have been the most famous person in Montana at one time, although that time has passed. He's famous enough to have a Wikipedia page, though. Here's what it says:

Hugo Hunter (born 1975) is a retired American boxer, best known for a controversial loss in the lightweight final of the 1992 Summer Olympics in Barcelona, Spain.

Early life
Hunter was born February 9, 1975, in Billings, Montana, to Helene Hunter. He attended public schools in Billings but dropped out of high school in 1993 to pursue a career in boxing.

1992 Summer Olympics
After winning a National Golden Gloves title as a lightweight in 1991 and then the 1992 U.S. Olympic boxing trials in Phoenix, Hunter went to Barcelona as a 17-year-old. He was not considered a pre-Games favorite to medal, but he gained attention at the Games with a counterpunching style.

His victory over German Horst Dorfschmedder, the world's top-ranked lightweight, in the semifinals resulted in intense media attention.

Olympic lightweight final

In the final, against Spaniard Juan Domingo Ascension, Hunter appeared to be well in control of the fight when he was disqualified for knocking out his opponent after the buzzer to end the second round. Subsequent television replays seemed to make clear that the knockout punch occurred just before the buzzer, and the U.S. delegation filed an official protest of the referee's decision. That protest was denied, and Hunter accepted the silver medal.

In 2000, a panel of boxing experts commissioned by ESPN listed the decision No. 5 among all-time boxing scandals of the 20th century.

Pro career

Hunter made his professional debut on May 15, 1993, against Leland Briggs. He won in a first-round knockout.

On Oct. 12, 1997, with a record of 20-0 with 17 knockouts, Hunter was scheduled to fight Rhys Montrose in London for the World Boxing Council welterweight championship. The night before the fight, however, Hunter reported falling in his hotel room and breaking his wrist. The fight was canceled, and Montrose went on to lose the title to Mozi Qwai three months later. In 2004, Hunter would lose to Qwai in their World Boxing Association super welterweight (154 pounds) title match. It was the only world title match Hunter fought.

Hunter's last fight was in 2013, a knockout loss to Cody Schronert in Billings, Montana. His record is 38-5, with 27 knockouts.

Drug problems and present day

Hunter has admitted to cocaine addiction. In 1998, he was charged with possession in Los Angeles but successfully completed a rehabilitation stint. The charge was dropped.

In late 2012, the Billings Herald-Gleaner and Sports Illustrated reported that Hunter had again entered drug rehabilitation. Afterward, he completed his general equivalency

53

diploma and began taking classes at Montana State University Billings.

Hunter's memoir, Hugo Hunter: My Good Life and Bad Times, *is scheduled to be released soon.*

Chronic traumatic encephalopathy

In March 2013, Hunter announced that his brain had been scanned by researchers at UCLA and that he showed signs of the progressive neurological disease chronic traumatic encephalopathy (CTE). There is no known cure for CTE, which has been cited in the deaths of several former National Football League players.

Holy shit, kid.

I'm writing this to you because although your father told you all about meeting his brother, I wanted to make sure you know just how important this is to him. Edward (you will call him Dad, or Daddy, or Father, or Pop, but you will not call him Edward—we will not be that kind of family) doesn't usually tip his hand when he's excited about something unless he really trusts you. I read everything he writes to you, and I think he's still holding back. I know he is. I know him well.

But he's writing to you as much as he can, and I think that says what needs to be said. He might argue that he can't love someone he doesn't know, but he loves you. It's obvious.

He was waiting for me at the door when I came home from work, and he couldn't even let me sit down before he blurted out that he has a brother.

As you can probably imagine, I was completely shocked by this, and I guess I'm still shocked, even though it all makes sense. I've heard the stories about his father, Ted, and the timeframe is right, so ... yeah, they're probably brothers. I'm going to let you make up your own mind about your grandfather as you learn the stories about him, but I can't say I'm impressed by him. He was mean to your grandmother (who is, I'll admit, a piece of work), and he was mean to your father, and now we find out that he probably had another son.

I didn't want to say anything discouraging tonight because your father is so excited about this, but I am worried. We don't know this person. We don't know if he wants anything. I mean, your father—we—have a lot of money, because your grandfather was a very wealthy man. Maybe Hugo wants some of it? I hate to even think like that. I'm not trying to influence how you feel about your grandmother, but that sounds like something she'd say. So distrustful. And that's why your father and I agreed that we won't be telling her until after the blood test confirms it. But you do wonder. Why did he show up now?

Your father is so over the moon about this. After he told me what happened today, he made me go into the computer room with him and watch clips of Hugo's fights on YouTube. He's so much smaller

*than your father is, and his coloring is different, but you know
... when you look close, they have the same eyes. You can tell. I
finally had to ask Edward to turn off the computer so we could
have dinner.*

*Just before your father went to sleep, he got all serious and
asked me if I was scared that Hugo will die soon. I asked him where
he got such a silly idea, and he told me about the head trouble
Hugo has. I said that from the sound of it he seems OK now, and
that we could just hope he's getting treatment. Your father went to
sleep after that, and now I'm downstairs in the basement and I've
had a good cry, and I'll fold the clothes before I go back up and
get into bed.*

*I'm happy for your father. I really am. But I'm sad for me. My
people are all gone. My mom and daddy have been dead for many
years, and they're in the ground now. I didn't have any brothers
or sisters. I don't know any cousins or aunts or uncles. Like your
grandparents, mine were dead before I came along. I have your
father, and I love him. I have you, and I love you. I wish I were
getting someone new in my life like your father is (besides you, of
course). Maybe I am. Maybe I'll grow fond of Hugo, the way your
father already is. But still, it's different.*

*I wish you were here right now, where I could touch you and
kiss you. I haven't even felt you kick yet. I guess you're not ready
for that.*

We're five weeks into this thing, kiddo. Thirty-five to go.

I love you so much.

*Your mother,
Sheila*

BIG TROUBLE

Your mother has become unpredictable. Strike that. She always has been a little bit unpredictable, which strangely is one of the things I like about her, but now she's erratic (a good word, but a bad quality).

Let me start at the ending and work backward so you can understand this: Today, February 3rd, your mother went to work at Purl Jam, as scheduled. I kissed her on the lips eight times and said goodbye, and she didn't say goodbye to me, which I thought was strange. She usually does. But I thought that maybe her mind was on work.

At 10:47 a.m., I received a call from the Billings Police Department. Your mother was in custody—she wasn't being charged with anything, the police officer who called me made sure I knew that—and I needed to drive downtown and pick her up.

Of course, I couldn't drive downtown to pick her up. Your mother took the Cadillac DTS to Purl Jam. So I had to call a taxi to pick me up and take me downtown.

What a shitburger of a day it turned out to be.

At the police station, I waited in the foyer for your mother to come out. The arresting officer, whose badge read "Gilluly," talked to me first.

"She's embarrassed," Officer Gilluly said.

"What did she do?" I asked.

"Tore the place apart."

"Purl Jam?"

"Yes."

"Why?"

"You'll have to talk to her about that. They don't want to press charges. They just wanted her out."

"OK."

"You can take her home."

"OK."

"I'll go get her."

"OK."

When your mother came out, I didn't recognize her. That's an imprecise statement. Of course I recognized her. She was wearing the green down jacket she had on as she left the house, and her hair was in the same style, and those were her eyes and her nose and her mouth. But she looked defeated. That's the best way I can describe it. I didn't recognize that look in her. I had seen it only once before, when she decided to close the motel.

"Hi, Sheila," I said.

"How'd you get here?" she asked.

"I took a cab. I forgot to ask him to wait."

"It's OK. I want to walk."

She brushed past me and pushed open a door and stepped outside, and I followed her. Cold air hit me in the face once we were on the sidewalk. Your mother walked to the corner and turned west up Third Avenue North. I jogged and caught up with her.

"What happened?" I asked.

"Nothing."

"Sheila, that's not accurate."

"I know."

Your mother walked faster and left me behind. I jogged again.

"Please tell me."

"I will. Not now. I want to go home."

At the corner of Third Avenue North and 30th Street, I took her hand, and I held it as we crossed the street. Once we were on the other side, she let go.

"I don't want to," she said.

"We like to hold hands," I said.

"Not today. Today, I don't."

"Sheila—"

"Just go ahead. I'll be home soon."

"No, I'm not leaving."

I fell back, so she was in front of me and I could watch her. We walked all the way home like that. It took twenty-one minutes.

It felt like a lot longer than that.

When we got to the house, your mother said, "I'm going to bed," and when I asked if she wanted me to lie down with her she said, "No. I don't."

She went into our bedroom and she closed the door.

I didn't know what to do. I knocked, but she didn't answer. I said her name, and she didn't say anything. I said, "I'm going to knock down this door," and she said, "Edward, just leave me alone. I'll talk to you later. I promise."

I was flummoxed, flummoxed, flummoxed.

I called the taxi company again and asked for a ride to the West End so I could pick up the Cadillac DTS. The dispatcher told me that it would be about forty-five minutes, so I looked for something to do to pass the time.

I did web searches for stories and photos and videos about your Uncle Hugo. Do you like that name, Uncle Hugo? I think it has a certain ring to it (idiom, and also a bad boxing pun), but that's a subjective thing. You might hate how it sounds. We'll see. You have to be born and learn to think and form opinions first. This will take a while.

Your Uncle Hugo sure has had a lot of things written about him, and some of it isn't flattering. He's been called a choker and a junkie and a disappointment. I found one article, on a sports website, that mentioned his book and wasn't very nice about it:

So Hugo Hunter has written a book. That begs two questions: 1. Was it written in crayon? 2. As this isn't 1993, does anybody really care?

I hate it when people write like they're know-it-alls. This writer doesn't know that much. He doesn't know that "beg the question" is an informal fallacy in which the question isn't important but the conclusion is. Also, it's not as if people cared about things only in 1993. That's stupid. He's stupid.

So I wouldn't continue to get angry, I stopped reading stories about your Uncle Hugo and instead just printed out pictures of him from his boxing days. When I see him again, I might ask him to sign them. That would be neat.

The taxi driver arrived at 2:43 p.m. and honked. I went to the bedroom door and said, "I'm going to pick up the car." Your mother said nothing. I went outside and got into the taxi and said, "Your dispatcher said you'd be forty-five minutes and you took sixty-three. Explain yourself." The taxi driver said, "Tough titties. If you don't like it, get out." To that, I said, "I don't like it, but I have to go to Purl Jam on 24th Street West, so let's go."

"Well, OK."

The cab fare came to $11.75. I got out of the car and counted out the exact change. "No tip," I said. "Tough titties." The driver gave me the finger and then left, and I suppose that's been the most satisfying interaction I've had with another human being today. That's a joke, kid. I'm pretty funny even on a shitburger day.

I arrived home at 3:16 p.m., and after I closed the front door, your mother came out of the bedroom.

"I called Dr. Haworth," she said.

"Why?"

"You know why."

"What did she say?"

"I'm hormonal, like I didn't know that."

"We're in Week Six now," I said. "The baby's face is beginning to form. Did she say anything about that?"

"She did not."

"Why did you get arrested at Purl Jam?"

Your mother sat down and invited me to sit next to her, which I did.

"I was going to quit anyway."

"I know. But on February 10th. And getting arrested is bad." I should know, kid. I've been arrested.

"I couldn't wait until February 10th. And I'm sorry I got arrested. But that's my problem."

I considered this. "We decided something. Decisions matter. And we said when we got married that we'll get through problems together. That's what we said."

Your mother took my left hand in both of hers. "I know."

"Do you?"

She wrenched her body around to where she was facing me, and then she grabbed my hand again.

"I feel like I'm waiting for everything," she said. "I was waiting to quit my job. I'm waiting for this baby to arrive. I'm waiting to feel better about being here, and about why we left Cheyenne Wells. I'm just tired of it. When Pam asked me to stock the shelves today…God, I just lost it. I don't want to just sit back and wait anymore."

"So you destroyed the store?"

"I didn't destroy the store," your mother said. "I pulled a few things off the wall. I might have screamed a little bit."

"You used to be happy," I said. "Why aren't you happy?"

"It's not that simple."

"I think it is."

"To me, it's not that simple."

"Something needs to change," I said.

"I know. I've made a decision."

"What?"

"I'm not ready to tell you."

"That's not fair."

61

"I know."

I started to cry. I'm ashamed to tell you this, but it's true.

"Don't you like me anymore?"

Your mother cupped her hands behind my neck and pulled me in and gave me kisses on my nose, which tickled. "I love you," she said. "My decision is a good thing, I promise. I'm going to tell you soon. I just need to work it out in my head. OK?"

"You love me?"

"Always."

"OK."

I don't want to sound like your father here, but I'm going to talk to you about words and phrases. When you get older, you'll hear this one a lot: "That breaks my heart." It's a terribly sad feeling that leads someone to say that. In most cases, the heart—the organ inside your body—doesn't actually break into pieces. It's the emotion that makes you feel broken. This is hard to explain.

Today, I felt like my heart broke twice. The first time, I broke my own heart by losing control at work. By the time I'd finished screaming, Pam Peppers had already called the police, and I felt as though I had to just sit there and take whatever was coming. The officer arrived, and he handcuffed me and took me to the police car, and that was as humiliated as I've ever been. I wondered what my parents would have said if they'd seen that. I wondered what I would say to your father. The officer was very nice to me. He talked calmly to me and said he didn't think I would be charged, and he asked how long I've lived here. I was touched by his humanness, even though I was so humiliated. I'll have to bear the burden of getting over that.

The second time was when your father asked me if I still like him, because I don't know if I can ever make it up to him that I caused him to feel that way. I haven't been nice to him in a long time, it seems, and I'm starting to fear I've forgotten how to do it. Which means I'll have to learn how again.

I don't know how I got to this place.

Dr. Haworth said I'm hormonal and that I should talk to someone.

I'm starting with you. And, I promise, I'm going to talk to your father.

This is on me. It's my mess to clean up.

I'm not proud of me, and I know your father isn't proud of me, and I suspect you wouldn't be, either.

I'll have to change that.

I love you.

A DAY LATER, A NICE SURPRISE

The smell of homemade spaghetti sauce—spaghetti is my favorite—filled the house this afternoon. Before I met your mother, I liked to buy Newman's Own brand spaghetti sauce, which is very good, but your mother makes her own from scratch, and she cooks it slowly for several hours. It's way better than Newman's Own, and I say that as a fan of Paul Newman as a man and an actor. He was excellent in the movie *The Hustler*.

At 5:02 p.m., your mother told me to take a shower and then put on some nice clothes. "Wear that checkered shirt I got you for Christmas," she said. I did as she requested, and after I was done, your mother took her shower. She slipped on my favorite dress of hers, a simple black dress that shows off her legs. She doesn't wear many dresses and doesn't really like them, but she wears this one for me because she knows it makes me horny. She smiled at me and said, "Might as well enjoy it before I have to start wearing those dowdy maternity clothes."

Your mother is pretty funny sometimes.

At 6 p.m., the doorbell rang.

"Answer it, please," your mother said.

I got up from the love seat and went to the door. I looked through the peephole and got a surprise.

"It's Scott Shamwell," I said.

"Let him in."

I opened the door, and though I knew it was Scott Shamwell, I remained surprised. He wore a blue shirt with a yellow tie and khaki dress pants. His bushy red beard had been trimmed, and his long hair was pulled back into a tight ponytail. He smelled really good, too, like the cologne Dr. Bryan Thomsen wears. He handed me a bottle of red wine, which I don't like, but still, it was nice of him to bring it.

"Am I late for dinner?" he asked.

Your mother walked over, stood next to me and took the wine.

"You're right on time, Scott," she said, and then she did the most astounding thing. She leaned over and she kissed Scott Shamwell on the cheek.

Holy shit.

Two times during dinner, which was excellent, Scott Shamwell asked me what was new. He didn't ask in the sense of wanting information about the world; had that been the case, I could have told him that our snowfall total for the year was new, or that our across-the-street neighbor, who lives in Donna Hays's old house, has a new Toyota. He was asking us how we were doing.

I giggled both times he asked, because I actually do have some big news, but your mother and I agreed that we wouldn't blab about your Uncle Hugo until blood tests confirm that we are brothers. So I giggled and said, "Nothing, Scott Shamwell," and then I looked at your mother, and she smiled at me, and Scott Shamwell said "What?" and I said, "Nothing, Scott Shamwell," and then we all laughed. We're pretty funny sometimes.

"This is really good, Sheila," Scott Shamwell said as he ate his fourth slice of French bread. "Thank you for inviting me."

"Why did you invite him?" I asked.

"Edward, that's rude," she said. Scott Shamwell laughed and pounded the table with his fist, until your mother told him to stop.

"I'm sorry," I said. "I just thought you didn't like him. That's what you said."

Your mother flushed a shade of red, and then she turned to Scott Shamwell and said, "Scott, Edward told me what you said to him."

"When?" Scott Shamwell asked.

"Right before he came to live with me in Colorado."

"What did I say?"

Your mother looked at me.

"You told me that people should just leave me alone and let me love Sheila," I said.

"I said that?"

"Yes," I said. "You did. We were sitting in my car in the driveway outside."

Scott Shamwell scrunched up his face and scratched his beard, and I couldn't tell if he was being serious or putting me on, so I waited.

"I think I remember that," he said. "I was kind of drunk."

Your mother dropped her fork on her plate and started gathering up the dishes. She was angry. I could tell.

"No, you weren't," I said.

Scott Shamwell smiled and gave me a little shove. "I was just kidding with you. Yeah, I remember that."

Your mother sat down again, but I could tell she was still annoyed.

"OK, listen," she said. "I don't think you're as funny as you think you are, Scott, but it's important to me that you said that to Edward, and I know you care about him."

Scott Shamwell's face took on a sober look. "I do," he said.

"Good," your mother said. "Now I want you both to listen to me." She looked us both in the eye, first Scott Shamwell and then me. "I've decided that I want to do something. I want to go to Cheyenne Wells. I want to go as soon as possible. And Scott, I want you to come with us."

Scott Shamwell and I looked at each other and then back at your mother, and what we said was identical: "Why?"

Your mother put her hands on the table and stiffened her arms. "Because I have some things I want to do—personal things that I want to do alone, but I can't make the trip by myself. You're a special friend to Edward, Scott, and I want you to be there for him so he's not by himself, and also so I can get to know you better."

Your mother is pretty smart sometimes. Scott Shamwell was no longer cracking jokes and irritating her. He looked like he was hearing something very serious.

"I can't," he said. "I wish I could, but I can't."

"Why not?" your mother said.

"My dad and brother are in jail," he said. "The feds have all our bank accounts locked up. I'm having to work cash jobs just to try to hold everything together for me and my mom. I can't just go off to Colorado now."

Now your mother looked sober.

"I'm sorry," she said. "That's too bad."

I'm going to interrupt here, kid, to tell you something important. I sometimes have good ideas. The problem with my good ideas is that they don't always occur to me at the best possible time. I'm often too early or too late with them. But tonight, when I really needed to have a good idea, one came to me at just the right moment.

"We could pay you," I said.

"What?" Scott Shamwell said.

Your mother knew what I was saying, though. She said, "Yes, yes. That's right, Scott. We could pay you for your time."

"That wouldn't be right," he said.

"Why not?" your mother said. "You would be doing something for us that we need done. That's a service rendered. It's not wrong to receive payment for that."

"I don't know."

"Plus, I'm fucking loaded," I said.

Your mother scolded me. "Edward, don't you cuss around me."

"Maybe," Scott Shamwell said.

Your mother moved to close the deal. "How much do you make for a day's labor?" she asked.

"I don't know," Scott Shamwell said. "If I'm lucky, maybe two hundred dollars."

"Fine," she said. "We'll double your rate. We should need you for five days. So will you do it for two thousand dollars?"

"I don't know."

"Please?" I said. I must acknowledge something: I was getting excited about spending some time with Scott Shamwell.

"OK," he said.

Your mother and Scott Shamwell shook hands on it. That made everything official.

CLOSING THOUGHT

There are 719.7 miles between Billings, Montana, and Cheyenne Wells, Colorado. I know this because I've made the drive three times: On December 20th, 2011, with my mother (your grandmother) when she came to Colorado to get me away from your mother; seven days later, when I drove back to Cheyenne Wells to tell your mother I love her; and on June 19th, 2013, when we moved here to Billings.

Each of those times, the drive was made in a single day, but your mother, Scott Shamwell and I decided to be a bit more leisurely (I like that word) when we leave tomorrow.

Here is our itinerary (also a nice word):

DAY	DISTANCE	DESTINATION
Wednesday	453.9 miles	Cheyenne, Wyoming
Thursday	265.8 miles	Cheyenne Wells, Colorado
Friday	None	Cheyenne Wells, Colorado
Saturday	444.4 miles	Casper, Wyoming
Sunday	275.3 miles	Billings, Montana

These distances don't include variances for finding gas

stations and hotels; that, unfortunately, is a limitation of not knowing every detail about your trip in advance. But you can rest assured, kid, that I will meticulously track every detail of the trip, including exact mileages and miles-per-gallon and time spent in transit. As you are my son or daughter, you will have full access to my data notebooks when you reach an age where such things interest you.

I am looking forward to this trip. Your mother says she needs it, that she has some personal matters to attend to, and that's good enough for me. But there's also something in it for me. I get to hang out with my friend Scott Shamwell. I don't have many friends, but he's a good one. I will also be traveling through country that my father, your grandfather, knew well. He used to be an oil man, and he spent a lot of time in places like Casper, Wyoming, and Cheyenne Wells, Colorado.

I know this won't make much sense, because there's no tangible proof, but I feel closer to my father, your grandfather, when I go to places he knew. I feel like there's some part of him still there. That maybe he knows I'm there and is looking out for me, or at least getting a chance to see how I've changed since he died. So much of what existed between your grandfather and me was broken at the time he died. I've managed to repair some of it, by getting to know more about him and by remembering that he loved me, even if he didn't always know how to show it.

I'd like to fix more of it, if I can.

I don't know how I'm going to survive five days with that Scott Shamwell. He's so cocky, so cartoonishly manly. I much prefer someone docile like your father. But I also know that your father reveres this man, and Scott has been a good friend to him even if he's irritated the you-know-what out of me.

It took me a long time thinking about it, but I finally figured out why I haven't been able to move on from leaving Cheyenne Wells. When we spent all of that money to make the motel better and we still didn't get any new customers, I became so depressed that I just wanted out of it, out of town, out of my life. There's this saying about how the grass is always greener on the other side of the fence. I never believed that, until I had to believe it.

I need to go back and make my proper goodbyes. I have friends there. I have parents in the ground there. For many years, I managed to keep that motel up and running. It wasn't easy, and I nearly lost it several times, but nobody ever shut me down. I shut myself down. I've let it become this shameful thing, and it's not. That motel is something I should be proud of, and I'm going back and holding my head up high.

I don't know if your father understands this. He hasn't asked any questions about this crazy plan of driving across two states in the dead of winter. I think he could tell how much it means to me, and now he's distracted with the pleasant idea of traveling around with his buddy Scott. That's good. I don't need a lot of questions.

I'm watching your father sleep as I write this. I should be mad at him that he falls asleep so easily, and once he does he's down all night, peacefully off in his own little dreamland. Sleep is never that easy for me, and I'm always up before him, too. But I can't be mad at him. He's so gentle and kind. A little irritating sometimes, yes, and I hate it when he cusses. (He's going to cuss A LOT after this trip. Believe me. That, unfortunately, is something Scott Shamwell brings out in him.) But he's such a good man. You're getting the best daddy in the world, I think.

Love,
Your mom

UNCLE HUGO

When my bitchin' iPhone rang, I was loading a case of bottled water into the trunk of the Cadillac DTS. When you're driving long distances in the winter, kid, you don't want to take chances with being stranded by weather. I'd also put a case of granola bars into the trunk.

I looked at the phone's screen and smiled. It was your Uncle Hugo calling me just two days after we first met.

"Hi, Hugo Hunter," I said.

Your uncle laughed softly. I like his laugh. "How long are you going to call me by my first and last names?" he asked.

This question flummoxed me. "Don't you like your names?"

"Yeah. I mean, yeah, fine, they're great. It's just a little formal."

"I didn't realize that."

"It's no big deal. How've you been?" he said.

I told your Uncle Hugo that I was doing well, and that we would be leaving on our trip in the morning. He wished us luck and said he wished he could go with us. I wish that, too. If I went on a trip with Scott Shamwell and your Uncle Hugo, I wouldn't have to say a word. I'd just sit and listen to them.

71

"My book came out yesterday," he said. "I'm going to be traveling, too. Flying to New York City on Thursday, and I'll be on a bunch of different shows Friday—the CBS morning show, that one with the ex-football player and the soap-opera star, a couple of others. You should watch if you get a chance."

"I will. We'll be in Cheyenne Wells, Colorado, that day."

"Listen, Edward, I want to warn you about something," he said. "They'll probably ask me about, you know, your dad and you. I don't name you in the book, but I knew who you were. I just want you to know that I'm going to be cool, OK?"

"OK." I didn't understand "be cool" in that context. I wondered if your Uncle Hugo was having an anger-management issue, or maybe he's been feeling feverish lately, but I didn't want to ask.

"You might also hear some other stuff about me because of this book. Bad stuff."

"Like the drugs?" I said.

The connection went silent for a couple of seconds. "You've already read it?"

"No," I said. "Wikipedia."

At that, your Uncle Hugo laughed long and loud. "OK. Well, if it's there, it must be true, right?"

I blurted out my next question. "Are you going to die?"

Your Uncle Hugo stammered, then recovered and said, "You mean ever, or—"

"From the CTE."

"Oh, that."

"It sounds pretty bad."

Your Uncle Hugo laughed again. He must use laughter as a coping device; Dr. Buckley explained this to me early in our working together, because I thought that people who laughed were making fun of me. Some of them were, of course, but not all of them. Dr. Buckley explained that laughter can be used in many ways: as an expression of joy, as a means of derision (fine word, derision), as a way of masking insecurity or doubt. I don't think your Uncle Hugo was making fun of me.

"Well, it is pretty bad. But I'm getting good care, and my symptoms aren't bad, at least not yet. I have to hope treatments improve before things get worse. All I can do, really."

I didn't say anything. A few moments of silence passed through our conversation, and then your uncle spoke again, softly this time.

"It's a hell of a thing, though, isn't it? I never got hit very much in most of my fights. That was my thing, defense. And here I am, almost thirty-nine years old—"

"Your birthday is Sunday!" I said. "That's the day I get back."

Your uncle laughed yet again. "How'd you know that? Wikipedia?"

"Of course."

"OK. Anyway, I've got this thing inside my head that could take everything away from me. It makes you wonder."

I think your Uncle Hugo was speaking rhetorically, but I had to ask.

"Wonder what?" I said.

"If I've got this thing, what is going on with all of the guys I knocked out?"

CLOSING THOUGHT

In one of the YouTube videos your Uncle Hugo appears in, he talks about the "controlled violence" of a boxing match. He describes how he can bring himself to inflict pain on another human being without actually disliking that person.

"I try to imagine that there's one thing in this world that both of us want," he said. "And it's either him or me who's going to get it. If he gets it, he's going to be happy for the rest of his life and I'm going to be miserable for the rest of mine. If I get it, i'm the happy one. If there were two things and we could be equally happy, I don't know that I could do this. But there's one thing, and I have to hurt him to get it. That's what I think about."

I like your Uncle Hugo, but this is horrifying to me.

73

I've never been in a fight. One time, I was in Bozeman, Montana, and a man punched me in the face for no reason. That wasn't a fight, though, because there was no provocation and no retaliation.

I can't imagine striking another man in anger. I don't want to imagine it. I don't know how your uncle did it.

TRAVELOGUE, DAY 1

Your mother had her doubts that Scott Shamwell would be on time—"He's such a knucklehead," she said, and I laughed because "knucklehead" is a pretty funny visual if you allow yourself to think of the literal parts of the word. But sure enough, he pulled up to our house at 5:46 a.m., and we were on the road by 6, as we planned. Your mother shouldn't have worried. When Scott Shamwell worked at the *Billings Herald-Gleaner*, he was a pressman. His entire job was to get the newspaper printed on time. Scott Shamwell is good at meeting deadlines.

It was decided that at each stop for gas or for food, I would alternate between riding in the front seat with Scott Shamwell and riding in the backseat with your mother. We hired Scott Shamwell to do all the driving, although I was not inclined to be rigid about that. After all, it's my Cadillac DTS and I'm a very safe driver.

Just outside town, Scott Shamwell turned the radio dial to his favorite station, which plays "nuclear-annihilation death metal," as he puts it. The frenetic (love that word) guitars and loud drums assaulted us in the backseat, and your mother began yelling above the noise, "No, no, no, no, NO!" Finally, Scott Shamwell heard her and turned down the volume.

"What's wrong?" he asked.
"We are not listening to that," she said.
"Why?"
"I'm carrying precious cargo," she said (she was alluding to you, kid), "and I'm not subjecting my child to that infernal noise."
"Ah, man. This sucks."
I tried to be helpful. "I've programmed a playlist for our trip on my bitchin' iPhone," I told him.
"Like what?"
"I have R.E.M. for me."
"Sissy-ass wimp pop."
I went on. "I have lots of old country music for Sheila. Merle Haggard. Waylon Jennings. Conway Twitty."
"Old-man hairspray claptrap crap." I had to giggle when Scott Shamwell said this. It's like he was just uttering random nouns.
"I have some songs for you, too," I said.
"Oh?"
"Yes. I know you like metal music, so I downloaded songs from bands like Warrant and Skid Row and Cinderella. I even have one from a band called Poison. That's a bad-ass name."
"Don't you cuss around me, Edward," your mother said.
"Are you fucking kidding me?" Scott Shamwell said.
"Scott!" Your mother sat up in the backseat and grabbed Scott Shamwell's head rest. "Now listen to me, you two. I will not have cussing on this trip. I'm going to start fining each of you a dollar when you cuss. Scott, your two thousand dollars will be gone by this time tomorrow if you don't watch yourself."
I sat back, chastened (also a fine word). Your mother stared down Scott Shamwell through the rearview mirror. Scott Shamwell waggled his fingers on the steering wheel.
"I should have asked for three thousand," he said.

At 10:07 a.m., we reached Casper, Wyoming, leaving us just 177.8 miles short of Cheyenne. We pulled off Interstate 25 to have a late breakfast at an International House of Pancakes restaurant. In the past year, I have lost forty-two pounds and have been able to control my Type II diabetes mostly through eating right, so restaurant pancakes are a rare treat for me.

Scott Shamwell tore into a steak omelet while I watched snow blow across the parking lot.

"Damn, the wind in this town," he said. He looked quickly to your mother. "I mean, darn."

She smiled. "You're forgiven."

"I drive through here a lot," I said, remembering my three trips dating to December 20th, 2011. "The wind's been blowing every time."

"Edward's parents used to live here," your mother said.

"Get out," Scott Shamwell said.

My mouth was full of pancakes as I protested. "No. It's too cold outside."

Scott Shamwell and your mother laughed at that one.

It was too cold. I wasn't kidding.

We were nearly to Chugwater (I love that town name), one hundred and thirty-four miles from Casper, when Scott Shamwell told us about his father and brother and their trouble with the federal government. It came in response to a question from your mother, who was typically blunt.

"Scott," she said, "are you a drug dealer?"

I cringed. I'm not one to talk around things—I hate when people do that—but I had to think there was a better way to approach this subject.

Scott Shamwell, though, didn't appear to be bothered by your mother's directness.

"No," he said. "I'm not. A lot of people think I am, though."

She didn't have to ask him anything else. The rest came out.

"I knew even when I was a little kid that I didn't want to stay in Musselshell County," he said. "That's probably the worst thing about being there now. I tried to go to college, but my mom got sick with the cancer, and I knew my dad wouldn't take care of her the right way, so I came home. Once I saw her back to health, I figured I'd better stick close, but I couldn't live there, so I got me a place in town and started working at the *Herald-Gleaner*."

He drove on, not saying anything. We didn't say anything, either.

"I knew what they were doing. I mean, a couple of dirt-poor farmers start buying new cars, you figure out pretty quick that they probably didn't get them with the crop money, you know? I didn't think it was any of my concern. It's not like they would have listened to me, anyway, if I'd told them they were doing something wrong. I just never figured the feds would put the finger on me, too, or try to. They must look at us and say, 'These hayseed dumbfucks are all the same.'"

He reached into his shirt pocket and pulled out a crumpled dollar bill. He put it in the center console of the Cadillac DTS.

"Sorry about the cussing, Sheila," he said.

"Keep your dollar," she said.

I reached for the bill and handed it back to him. "I'm sorry this is happening to you."

"It's just weird," he said. "You know, we've talked before about our old men, how different they are from us. I'm probably more disappointed in my brother. You know, I looked up to him. I wanted to be like him. It sucks ass to be ashamed of your own brother."

He pushed the dollar back into the console.

"Sorry again."

CLOSING THOUGHT

We stopped for the night at the Little America resort on the south side of Cheyenne. That will put us in good position for the drive across the state line and into Colorado in the morning.

By the time you read this, you may well already know what I'm about to tell you. Cheyenne is the capital city of Wyoming. You would think Billings, where we live, would be the capital of Montana, since it's by far the largest city. But the capital of Montana is Helena, which doesn't make sense to me. It's way smaller than Billings and isn't even on the main highway that runs through the state. I don't like Missoula, a place where people wear a lot of sandals and are kind of snobby, but it would be a better choice than Helena. Billings, though, would be the best choice. Get used to it, kid: A lot of things in this life don't make much sense.

CHEYENNE FACTS

Population: 59,446

Square miles: 24.63

Density: 2,425.2 people per square mile

Elevation: 6,062 feet

Motto: Magic City of the Plains. (Interestingly, Billings, Montana, where you will live, is called The Magic City. Personally, I think whoever came up with that name promised too much.)

I'm up again, little one.

Your father is snoring, which he tends to do when he's not in his own bed. He's what we call a creature of habit. I'd like to blame him for my sleeplessness, but it's not his fault. I think I would be awake anyway.

We got into Cheyenne early, and that was nice, because I was able to go for a swim. It felt so good, letting the water do all the work of carrying us for a while. You're not even the size of a peach, but even that small size added to my body makes a difference. I'm not heavyset like your father, so every little ounce taxes me in ways it wouldn't tax him. I will spare you the hundreds of other ways that pregnancy is disproportionately hard on the mother, because I know the one way that it brings me joy: I can talk to you, like I did in the pool, and really feel that you know what you're hearing, because you and I are connected in a way that your father will never know. I will not lord this over him, but it's true. And that's why I got so angry with Scott about the loud music. I have this monster urge to protect you from all things scary and disturbing during this special time we are having together. How I long to feel you move inside me. I know that's coming, and I'm so ready for it.

Your father has taken the lead in imparting life lessons to you, and he's doing a fine job, but when I think of Scott, I'm reminded of something I think it's important for you to know. I was wrong about him. He's a good man. I may never accept his manners, but I feel like I'm getting to know his heart. Your dad was a little rough around the edges when I met him, too, and look how that's turned out.

We'll be in Cheyenne Wells tomorrow, and I'm nervous. But I'm also at peace, if those two things can co-exist.

I love you,
Your mother

TRAVELOGUE, DAY 2

Seven minutes into our drive, we reached the Wyoming Colorado
state line, and your mother asked Scott Shamwell to pull over
so we could get some pictures. The shoulder of the highway was
iced over from all the storms we've had this winter, and I held
your mother's hand so she didn't slip and fall. She's not usually
one to let me be protective of her like that, but we've both been
much more careful since we found out about you.

We took three pictures. In one, your mother and I kissed in
front of the WELCOME TO COLORFUL COLORADO sign, and then after
Scott Shamwell snapped that picture, I stole seven more kisses
from your mother so we could stay consistent. Your mother took
a picture of me and Scott Shamwell with our arms around each
other and both of us on our tippy-toes, trying to be taller in the
picture. Scott Shamwell had no chance. I'm six feet, four inches
tall, a good six inches taller than he is. Finally, I took one of Scott
Shamwell with his arm around your mother. We will put them in
a scrapbook for you.

After that bit of tomfoolery (odd term meaning "silliness"),
we settled into mostly quiet. Your mother napped against my
shoulder. I don't think she's getting much sleep, and this morning

she threw up again. You're a lot of trouble, kid. I hope you're worth it. I think you will be. Scott Shamwell did his part by driving, and I think he's even starting to like the R.E.M. music that shows up on my playlist. I gave him full control of the bitchin' iPhone, and he started skipping the songs I picked out for him. However, I did catch him humming along to "It's The End of the World As We Know It (And I Feel Fine)." He looked in the rearview mirror and saw that I was grinning, and he said, "I still hate these guys. They suck donkey butt."

"I know you do, Scott Shamwell," I said. "Way to avoid a one-dollar fine." He and I cracked up about that.

I looked out the window a lot and remembered another time that I drove along this route, on December 14th, 2011, with my good friend Kyle Middleton. He was just twelve years old then, and his parents, Donna and Victor Hays, had allowed him to visit Colorado with me because he was going through a hard time and needed to be with a friend. We argued about Tim Tebow, because Kyle claimed at the time that he was the best quarterback in the NFL, which was laughable then and is even more laughable now because Tim Tebow isn't even in the league anymore. That was a good time with a good friend, and I liked that I was being made to think about him on this trip.

Kyle is almost fifteen years old now—in fact, I just remembered that he will turn fifteen on Sunday, the same day my brother Hugo Hunter turns thirty-nine. I will have to send him a present while we're on this trip. Anyway, now that Kyle is almost fifteen, he's smart enough to know how wrong he was about Tim Tebow. Kyle has turned into a star athlete; he was the quarterback of his freshman football team and the leading scorer on his basketball team. His mother sends me pictures of him from time to time, and it's astounding how fast he's grown. She tells me he's just an inch shorter than I am now, and as I thought about him, it made me wistful for when Kyle and his mother lived across the street from me and we would measure him monthly against the side of my garage, recording his growth. I haven't thought about that in a while. Kyle and his mother and his stepfather moved away to Boise, Idaho, and then I moved to Cheyenne Wells to be with your mother, and then she and I moved back to Billings, Montana.

I remember a time when I had no greater desire than for things to just remain the same. They never do, of course. I wonder what your mother expects to accomplish in Cheyenne Wells. That's probably not the same, either.

We drew closer to Denver, and Scott Shamwell pulled over at a gas station along Interstate 25 so I could pee. When I got back in the car, I moved to the front seat opposite him. Your mother was coming out of her sleep.

"I feel better," she said. She drummed her fingers on the leather seats. I guess she was anxious. I would be.

Scott Shamwell was looking through the sunroof at the sky. We'd been fortunate with the weather so far; a driving trip in this country, in the heart of winter, wasn't always this smooth. I was getting by with a light jacket, and sunlight had broken through the cloud cover that had hovered over us from Cheyenne.

Scott Shamwell pushed his sunglasses onto the tip of his nose and arched his eyebrows twice to move them up the bridge. "A good day for driving," he said.

"Let's get to it, then," your mother said.

Yep, she was anxious, all right.

We swung east around Denver on I-470, brushing past the airport and on to Interstate 70. Now that I've been to Colorado several times, I have to say that my favorite part of Denver is how the vast flatlands to the east run toward it, colliding with the mountains that people (well, not everybody, but most people, although I can't prove that empirically) think of when they hear the city's name. We headed into a wide prairie, filled with scrub brush and dirt and dustings of snow here and there. I turned in my seat and reached for your mother's hand. I wished I'd remained back there with her.

Just outside Limon, your mother pointed to the westbound lanes of I-70 and said, "There. There was where you crashed the car," and Scott said, "Oh, yeah, I forgot about that." I wish I could forget about it. I ran into the back of a snowplow during a heavy snowstorm on December 16th, 2011, and I got hurt really bad. I broke my ribs, which is just about the most painful thing I've ever experienced, and I lacerated my spleen and had some other minor injuries, like a concussion. To make matters even worse, I received a $562 traffic ticket from Officer Jonathon Hunter of the Colorado Highway Patrol for my accident, which seemed excessive.

I don't recommend any of it, kid.

I'm pretty funny sometimes.

After leaving the interstate at Limon, we passed through the towns of Hugo—which made me think of my new brother and almost caused me to spill the beans (idiom) to Scott Shamwell—and Kit Carson. We were getting close now. As we continued on, I counted off the twenty-five miles remaining to Cheyenne Wells. At the fifteenth of those miles, I turned to your mother and said, "Are you going to want to stop?"

"Why?" Scott Shamwell said. "There's nothing here."

"No, just go." Your mother had a different look about her, a nervousness that I don't often see. I get nervous sometimes, but it's a rare display from your mother, who really is a fearless woman. I didn't know what was occupying her thoughts, but I could make a good guess. Guesses generally fall far short of the mark I demand for information, but an informed guess can often be trusted. This was such a case.

Seven miles from Cheyenne Wells, on August 7th, 1997, your mother's parents—your grandparents, Raymond and Ruby Renfro—died in a car accident, and that left your mother alone. It's a terribly sad story. It's worse than losing my own father, and that really hurt me and continues to hurt me. At least I still have my mother, and now I'm getting a new brother, too. Your mother didn't have anybody for a long time. That's one of the big reasons she's looking forward to your arrival.

I reached over the seat and held your mother's hand until we drove into Cheyenne Wells.

We came into town on the main drag, and that's when I saw something I hadn't expected: Our motel, The Derrick, still stood there. It was empty, of course, and weeds had pushed through cracks in the parking lot, but I had assumed that the railroad would level the building as soon as it was acquired. I'm usually not so lazy as to assume anything, and you can see from this anecdote why I try to avoid such things.

"Why?" I said to your mother, as if she would know what I was talking about.

"I figured," she said. "Land grab. They'll knock it down when they need the space."

She directed Scott Shamwell to the pizza restaurant and had him park there.

"You guys go eat something," she said. "I'll take the car."

Scott Shamwell handed over the keys. "I'm hungry enough to eat bigfoot's—" He looked at your mother. "—butt."

"Nice save," she said. "I'll be back for you in a couple of hours."

Scott Shamwell and I got out of the car. He headed for the restaurant door, but I lingered in the parking lot. Cheyenne Wells has a particular smell. It's not petroleum, exactly, nor is it the smell of a farm, of dirt and manure and plant life in equal measures. It's something different from that, something clean. It's a smell I don't get in Billings, Montana, with all its people and cars and industry. I closed my eyes and breathed it in. It wasn't my home for long, but it was home as long as I was here with your mother, and I realized as I stood there that I had missed it. I missed the open space and the big sky cut only by clouds and jet streams, and I missed how everything was just a short walk away. I knew your mother would be dealing with her memories now that she was back. I was surprised by how strongly mine had come on, too.

"Come on, white boy," Scott Shamwell said, and that put an end to my daydreaming. I jogged over to the door, where he stood, and we went inside.

The first person who recognized me was Sheriff Pete Amblin,

who came into the restaurant to pick up a to-go order and spotted me and Scott Shamwell at the corner booth, having some pizza. He came amblin' up (I'm pretty funny sometimes).

"Didn't expect to see you here."

"Hello, Sheriff," I said.

Sheriff Pete Amblin moved on from me to Scott Shamwell and looked him over in a way that clearly bothered my friend. That wasn't a surprise; it bothered me, too.

"Who's this?" the sheriff asked.

"King of Norway," Scott Shamwell said, offering a handshake that Sheriff Pete Amblin did not accept.

I'm pretty sure Scott Shamwell has Irish heritage, but it was still a funny thing to say. I giggled, and Sheriff Pete Amblin turned back to me.

"Your little spitfire with you?" he asked.

"Somewhere," I said.

He tilted his hat back. "I thought once she kicked the dirt of us from off her shoes, that'd be it. We'd never see her again around here."

You can see here, kid, what I've been telling you: Not many people are willing to say what they mean directly.

Scott Shamwell took a bite of pizza and then wiped his mouth with the back of his hand. "You know, Edward," he said. "I like this place. Good pizza. But there's too much pork. I don't like a lot of pork with my pizza. What do you suppose it is about this place that there's so much pork?" Every time he said the word "pork," he looked directly at Sheriff Pete Amblin, as if to punctuate the word. I wonder if Scott Shamwell was a member of Toastmasters at some point. It was an effective oratory (good word).

"This is a taco pizza," I said.

Sheriff Pete Amblin looked agitated. "You boys enjoy your lunch," he said. "Don't do anything I wouldn't do." And then he picked up his food at the counter and left.

After he left, Scott Shamwell said, "I'm gonna get laid this decade. Sorry, Sheriff."

That made me laugh.

After we ate, Scott Shamwell asked if we could take a walk. Some sunlight had broken through the clouds, and the wind—which I remembered from my time living here as an almost relentless force—was down. I said that sounded nice.

We moved out of the business district and into the clusters of houses in town. Cheyenne Wells had a neat, tended look to it that I always enjoyed when I lived here, and I think Scott Shamwell found it pleasing, too. I'd steal glances at him as we walked along, and he was giving everything we saw good consideration.

"Nice town, overbearing police aside," he said.

"Yes, it is."

It didn't take us long to clear the neighborhood and find solitude beyond the town's boundaries. Given enough time, we could have walked the fourteen miles to Kansas with no difficulty. Cheyenne Wells really is a small place. As the town dropped farther behind us, and just as I was about to suggest we turn around and go back, Scott Shamwell veered off the road and leaned against a fencepost.

"I could get used to this silence," he said.

I didn't say anything. I didn't want to intrude.

"Although," Scott Shamwell said, chuckling, "maybe I should get some cuss words out of my system before your wife the language cop gets back." He looked at me and smiled.

"TITTY-SUCKING COCKBAG!" he yelled.

"That was funny," I said.

"MONKEY-RAPING GOAT FUCKER!"

He looked at me. "You try it, Ed." Nobody calls me Ed, except Scott Shamwell. I'm not sure why that's OK, but it is.

"BALLS!" I yelled.

"Come on, man," he said. "You can do better than that."

"BALL-GOBBLING SCROTUM-SNUGGLER!"

"Yeah!" Scott Shamwell said, and then he yelled "PENIS CHEESE!" That made me break out laughing.

We're strange sometimes.

On the walk back to the restaurant, I thought about what Scott

Shamwell said about the quiet. Of course, in the next moment he was shouting funny curse words, so I had to wonder how much he valued silence. Scott Shamwell is hard to figure out sometimes.

I thought about something I'd read, about this laboratory in Minnesota that has something called an anechoic chamber. It's a room built in such a way that almost all ambient (look it up) noises are absorbed, and if you're inside the room, you can hear your own heart beating. The article I read said that in such an extreme absence of sound, people begin to hallucinate within forty-five minutes—that the mind literally begins to fall apart.

The idea of that scares me.

The article said that people need the sounds of everyday life, no matter how slight, to remain sane, whether it's the drip-drip-drip of a leaky faucet or the sound of a clock ticking or a refrigerator running or whatever. When all sound is gone, the mind struggles to orient itself.

When I read the article, it made me think of the silent treatment, something my father used to do to me when he was angry. He just wouldn't talk to me or acknowledge me for some amount of time, which was his immature way of demonstrating his displeasure. Silence is a form of torture, just like extreme noise can be. I don't need someone to talk to me much, but I do need some interaction.

There was a time in my life when I could go nearly a week without speaking to anyone. I would see Dr. Buckley, and then I'd be alone for six whole days until I saw her again. When people started coming into my life, like Donna Middleton (now Hays) and Kyle, and then Victor, her husband, and Scott Shamwell and your mother and now your Uncle Hugo, I wondered sometimes how I could handle all that noise where once I had nothing but solitude. What I came to realize is that I needed that activity, that motion from other people. I wanted it, even when I didn't know that I wanted it. It's like the article said: I need the noise to stay sane. Soon, kid, you'll be coming, and if I've learned anything about babies in my reading these past few weeks, it's that you're going to be noisy. I may have to bring out the silent treatment if you get out of line.

I'm just giving you shit, kid. I would never do that.

When we got back to the restaurant, your mother was already there, sitting at the wheel of the Cadillac DTS. She got out when she saw us approach.

"I'm done," she said. "Let's leave." She opened the backseat door and climbed in. I joined her from my side of the car.

"Already?" I said. "I thought we were going to stay another day."

"No. I don't want to. Let's go to Denver and do something fun, and then we can go home Saturday. I want to go home."

Scott Shamwell slipped into the driver's seat. "Onward to Denver," he said.

As we left town, your mother turned around in her seat and watched Cheyenne Wells fall behind us. When it was gone, she faced forward again.

"What did you guys do?" she asked.

"We took a walk," I said.

"Got harassed by the po-po," Scott Shamwell said.

Your mother nodded. "Sheriff Pete. He found me, too."

"What did he say?" I asked.

Your mother pursed her lips and shook her head. "Nothing important. I haven't listened to him in years."

"He's penis cheese," Scott Shamwell said.

That confused your mother. "What?"

"Nothing," I said. "We were being silly."

"You guys?" your mother said. "Never!"

That was sarcasm. Scott Shamwell got it before I did, and when he laughed, I laughed, too.

CLOSING THOUGHT

I hate loose ends, but I love your mother, so I have to accept that she felt compelled to change our travel plans.

Here's the new outlook, with precise mileage totals from the days already behind us:

DAY	DISTANCE	DESTINATION
Wednesday	455.8 miles	Cheyenne, Wyoming
Thursday	266.4 miles	Cheyenne Wells, Colorado
Thursday	182.7 miles	Denver, Colorado
Friday	None	Denver, Colorado
Saturday	552.1 miles	Billings, Montana

We arrived in Denver in the middle of rush-hour traffic, so it was nearly seven p.m. before we made it to a nice Marriott on California Street. I paid for a room for your mother and me, and I got Scott Shamwell his own room. It came to $537 for the two rooms, which is a lot of money, but as I've told you before, I'm fucking loaded.

Your mother and I came up to our room, showered, and engaged in sexual congress. She won't be happy that I told you that, but it was the first time since we found out about you, so it was something of a noteworthy occasion. Your mother said she wanted to engage in sexual congress while she still had the drive for it; she warned me that soon she would want to rip my face off rather than engage in sexual congress with me. I hope she was being hyperbolic about that, but if not, I will invest in a facemask.

Scott Shamwell said he was going out for something to eat and "a piece of tail, if I can find one." Your mother rolled her eyes, but more important, she smiled and she did not dock him a dollar.

He got lucky. Not in the way he was hoping, though.

Did you get that, kid? I'm pretty funny sometimes.

My beautiful child:

After I dropped off your father and his friend, I drove out of town on County Road 44, to the Fairview Cemetery. I hope it doesn't sound cold when I tell you that I don't visit my daddy and mom's graves very much. What's the point? They're dead and in the ground, and seeing where their bodies are parked is not going to make my memories of them any brighter or take away the occasional sadness I feel for having lost them.

But when we moved up to Montana last June, I was in such a state of despair that I didn't even think that I should go see them, and so we left without having done so. These several months have been, in their own way, harder on me than the actual leaving, and I've missed my parents more acutely than I have in a long time. I wanted to at least talk to them again, even if they cannot talk to me ever again.

At the cemetery, I pulled weeds from the around their double headstone, and I told them about you (they would have been so excited about you, and you would have loved them, I think). I told them that I have a good man, and that I think I can finally make a go of it in Billings. It may never be home to me the way Cheyenne Wells was, but then again, it's hard for me to imagine a home without you and your father. The where isn't so important.

I didn't have what I would call close friends. I knew a lot of people—well, pretty much everybody in such a small town, and many of them said hello to me when I got back to town. I even saw Bradley Sutherland, who might have been lucky enough to marry me if he'd been able to let go of his beer once in a while. I'm glad I recognized that he wasn't the special man for me, and I'm glad I waited for your dad. I was feeling good, and I told Bradley Sutherland he'd missed his chance, and he just laughed and wished me luck. That felt good.

I did one last thing, and here I have to admit that I technically broke the law. I went to The Derrick, the motel I owned, and I found one of the keys I'd hidden on the property in case I locked myself out. I figured the railroad wouldn't have done anything with the property by now, and I was right. The key was where I left it, and once I got inside, I was able to flip on a few lights. I guess the railroad has so much money that it doesn't mind paying the electric bill on a place that sits empty all the time.

It was strange to go through all the rooms and see them emptied of beds and furniture and TV sets. We bought all new stuff when your father moved to Cheyenne Wells to be with me, and so we were able to sell a lot of that when we decided to give up the motel, allowing us to recoup at least some of the money we'd put out. I just wanted you to have been there, even in your gestating state. My parents built the place, and I ran it for a long time, and whoever you end up being will be influenced, at least in part, by the fact that this was my home and my passion.

At the front desk, or where the front desk used to be, I left a short note:

To whoever finds this:

From 1968 to 2013, my family owned this motel. It was very important to us. I write this to let you know that we existed.

Sheila Renfro Stanton

That sounds kind of silly now that I say it out loud to myself, but it seemed important to do at the time. I was actually relieved to see your father and his friend Scott return to the restaurant so we could leave. It's strange that I was so compelled to return to Cheyenne Wells and then was so eager to leave again. I can explain it only by saying that I felt like I would get trapped by the past if I spent another minute there.

Someday, when you're old enough, I bet you'll know what that feels like.

I love you,
Your mother

TRAVELOGUE, DAY 3

I received an e-mail message from your Uncle Hugo on my bitchin' iPhone at 5:59 a.m., telling me that he would be on the CBS morning show segment at about 8 a.m. Mountain time. I wouldn't have known about this if your mother hadn't already been awake, so that was fortunate. I woke up, put on some fresh clothes and deodorant and went to Scott Shamwell's room at 7:02 a.m. to see if he would like to have breakfast with us. I didn't knock, though, because Scott Shamwell had put out the DO NOT DISTURB sign and had affixed a sticky note to it with this handwritten addendum: "MONKEYSPANKERS!"

I guess he didn't want breakfast.

I went back downstairs to our room and collected your mother, and we had a nice breakfast in the hotel restaurant. Blintzes. That's "a thing," as Kyle Middleton tells me sometimes when I talk to him on the phone. I reminded your mother that Kyle's birthday is just two days away (as is your Uncle Hugo's), and she said we could send him a card with some cash, then call him Sunday. I used to get Kyle really nice presents—I even made him an awesome three-wheeled vehicle several years ago, when he was just a little boy—but he's become difficult to shop for as he's gotten older. Cash will probably mean more to him than any present I could find. That's what your mother said, anyway, and she's a very smart woman.

At 8 a.m. sharp, we turned on the television and turned the channel to the CBS morning show. After a few minutes of commercials, the show came back on, and there was your Uncle Hugo, sitting at a round table with the hosts of the show. He looked good. His hair was slicked back, and he had on a gray suit with a gray shirt and a gray tie. Your mother called that "monochromatic," which may be the best word I've heard this year.

One of the hosts held up his book and talked about how your uncle was an Olympic medalist, how his book had just come out and that the reviews had been good. The host said it was an "unflinching" look at boxing and drug addiction.

The interview went like this:

Host No. 1: "Now, you've been scanned by researchers who say you probably have CTE."

Your Uncle Hugo: "That's correct."

Host No. 1: "But they don't know for sure?"

Your Uncle Hugo: "No. The only reliable test can be done only after death. So I'm going to wait to take that one." Your Uncle Hugo is pretty funny sometimes.

Host No. 2: "So here you are, you're not even forty years old, and you're looking at the possibility of debilitating neurological disease. What's that like? Is it scary?"

Your Uncle Hugo: "Sometimes it is. I like where I am right now. I've worked hard to find a peaceful place in my life. The idea that something could unravel that—and that I caused this to happen some time ago—that's pretty disturbing, if I allow myself to think about it too much."

Host No. 1: "So, what, you just don't think about it?"

Your Uncle Hugo: "I try not to."

Host No. 2: "In the book, you write movingly about what it's like to grow up raised by women, your late mother and grandmother. Did you ever know your father?"

Your Uncle Hugo: "I know who he is, yeah. I guess I even met him once. But, no, I didn't know him."

Host No. 1: "The book alludes to a brother you didn't know you had. One of the intriguing things is that, as of the book's writing, you were wrestling with whether to contact him. Have you?"

Your Uncle Hugo: "Yes, we've met once. I like him, very much."

Your mother wrapped an arm around my back and hugged me as we sat on the edge of the bed, watching.

Host No. 2: "Can you tell us about him?"

Your Uncle Hugo: "He's a private man, with a family. I think I'm going to let him remain private, if you don't mind."

Host No. 1: "Finally, we have to ask you about this."

Your Uncle Hugo: "Sure."

Host No. 1: "The sports press has focused on what you wrote about your two title fights. The first one didn't happen because you succumbed to cocaine the night before the fight and faked an injury—"

Your Uncle Hugo: "There was no faking. I intentionally broke my wrist."

Host No. 1: "Right. Sorry. And the second one, you had to lose several pounds the day before the fight to make weight because you'd been binging on food so you didn't go after cocaine again. You were sluggish in the ring and got beat. Some columnists are saying that you defrauded fight fans. What's your response to that charge?"

Your Uncle Hugo: "I guess if I was someone who bought a ticket to one of those fights, or ordered it on pay-per-view, I'd be mad. But you know, the first one, all those people got their money back. In the end, I only cheated myself. The second one is a little trickier, because I did show up, but I didn't fight very well. If anybody wants an apology, I'm happy to offer it, but I'd ask who really got hurt by my addiction. I did. My son did. My relationships did. And we're all still trying to rebuild the damage done. Everybody else has moved on to other diversions."

Host No. 2: "Knowing what you know now, if you had to do it again, would you be a boxer?"

Your Uncle Hugo: "No."

I leaned into your mother. I said, almost whispered, "I'm proud of my brother." *My brother*. I never dreamed I would utter those two words together. Why would I have dreamed that? Dreams are unreliable anyway. I'd rather have one good fact than a million dreams.

I didn't see Scott Shamwell until 1:13 p.m., and by then your mother had left the hotel to go shopping for some maternity clothes. I asked her if she wanted me to go with her, and she said, "I do not. You'll see me in those dowdy clothes soon enough." Your mother likes the word "dowdy." It is a good word.

When Scott Shamwell came into the room, it was obvious he'd showered, but he didn't look refreshed. His eyes were bloodshot, and he moved slowly into the room, plopping onto the bed and dropping his torso until his head came to rest atop the mattress.

"Long night?" I asked, even though I was sure I knew the answer. Also, this has nothing to do with physical measurements. In fact, no one night is any longer than another. It just seems that way if you're emotional.

"I got whiskey-drunk," he said.

I'd never heard that phrase before. I like it, although Scott Shamwell didn't seem to be fond of the effects of it.

"I need to eat something," he said. "Have you had lunch?"

"No."

"I'll buy you lunch."

"I'll buy it, Scott Shamwell."

He sat up and looked at me with his red eyes.

"I'm buying lunch," he said.

I withdrew from the fight.

We walked a block down California Street and found a place that made big burritos. Scott Shamwell said he needed something "big and spicy and thermonuclear" dropped into his gut to neutralize the alcohol. I think Scott Shamwell says such things for attention, and he certainly got it while we were in line at the burrito place.

The couple in front of us gave Scott Shamwell a nasty look, and the person who prepared his burrito wasn't happy, either, because Scott Shamwell kept haranguing him about his building method.

"Dude, you're making that thing look like a bunch of rail cars. I don't want the sour cream as a damn caboose! Slather that stuff on top of each other."

I really like the word "slather."

We sat down, and Scott Shamwell put his arms around his tray like he was protecting it from a marauding horde.

"I'm too old for this shit," he said.

"Burritos?"

"No, drinking myself silly." He used his fork to wrench off a corner of his burrito, and he lifted that into his mouth. I sipped my diet soda through a straw and watched him. "Thank you for asking me to come on this trip, Ed buddy. You know, I thought it was just going to be fun to get away from all the shit for a few days, but it's been a lot more than that."

Scott Shamwell caught me mid-bite with that observation, one that demanded my participation. I held up my left index finger, letting him know I'd be with him soon, while I chewed my food, swallowed it, and chased it down with more soda.

"What happened, Scott Shamwell? Is that why you got whiskey-drunk?"

He dug into his burrito with more vigor. "Yeah, I guess it was, kind of. I found this bar down the street, and I did a shot to my health. I always do that. And then I did one for my mom's health, and then one for my father, and one for my brother. I'm four shots in at this point, you know, and I've been there maybe twenty minutes. The room got a little blurry."

Scott Shamwell put his fork down.

"And so I'm sitting there thinking, and I'm like, 'Why am I drinking for those two dumb assholes?' You know? They've got me in a big mess, one I didn't ask for, so why do I feel this pull of loyalty toward them? That's what I started thinking about last night, only by the time I thought of it, I was in no condition for thinking. So, really, all I could do was drink some more."

That was some strange logic from Scott Shamwell. Even more strange: I completely understood what he meant. Scott Shamwell was wrestling with the obligation to family versus the obligation to self. Dr. Buckley and I talked about this many times, especially after my father died, when I wanted to understand him with an urgency I didn't feel when he was alive. I struggled with that because it made me feel guilty. Dr. Buckley explained to me that it wasn't my fault, that I had come to realize only after his death that this was something I needed. I was in no position to diagnose what Scott Shamwell's needs were—I would rather let Dr. Bryan Thomsen or another qualified psychologist do that—but as I sat there, I had this thought: Scott Shamwell can't save his father and brother from the consequences of their actions, but he can save himself.

The next time he spoke, I realized I was correct.

"I'm getting out of there," he said. "Mom'll probably want to stay on the farm for as long as she can, but those asshole feds are going to take it away. My dad and brother can reap the whirlwind, for all I care. I'm getting on with it."

On the walk back to the hotel, I pulled out my bitchin' iPhone. I had two text messages waiting for me. The first, from your Uncle Hugo, asked if I'd watched him on TV and how he did. I wrote back: "You were great." The second, from your mother, wanted to know where I was. I called her.

"We're just coming into the lobby," I said.

"Scott's with you?"

"Yes."

"How's he doing?"

I looked over at my friend. "He's doing OK." Scott smiled from behind his sunglasses and kissed his own bicep.

"I went up to his room looking for you. Nice note on the door. Tell him he owes me a dollar."

I turned to Scott Shamwell as we waited for the elevator. "She says you owe her a buck."

He took the bitchin' iPhone from me, held it up to his mouth, and said, "Pishposh."

That's a word meaning "nonsense."
Scott Shamwell is pretty funny sometimes.

While your mother was shopping, she found a suitable birthday card for Kyle, and she suggested I give him a hundred-dollar bill. That was easy enough, as I am fucking loaded. Donna will get on my case about the gift and say it's too much, but it really isn't, and besides, what can she do about it now? These past several years have taught me much about how we move through each others' lives. Five years ago, I couldn't have imagined a time when Kyle and I wouldn't be the closest of friends—I wouldn't have even wanted to imagine it, because imagination is a poor substitute for verifiable fact. But this June, it will be three years since he and his parents moved away from Billings, Montana, and it's been a year and eighteen days since I last saw him. He's growing up now, and he has other friends, and that's the way it goes. The great likelihood is that you will pull away from me, too, once you get to an age where you're a little more independent and I don't seem all that wise.

I'm thinking about that now, and this further thought occurs to me: I don't want to see that day with you. And still another thought crashes in: I'm wishing the days away now, hoping you will arrive so you're a real baby, someone we can hold and love, someone who poops and pees and cries and sleeps, and as soon as you're here, I'm going to want the days to slow down, so I don't miss a thing and so I can savor the moments I have with you. I'm going to want time to slow to a crawl so I don't get old too fast, so I'm not this ancient man watching as you receive your high school diploma, go off to college, get married, have your own children. I don't want to die and leave you, the way my own father left me.

And, finally, I have still another thought: If I'm thinking all of these things, I must love you after all.

How the hell did that happen?

I have no closing thought.

I'm all thought out.

My beautiful child ...
Can I say it? YES! I knew he would figure it out. I just knew if I gave him time, he would figure it out.

I don't know how old you'll be when you finally read this, or if you'll read it all, but I want to say this: Your father always figures it out. He has his own methods, and he thinks in some mighty peculiar ways, but he always arrives at the answer he needs. I told him one time that he wasn't the special man to understand my specialness. It killed me to say those words, but it's what I thought at the time. And I was wrong. He did understand. He just had to get there in his own way.

You're going to be so lucky to have this man as your father.

Love,
Your Mom

TRAVELOGUE, DAY 4

An hour and forty-two minutes after we left downtown Denver, we crossed the state line into Wyoming. I searched your mother's face for some indication of her feelings at leaving her home state for a second time, but she didn't show me anything.

"Do you think we'll go back to Colorado?" I asked.

"Maybe," she said. "I don't know. I'm just ready to get home."

Her invocation (nice!) of the word "home" pleased me. For a while, I'd been laboring under the fear that she would never warm up (idiom) to living in Montana with me. I found hope in her statement. Hope isn't an indication of fact, of course, but I've learned that it can be a good thing. It can be the best thing, sometimes.

"No more crying downstairs?" I asked.

She looked into the rearview mirror at Scott Shamwell's face, and he did the smart thing by keeping his eyes fixated on the road. She turned to me.

"Edward, I'm pregnant," she said.

"I know."

"No, you may be aware of this fact, but you don't know." She wheeled herself around in the backseat and faced me. "You don't know what it's like to barf every morning. You don't know what it's like to just break out crying because your stupid emotions are all over the place. You don't know what it's like to feel contented, and then violent, and then ill, all in the space of an hour. You just don't know, OK? I can tell you, but you'll never know, goddammit."

My eyes must have opened wide, because your mother stopped short on her harangue (good word) and said, "Did I just cuss?"

Scott Shamwell opened the console where he'd been stashing dollar bills to satisfy your mother's penalties and said, "I'll just take this one back, I guess."

"Yes, you cussed," I said.

"Shit," your mother said, and Scott Shamwell retrieved another dollar bill.

"You know what it is?" your mother said. "I've been hanging out with you guys too long."

Scott Shamwell boomed out a laugh from the front seat. "My work will not be done until you're wearing a Black Sabbath T-shirt," he said.

I wasn't sure what he meant by that, but it drew a giggle from your mother, so I decided I had better laugh along, too.

"This is why I call Wyoming the state in my way," Scott Shamwell said, pounding his fist on the steering wheel. "Look at this. Nothing but flatland and blowing snow. How am I supposed to see in this slantwise stuff?"

We had moved up into the interior of the state through the morning hours and the early afternoon, and then the weather had turned on us. When we reached Casper, I'd wanted to have Scott Shamwell drive us past the old house where my mother and father lived right after they got out of college and my father went to work for an oil company. By then, though, the snow was turning heavy and clumpy, and Scott Shamwell suggested that we push on before things got worse.

As it turned out, we had no way of avoiding that. Snow accumulated in the roadway, and visibility eroded. We needed four hours to cover the one hundred and twelve miles between

Casper and Buffalo. The sun was down, and the Highway Patrol was closing up the interstate. We had no choice but to find a place to stay in Buffalo.

We were able to get a single room at a motel right off Interstate 25, and after we checked in Scott Shamwell fought the wind as he walked across the street to a convenience store and bought us beer (non-alcoholic for your mother and me) and Funyuns and saltwater taffy and beef jerky.

"The kid's gonna pop out of there a junk-food junkie," he said as he spread the food out on his double bed. I made some mental calculations. The salt and sugar would mess up my blood glucose readings, I was sure. Well, that's not true. I suspected. I would find out the facts of the situation soon enough.

Scott Shamwell lifted his can of beer. "To a successful adventure." I clinked cans with him, but your mother did not.

"It's not successful yet," she said. "We still have to make it back home."

"We will," Scott Shamwell said. "Guy on the radio said it'll be clear enough tomorrow."

"I hope so. As much as I wanted to get to Colorado, that's how much I want to get home."

It made me feel good to hear your mother say that, especially the word "home" again.

"Big changes," I said.

"No," she said. "Little ones. Little ones all the time. They get big when you put them all together." I think she was describing you, kid, and the effect you're having on her. On us. We're in the seventh week now. I looked at your mother's boobs, which are supposed to be getting larger. I couldn't tell with the heavy sweater she had on, and I probably won't be able to get a look at them while Scott Shamwell is here. Suddenly, I wanted to be home, too.

Scott Shamwell was on his third beer, having gulped down the first two and then crushed the cans with his fist.

"You want to know what I'm gonna do?" he asked us.

"Tell us, Scott," your mother said.

He set down his beer.

"I'm going home," he said, "and I'm telling those assholes that I'm not covering for them anymore. I'm not going to throw them under the bus, but they've gotta face what they've done. I'm putting my stuff in a trailer, and I'm moving to Billings, and I'm gonna open me a small-engine repair place, and I'm gonna do for me for once in my life."

Your mother broke into a big grin.

"Sorry about the 'assholes,' Sheila," Scott Shamwell said.

She reached across to him and clutched his hand.

It was a nice thing for her to do. It was a compassionate thing, and I think Scott Shamwell needs compassion even though he likes to act like he's tough. You're getting the best mother in the whole world, kid.

Scott Shamwell finished off a six-pack like it was nothing, and then he clambered into his bed and fell fast asleep. Your mother and I, on the other hand, remained awake late into the night as his snoring kept us from finding our own sleep. He must have adenoids the size of the moon (this is hyperbole).

"My fingers smell like onions," I whispered.

"Maybe you should have let someone else have some Funyuns," your mother said, also in a whisper.

"Didn't I?"

"No."

"That was rude of me."

"This is my point."

I giggled and then snuggled down into the covers. I don't like motel rooms. The beds are too soft or too hard, and the blankets are too rigid. For the second time that night, I wanted to go home.

I put my hand on your mother's tummy, and she slipped her own hand over mine. You're definitely in there, kid. Unlike me, your mother has a flat, muscular belly—at least she does when she's not pregnant. The little lump I felt was you.

"I've been thinking," your mother whispered. "What do you think about joining up with Scott on this business idea of his?"

Scott Shamwell, at that very moment, emitted a snort, and then he flopped over in bed. Your mother tried to cover up a sputtering laugh.

"See?" she whispered. "He thinks it's a good idea."

I'll tell you what I was thinking: I was thinking that your mother is a very smart woman. Scott Shamwell and I could open an engine-repair business together. I had the start-up money for tools and a work space, on account of the fact that I'm fucking loaded, and Scott Shamwell already had some customers.

And if we did this, I wouldn't have to go to work for Jay L. Lamb's law firm, which I knew I didn't want to do. Jay L. Lamb is married to my mother now, and while I don't dislike him the way I once did, I'd prefer to limit my interaction with him. That's just smart business, I think.

"I will talk with him," I whispered. Home lay 164.8 miles away. I couldn't wait to get there and start something new with Scott Shamwell.

"Good."

I moved my hand up your mother's stomach to her left boob. She slapped at my hand with hers.

"Edward!"

I kissed her on the cheek. "Your boobs are a little bigger, I think."

She kissed my nose. "You're bad."

I'm not really bad.

I'm just pretty sneaky sometimes.

CLOSING THOUGHT

This will be of the knowledge-that-cannot-be-empirically-proven variety and not so much of the factual variety. I'm sorry about that, kid. It happens.

My thought for you is simple. It goes like this: You never know how quickly something can change, so it's best to be prepared for anything. This is a difficult thing for me. I would rather control everything in my immediate vicinity and leave nothing to chance. This compulsion is with me every day, and it will be with me for every day I have left. It's part of who I am, Dr. Bryan Thomsen says.

And yet, I know that many of the things that are wonderful about my life have come about because of chance. I became friends with Donna and Kyle because I took a chance on letting them get to know me. I married your mother because I took a chance on living somewhere else. Scott Shamwell is ready to take a chance on living somewhere new and trying to build a new business.

Chance is hard to define with numbers and hard data.

I will never get used to that.

My hope for you is that you can find a way to embrace chance. I think you will get a lot more out of your life if you do, and I've never wanted something as much as I want that, for you.

MARCH

SEVEN WEEKS (ALMOST)

Kid, it's almost unbelievable that I haven't written to you in forty-one days. I say "almost" because it is, in fact, entirely believable. Once you look at my notebooks and see that the last entry occurred on February 9th, and once I vouch for the fact that I haven't written any other letters to you in other notebooks, you cannot reach any conclusion but this one: I went forty-one days—from February 9th to March 22nd—without writing to you.

I didn't mean to go this long, but I don't think it could have been helped. However, so I don't leave you hanging, I will fill you in on the many things that have been going on since I last wrote to you.

First, and most important, there's your ongoing development. We've been to see Dr. Arlene Haworth two times since we returned from Colorado, and you're progressing nicely, she said.

You're in Week Fourteen now, and you know what that means, right? We've crossed into the second trimester. That happened yesterday, after we saw Dr. Arlene Haworth for the second time. She said everything that should be happening with you is coming right along. You've been kicking at the insides of your mother for several weeks now—the first time happened at 7:08

p.m. on February 18th. You should have been there. (I guess you were, technically.) Your mother's eyes went wide open, and she said, "The baby! The baby! The baby kicked!" I dashed in from the kitchen and sat down beside her, and I put my hand on her tummy, and I could feel you moving around. In subsequent days, you became much more active in the womb, and your mother can certainly tell you're getting stronger. That's not a surprise, as the ninth and tenth weeks called for you to be adding muscle, bone and cartilage.

In the eleventh week, we saw Dr. Arlene Haworth, and she did a scan (called an ultrasound) of your mother's womb, and she showed us your face. Your mother said you are beautiful, but I'll be honest: It was hard for me to detect beauty in the grainy black-and-white image I saw. But you do look like a person, so that's outstanding. We asked Dr. Arlene Haworth not to tell us whether you're a boy or a girl. Your mother wants that to be a surprise, at least for us, when you're born.

Now that the first trimester screen is done and you're looking like a real person, your mother said it's OK if we start letting people know that she's pregnant. I told Scott Shamwell first, because I see him nearly every day with our new business (I can't wait to tell you more about this), and he wasn't surprised in the least because he heard us talking about it on the trip to Colorado. But now he's really embraced the news. He's started referring to himself as Bad Uncle Scott—as in, "Bad Uncle Scott wants barbecue for lunch today." I think he's pretty funny when he says things like that, and he can be your uncle if you want him to. By the time you read this, you'll have probably made a decision already.

I haven't seen your Uncle Hugo since that day at his house last month. His book has done really well, though, and for a couple of weeks he was showing up on TV talk shows and ESPN and other sports shows. *Sports Illustrated* did a big write-up about him, and so far he's kept his word about not saying anything about me. He's in California now, working with a man who wants to write his story for the movies. That would be something, wouldn't it? Your Uncle Hugo has written me six emails while he's been traveling, telling me whom he's meeting and what he's doing. It sounds like he goes to a lot of parties and dinners and has to meet a lot of different people, which I think would exhaust me. But he seems to like it. We still haven't had the blood test to determine if we're really brothers, and while I would like to square that detail away—facts are always better than supposition, after all—I'm not sure it would make a lot of difference. We think we are brothers, and we're trying to learn how to be brothers even though it's hard because we both thought we had no siblings, so what the blood test says is just a formality. For now, we're keeping it to ourselves. I haven't told Scott Shamwell or even Dr. Bryan Thomsen. I certainly haven't told my mother. My father's dalliance (I love that word) with your Uncle Hugo's mother was a source of despair for my mother, and so I've been avoiding the subject. If I find out that your Uncle Hugo is truly my brother by blood, I suppose I will have to tell her, as I will want him to come to family dinners and other events where my mother is likely to show up. She lives most of the year in Texas with Jay L. Lamb, but she does come back to Billings for special events and charities that she supports.

Oh my goodness! I can't believe I forgot to tell you that my mother, your grandmother, now knows about you.

It was actually an uncomfortable phone conversation, because she started crying and saying how happy she is. She said she's going to come to Billings so she can be here for your birth, which is scheduled for September 8th. I think that's a funny way of using the word "scheduled," since you could be born anywhere within a five-week window even in a normal pregnancy. In my world, nobody uses "scheduled" for a date that uncertain. Better to say that you're "targeted" for arrival that date, or even "possible." But not "scheduled." That's just dumb.

Your grandmother insisted on talking to your mother on the phone, and that's unusual. You might as well know the family dynamics; it will make navigation through our issues easier for you. (Incidentally, "navigation through our issues" is a Dr. Bryan Thomsen phrase that unfortunately I have adopted.) Your grandmother and your mother aren't very close. About all they have in common is that they love you and they love me. But on this phone call, I could hear your grandmother's voice, and she was still crying and telling your mother how happy she is, and your mother did her best to be nice even though your grandmother was giving her a lot of unsolicited advice about how to deal with being pregnant. Your mother doesn't like being told what to do.

Now, I must tell you this about your mother. She still cries a lot, and it's still your fault. Two days ago, I came home from a long day of putting up the sign on the shop I own with Scott Shamwell, and she was crying in the kitchen. I asked her what was wrong, and she just cried some more. She said she had been crying for two hours. I asked her why, and she said she started crying because her clothes aren't fitting well, but she kept crying for reasons she isn't sure of. (By the way, kid, teachers are probably going to tell you that you shouldn't end a sentence in a preposition, the way I just did. You have my permission to tell those teachers they are full of shit.) When we saw Dr. Arlene Haworth yesterday, I asked her about your mother's crying. Your mother wasn't happy I did that, but I felt helpless about the situation and needed to hear from an expert. Dr. Arlene Haworth said pregnancy is like dumping every emotion you've ever had out onto a table and then playing with them randomly. That was an odd and interesting way of putting it. She told your mother that it's normal, but also that if it happens too frequently that she should be notified. Your mother assured Dr. Arlene Haworth that she's fine, and I think we have to take her word for it.

Dr. Arlene Haworth did sound one note of caution. She said your mother's blood pressure is running a little high. She said it's nothing to worry about right now, but that it should continue to be monitored. I must have looked worried, because Dr. Arlene Haworth took me by the arm and said, "Don't worry, Edward. Women's bodies undergo many changes during pregnancy. Are you surprised? They're carrying a whole other life besides their own."

That's you, kid. Your mother is keeping you alive and herself alive. It makes what I'm doing—going to work every day and trying to build a business with your Bad Uncle Scott Shamwell—seem insignificant.

Insignificant or not, I must tell you about the business. When we were driving home from Buffalo, Wyoming, on February 9th, I asked Scott Shamwell what he had in mind for his business idea.

"Small engines," he said. "Boats, lawnmowers, motorcycles, ATVs, stuff like that. I've been reading up on this." Scott Shamwell was starting to get excited. He squirmed in his seat a little bit and was looking back and forth between me and the road. "There's this huge shortage of people who can fix junk like that—nobody knows how to do it anymore, and everything is so disposable these days that people just buy new things. Well, I know how to fix that stuff. Been doing it all my life. I think I can make a living and help people save some money, too."

"Where are you going to work?" I asked.

Some of the bounce went out of Scott Shamwell. "I don't have that one figured out all the way. I think I'm going to have to rent me a house and work out of there for a little while, till I get the scratch to buy or rent a workshop."

I smiled at him. He looked at me.

"What?" he said.

"I have an idea."

"What?"

"It's a great idea."

"What?"

I was just thinking about where I wanted to start when your mother said, from the backseat, "He wants to go into business with you, Scott."

I turned around and glared at her. That was a dirty trick.

"You do?" Scott said.

"Yes," I said. "I think I can help with the work, and I can definitely help find a place where we can do the work, because I'm—"

"Fucking loaded," your mother and Scott Shamwell said simultaneously.

Scott Shamwell put a dollar bill in the center console, and then your mother did, too. And then we all laughed, because that was really funny.

Two days after we got back, I drove up to Roundup to help Scott Shamwell pack up his belongings and move to Billings. His father and his brother, Studd and Studd Jr., were there, as they're out of jail on bond while waiting to be sentenced on federal drug charges. They didn't help us load the trailer Scott Shamwell had connected to his Ford pickup. They just followed us around and gave Scott Shamwell a hard time.

"You're breaking your mother's heart," Studd said to his son at one point.

Scott Shamwell never broke stride. He kept lugging boxes out to the trailer and packing them into it.

"I know for a fact that's not true," he said. "She told me herself to do what I needed to do."

Neither Studd nor Studd Jr. talked to me, which was all right, as far as I was concerned. I wouldn't have known what to say. When we got everything packed up, Scott climbed into the driver's seat of his pickup.

"I'll be back a couple of times a week to check on Ma," he told them. "And I'll be in court on the twenty-eighth of next month."

"Don't do me no favors," Studd Jr. said. He looked like a shorter, more corpulent (good word) version of his brother. Same red hair. Same arms that looked like giant freckled hams.

"Don't you worry," Scott Shamwell said. "I won't."

I ran over to the Cadillac DTS and climbed in, and then I followed Scott Shamwell out to the highway. I can tell you this now, kid: I wasn't sure Scott Shamwell had it in him to leave, but he did it, and I was proud of him. Family can be a powerfully persuasive factor for some people, and I knew that to be the case with Scott Shamwell. Kid, that's the case with me, too. My father used to have Jay L. Lamb send letters scolding me for how I spent money. My mother tried to control my love life when I was old enough to make my own decisions. Just because someone loves you, it doesn't mean that person will act in your best interest. Just because you love someone, it doesn't mean you can help them with their troubles. I think that's the decision Scott Shamwell finally came to with his own family. Studd and Studd Jr. are going to prison. He can't stop that for them. Moreover (also a nice word), he doesn't want to. That's a hard but necessary decision on his part.

Scott Shamwell moved into our basement for three days, until we found a nice garage on the industrial end of town that we could rent. We had a difficult time finding Scott Shamwell a house to rent, because he didn't have much money or good credit, and unfortunately his surname is well-known in Billings for all the wrong reasons. After we found the garage and paid a year's rent on it, he said he would throw up a hammock in the office and be just fine. That turned out to be a good solution, because Scott Shamwell doesn't sleep well, so he was able to work on getting the place ready at all hours.

We named our business S&S Motorworks (Shamwell and Stanton on the official paperwork filed with the state, because Scott Shamwell had the idea so he should go first). We bought a big sign that went on the front of the garage, we bought tools, a cash register with a credit-card reader, business cards, and advertising in the *Billings Herald-Gleaner*. One of the best things that happened is your Uncle Hugo put something on his Facebook page, which has several thousand people watching it. It said, *If you're in Billings and need small-engine repair, go to S&S Motorworks on North 14th Street.* That simple line brought fifty-two people in the first week we were open.

I come home sweaty and greasy and tired most nights, and sometimes I come in late. Sometimes I come in and I find your mother crying. Sometimes I come home and find her asleep, and I'm happy for that, because I know she doesn't sleep enough. I worry about the crying. Of course I do. But on the nights when I come home and I'm dirty and yucky, and your mother has dinner ready and she laughs with me and asks me about my day— when that happens, I feel really good. I feel like we're heading somewhere good. And you're coming along with us, kid. When we go to childbirth classes and learn what it's going to be like on the day you arrive, I sometimes look around at the other couples there and realize how much we all have in common. There are fathers and mothers and, inside the womb, gestating children like you. I haven't often felt like I had things in common with other people, kid, so thank you for changing that for me.

CLOSING THOUGHT

It costs a lot of money to start a business. Most people aren't as fortunate as Scott and I have been. They have to borrow money—which means they have to pay it back, with interest—when they start a business. I had the money to start S&S Motorworks, on account of the fact that I'm fucking loaded.

Here's a look at what it cost to start our business:

	AMOUNT		AMOUNT
Security deposit	$3,000	Signage****	$1,050
One year's rent	$16,000*	Newspaper ad	$860
Tools	$37,225**	Uniforms	$100
Cash register	$3,600	Supplies	$1,210
Business cards (500)	$85***	Grand total	$63,130

*—Rent is actually $1,500 a month, or $18,000 a year, but I got a discount for paying an entire year in advance. You'll often hear people say that the easiest way to save money is to have money. This is what those people are talking about. (Also, remember what I said about prepositions at the end of a sentence.)

**—I got 74.2 percent of our tools at an estate sale. Had I paid full retail price for all of our tools, this number would have been much higher.

***—I could have gotten five hundred business cards for twenty bucks, but they would have been flimsy cards on a weak paper stock. Here's something you need to remember, kid: If you're going to do something, do it right and do it with class. This is why I drive a Cadillac DTS, and it's also why I bought business cards on heavy stock with a matte finish.

****—"Signage" is a stupid word.

My dear child ...

I'm glad your father is writing to you again. He would have never forgiven himself if he'd dropped the ball on this. If you're reading his letters in order, you're probably picking up on the fact that he's getting more comfortable with you all the time. I'm glad he's seeing it through.

I want to tell you a little bit about my emotions. Your father talked about them some, and he got things right as far as I told him, but these feelings that overwhelm me are just so much bigger than anything I can describe to anyone. It's sometimes like any task, no matter how mundane, becomes THE BIGGEST THING I'VE EVER FACED IN THE WORLD. "Overwhelmed" is the right word. Sometimes, I just have to sit down and cry until I feel like I can face things. Sometimes I have to call your father and tell him to bring me something a milkshake from Sonic, a pair of extra-large yoga pants, pistachios. He fought me the first couple of times—"Sheila, I'm busy"—but I screamed at him and he brought me what I needed. I hate to be manipulative, but it works, so I do it.

Having Scott in our basement was tough, even though it was only three days. For one thing, that's my sanctuary. For another... well, let's just say a little bit of Scott goes a long way. He's so crude, so dirty in his speech. He's a very bad influence on your father in that way, and things are getting worse because I'm just too tired sometimes to fight your father on things like saying he's "f****** loaded" (which is just stupid to point out anyway) and the casual way he talks about sex. That's all Scott's influence right there, and now that they're working together all the time, there's more of it happening. Someday, though, I'm going to drop this load, feel more like myself, and I'm going to start cleaning things up, especially your father's speech.

(I'm sorry. You're not a load in the sense of a burden. But you are becoming a load in the physical sense of weight. Goodness, but you're growing!)

Oh, and by the way, if you EVER tell a teacher he or she is full of shit, you will be punished. I'm going to be talking to your father about that, because you are NOT allowed to talk that way. I know your father likes to show off what he knows about grammar, but he's gone too far this time.

OK, I can feel my blood pressure rising, and that's not good.

It's good to be writing to you again. Now, I'm going to have a jamoca almond milkshake, just as soon as your father gets here with it. I never liked that flavor before. Maybe you like it and I'm just the delivery vehicle. I don't know. I'm eating a lot of weird stuff.

Love you,
Your mother

I HAVE BEEN WAITING FOR THIS

Your Uncle Hugo came home today. He called me from Los Angeles at 7:38 a.m., which is weird because that's my most common waking-up time, and he asked if I would pick him up at the airport at 3:25 p.m. He said his friend Mark Westerly couldn't do it because his baby has been sick and has to go to the doctor.

That request filled me with excitement and dread all at the same time. "Of course I'll come pick you up," I told your Uncle Hugo, even though by then I was wondering what I would do if you got sick. To be honest, kid, I got a little queasy in my stomach just thinking about the possibility. I've been reading a lot about the birth experience from the standpoint of the father, and one writer said the arrival of his kid imbued (good word) him with the feeling that there was nothing he wouldn't do—including acts of savage violence—to keep his child safe and happy. I know what he means. I just thought about the possibility of your being sick, and it made me want to tear apart the room I was standing in.

I arrived at the garage at 9 a.m. on the dot—I love simultaneously watching the digital display on the car's clock and slowly easing into my parking space, and shutting off the car just as the fifty-nine morphs into a double-zero. I'm really good at it, too.

Scott Shamwell was already there—he lives at the shop, you know—and had just finished replacing the carburetor on a riding lawnmower. That would make Gene Rawlings, the owner, very happy, and it would put $179 in our pockets, minus whatever we needed to hold out for taxes. (Your grandfather—my father—hated taxes. We may or may not get into this more later.)

I told Scott Shamwell that I would be leaving early, although I did not tell him why, in keeping with my agreement with your Uncle Hugo that we wouldn't reveal we were brothers until we had the blood test results in hand.

Scott Shamwell had a glum look.

"What's wrong?" I asked.

"We'll both be gone. Will have to shut things down, I guess."

"Why?"

"Court."

One word, and I felt stupid. Today was when Scott Shamwell's brother and father were going to be sentenced.

"I'm sorry, Scott Shamwell," I said. "I forgot."

He pulled a bandanna from his back pocket and wiped his face. "It's OK. I've been trying to forget, too."

"I guess we'll just have to close early," I said.

"I guess so."

It wasn't an ideal situation. It's hard to complain about having too much business, but the fact is that we have a big backlog of work, with more coming in the door every day. Closing our doors early would limit how much we could get done and might dissuade walk-in customers. We're going to have to coordinate better from now on.

"Well," Scott Shamwell said, standing up, "let's get to it while there's still time for getting."

At the airport, your Uncle Hugo came out of the turnstile with a duffel bag in one hand and a smaller bag in the other. He looked around a couple of times before I realized he wouldn't know my car—the only time I met him, I was driven to his house in Mark Westerly's car—so I honked the horn twice and leaned out the

window. That got his attention. I hit the trunk-release button, and
he walked over and loaded his bags.

"Nice ride," he said when he slid into the passenger seat.
"Aren't you a little young for a Cadillac?"

I laughed and told him I was older than he was, anyway.

"My father liked Cadillacs," I said. "He used to call them
'the greatest negotiating tool ever made.'" I looked at your Uncle
Hugo, who was staring out the front window, and then I winced.
"Our father, I mean. Sorry."

"Don't worry about it." He waved his hand. "You're used to
saying it that way."

He was correct about that, but I still felt bad.

I put the car in gear and drove out to the west, looping around
the parking lot and then heading back down the face of the
Rimrocks toward downtown.

"You look tired," I said. Your Uncle Hugo's face was gaunt in
a way that I didn't remember from our previous meeting. He had
big baggy pouches of skin under his eyes.

"I am tired," he said. "Four weeks in L.A., man. I'll never get
used to that place. Ever been?"

"Once," I said. "I tried to see some of the places mentioned
in *Dragnet*."

"What's that?"

"My favorite TV show."

"Never heard of it."

"You should watch it. It's great."

"OK."

We were in the middle of downtown now, at a stoplight right
beside the county courthouse. I used to work there, in the clerk
and recorder's office. My father's—our father's—office was there
when he was a Yellowstone County commissioner. And just
across the street, on the courthouse lawn, your Uncle Hugo was
celebrated by thousands of people when he came home from
the Barcelona Olympics in 1992. It's so strange to think that we
crossed paths here and didn't know each other, and now we find
out that we're brothers.

"Green light," your Uncle Hugo said, and I broke out of my trance and got the car moving again.

"I used to live in L.A.," he said. "It was uncomfortable being back there."

"I didn't know that."

"You didn't read my book, then?"

Uh, oh. I stepped directly into that one.

"I feel dumb," I said.

"Don't." Your Uncle Hugo waved his hand again. He must like doing that. "Let's say I had some bad habits when I was living there. Some of those people, you know, they're still around. Luckily, there's a meeting any time you want in L.A."

"A meeting?"

"Yeah," he said. "AA. You know. Addiction."

"Oh," I said.

We crossed the railroad tracks into the South Side and continued down 27th Street.

"Turn here," your Uncle Hugo said, pointing to his right.

The houses in his neighborhood, the oldest in Billings, ran the gamut. Tidy frame houses with neat yards and well-tended fences next to shambling structures that looked as though they wouldn't stand up to a harsh wind next to empty, weed-filled lots. My father—our father—held the South Side in contempt, mostly. County business was limited within the city limits, confined mostly to matters of taxation, but as a private citizen and as a powerful member of government, he abhorred the crime and the poverty on the south side of the tracks. I don't think he was a serious man about why those things exist. It's hard for me to say that about my own father, but that's the truth as I see it. I can drive down State Avenue and see the shells of what used to be businesses, and now the weeds have taken over. Some cities promote what's called "in-fill" development, where as old businesses and houses get knocked down, new ones come in. That doesn't happen here anywhere but downtown. Mostly, the city grows to the north and to the west. The South Side doesn't even have a grocery store anymore.

How ironic that my father felt such animosity for this place and his own son lived here. That's real irony, kid, not the Alanis Morrisette kind.

Your Uncle Hugo dug into a box on the floor of his grandmother's bedroom. "I think it's in here," he said. "Give me just a second."

I sat on the bed, looking around the room at all the pictures on the wall. All of them were of your uncle, covering most of his life. Baby pictures, youth sports teams, high school prom (I didn't go, so I'm not sure what that would look like), wearing his silver medal from the Olympics. There was a photo of him and a little boy. That must be Raj. It was like a shrine.

"Here it is." He stood with a photo album in his hands, and he blew the dust off it. Then he sat down next to me.

"This is my mom," he said.

He opened the album to the first page and a full-size portrait of a young woman with long black hair. She was one of the most beautiful women I've ever seen.

"Wow," I said.

"I know. You were asking me how I could be so much smaller than you. Well, meet my mother."

"She's gorgeous, Hugo."

"She was a high school senior in this one," he said. He flipped a few pages more and stopped. "This is her just after she graduated from U of M. This is what she would have looked like when she was working for your dad."

She wore a yellow dress and had her hair cut much shorter than in the first picture. The beauty was still there, but it was enhanced—maybe even ruined, to be honest—by a heavier application of makeup. Only four years older in this photo, she looked ten years more world-weary. That's a lot to interpret in a photo, I know, but that's what I saw.

"He's your dad, too," I said.

"No, he can only be dad to you," your Uncle Hugo said. "You know what I mean? I didn't know him, and I'm not going to get to know him. I can't think of him in that way."

"I understand."

He closed the album and set it on the floor near the box he'd pulled it from. "When do you want to do this blood test?" he asked.

"You still want to?"

"I think we should. Just to know."

"Any time. I can make the appointment. Will you be in town for a while?"

"Yep, I'm back for good."

I looked at your Uncle Hugo for a moment, trying to formulate what I wanted to ask him, and then I just blurted it out. "What if it says we're not brothers?" I've been secretly dreading this possibility. Like your uncle said, it's better to know for certain— it's absolutely better if I want to tell my mother, your grandmother, about this. She'll want there to be no doubt. But now I'm invested in a certain answer; I want to be Hugo Hunter's brother.

"I don't know," he said. "Seems unlikely. Mark said my grandmother told him right out there in the front yard that Ted Stanton was my father. I don't know why she'd make that up. From what you told me, the timeline fits."

"OK. But hypothetically, what if?" This is an indication of how addled I am by this, kid. I have a fact-loving brain, and I was asking for your Uncle Hugo's imagination. That's pretty ridiculous.

"Well, I guess we're friends, anyway," he said. "What do you think?"

I didn't hesitate to answer his question. "I think we're brothers, Hugo."

He smiled at me. "I think we are, too."

Eventually, your Uncle Hugo fell asleep. He didn't excuse himself or ask me to leave, he just fell asleep on the couch while we were talking. The funny thing—not ha, ha funny, but just interesting—is that he had just been telling me how difficult it is for him to sleep for long stretches. He said he has to have total darkness in a room when he sleeps, that the sunlight gives him intense headaches. I asked if doctors could fix it, and he just said no. He didn't say so, but I think this might be related to his probable chronic traumatic encephalopathy.

When he fell asleep, I didn't realize it immediately. I kept talking about the new business with Scott Shamwell, and telling him that he needed to meet people like your mother and Scott Shamwell, when I heard him snore. He had pitched sideways against the arm of the couch, and so I got up, crept over to him, eased his feet onto the couch, and took his shoes off. The back of the couch was draped in knitted blankets, and I took one and placed it over him.

After that, I made sure all the curtains were drawn down, to keep out the light. And then I left.

I found Scott Shamwell at the shop when I went there to close up. He was in his bedroom, although that's a generous word. It's really just a hammock strung up between two walls and cordoned off with room dividers. He offered me a beer, which I declined. Four empty and smashed cans were scattered on the floor.

"What happened?" I asked him.

Scott Shamwell tried to get out of the hammock. It was a comical sight, and I tried hard not to laugh because I knew he was upset. He finally made it to his feet after falling back into the swing a couple of times.

"Maybe I should get a cot," he said.

"Maybe."

He paced around. He looked like a bear in a cage.

"Thirty years each, ten years suspended," he said. "Twenty years. Federal conviction, so there's no parole. Dad'll die in there. Studd will be retirement age. Fuck me."

"I'm sorry," I said. And I was.

"Feds are selling the farm. Mom said she'll go up to Havre and be with her sister, so that helps. I'll need a few days to move her up there."

"Of course."

"I'm drunk."

I put my hand on his shoulder. I don't like to touch people, but I think Scott Shamwell needed it. "You seem all right, considering."

"I'm gonna get drunker."

"OK."

He looked at me. "And then I'm going to get over it. OK?"

I smiled and nodded. Scott Shamwell went back to his hammock and got in much more expertly than he got out. I pulled up a chair and I sat with him, wordless, while he finished off three more beers.

For the second time today, I saw someone important to me off to sleep.

I made it home just as your mother was serving up dinner. These days, when I come home, I pause just for a second outside the door and I try to prepare myself for what I might encounter. I won't pretend that I understand what's happening with your mother's body and emotions as she goes through this process of carrying you to term. I can read about it, I can try to imagine it, but it's like your mother told me on our trip to Colorado: I just don't know.

Tonight, I found her in a wonderful mood. She had one of my favorite albums, R.E.M.'s *Automatic for the People*, playing on the stereo, and she was singing along with "Monty Got a Raw Deal" as she filled our glasses with water and brought in a salad from the kitchen. The music was playing loudly, and so I don't think she heard me come in. I just watched her from the living room for a minute. Your mother is beautiful, and I was so glad to see her.

When at last she saw me, she said, "Put that coat in the closet and come in here." I did what I was told to do, and when I reached her, I wrapped my arms around her waist and I kissed her on the mouth. And then I kissed her seven more times. That's the way we do things, kid.

"How'd it go today?" she asked me.

I sat down at the kitchen table. Your mother had made chicken parmesan for dinner. That's one of my favorites.

"It was an extraordinary day," I said.

Your mother dished up my food, giving me an extra-large helping of spaghetti. I've maintained good control of my Type II diabetes, so this was probably OK. "Do tell," she said.

So I did. I told of the seventeen outboard motors we needed to finish this week, of the afternoon spent with my brother, of Scott Shamwell's sadness, and of the blood test I needed to schedule.

"Are you scared?" your mother asked, and this made me feel good because she knows I get scared of a lot of things, and she likes to protect me if she can.

"No. Just nervous. There's a difference, right?"

"Yes."

"I've been thinking," I said.

Your mother cut in on me. "Ho, ho, that's dangerous!" She's pretty funny sometimes.

"No, I'm serious," I said. "We need to get everyone together. You need to meet Hugo. I need to meet his son. And then there's Mark Westerly and his wife."

"Who's that again?"

"The sportswriter. Well, former sportswriter. He's the man who introduced me to Hugo."

"Right."

I swallowed a bite of my dinner. "What if we had a party?"

"Here?" your mother said.

"Sure. Why not?"

"I don't know if I'm up to a party."

"We could have it catered, so you wouldn't have to do any work."

Your mother didn't say anything immediately, but I could tell she was working the situation out in her mind. A slow smile crossed her face.

"You're smiling," I said.

"I know. I think I'd like a party."

"Really?"

"Yes. I'm kind of shocked that you would, though. I can't even get you to go to the mall with me."

I took another bite. "Things are changing fast, I guess." It was a tossed-off line. Things are changing fast, but my aversion (nice word) to crowds won't ever change. I can't explain why I was willing to set it aside for this party idea. My life is filling up with people, and I'm just trying to keep them sorted out.

I can't believe I'd ever say such a thing, but what a good problem to have.

CLOSING THOUGHT

Your mother cracks me up sometimes, because almost everything she does is with certainty. She makes a decision, and she goes. She draws a conclusion, and she commits to it. I'm envious of this ability. Outside of concrete fact-or-fiction things, I have no such certainty. When I have to evaluate options that don't come with hard data, I sometimes freeze up. Your mother never does.

I'll give you some examples of what your mother said at dinner tonight:

On Scott Shamwell: "He just needs a girlfriend, if he can find someone who can handle him."

On your Uncle Hugo and his sleeplessness: "He needs forty-eight hours of complete solitude. Come to think of it, I need the same thing."

On being pregnant: "It's the most wonderful thing ever, and the most challenging thing ever. More challenging than wonderful, on the balance. I may never let you touch me again."

I think she was kidding about that last part.

I hope so.

I'm kind of horny.

My child ...

I was kidding about that last part. Also, you are never to use the word "horny" until you're grown up, OK? And be sparing with it even then, please.

You woke me up again with your kicking. Are you going to be a soccer player? Maybe a mixed martial arts fighter (no, you can't be a mixed martial arts fighter, sorry)?

I sat on the couch and I sang to you softly, so I didn't wake up your father, and I told you how much I love you, and I do. And then you stopped kicking, as if you could hear my voice and understand what I was saying to you. Maybe you can. Maybe you do.

I want you to know something else. Your father is very sweet and very kind, but I'm not nearly as certain as he seems to think I am. It's just that certain situations demand immediate action—someone is in trouble and needs help, or standing still will just let a bad thing get worse. What I'm good at is taking action. Not so much at being certain that I'm doing the right thing.

Scott does need a girlfriend. I am certain about that. He's too rough around the edges, too impulsive and argumentative. I think a girlfriend, the right girlfriend, could sand down some of those edges. And it's not just what she could do for him. He's a good man, beneath it all. He has something to offer. I could see that in him, and that's why I've tried to get to know him better. But, goodness, he's a handful.

I want to tell you a story. When I first met your father, and as I got to know him, I thought he was the special man for me, the one who would understand my specialness, the man my daddy told me would come along someday. But then, I thought, I found out that he wasn't. He didn't stand up to his mother when she came to Colorado and fetched him, and he came back to this house in Montana. I've never chased a man, and I wasn't going to start with him.

I was heartbroken—I was truly heartbroken—but I decided to go on. It was simple: Your father wasn't my special man. At least, that's what I thought.

And then, one morning, your father called me from the road and said he was on his way, that he was coming to live with me.

And I will admit that I told him then how happy I was, and how he really was the special man for me.

Here's my secret: I wasn't sure. I told him I was excited— and I was, but I was also nervous—because I knew if I said a discouraging word, he would turn right around and go home and I'd never see him again. But I was not certain it would work. He didn't arrive in Cheyenne Wells until late that night, so I had plenty of time to think about things and worry. I finally said to myself: "Sheila, he's coming, and you're going to have to give this a try." And guess what? It worked. I fell deeper in love with him, and he's the wonderful man I always hoped I'd meet.

But there's a difference between trying something and being certain of something.

I hope this makes sense to you.

Love,
Your mother

IT IS OFFICIAL

I have a brother! I have a brother!

This may seem like old news, but today marks the first time I can say it with certainty: I have a brother, and his name is Hugo Hunter.

Your Uncle Hugo and I went to St. Vincent Healthcare on Friday, exactly two weeks after he returned from Los Angeles, and we had blood drawn for a DNA comparison. The technician told us it might be the following Wednesday before we heard anything, on account of the weekend. So I was not expecting the phone call I received first thing this morning, telling me that our DNA test was a positive.

"Did you call Hugo Hunter?" I asked the woman who called my bitchin' iPhone.

"I'm calling him as soon as we hang up."

"OK," I said. "Please hurry. I have another appointment this morning, and I want to talk to him about this."

The woman said she would hurry because I asked so nicely. That made me feel good.

I sat at the kitchen table and I gazed at my watch, determined to count off exactly five minutes before I tried calling my brother (my brother!). I started watching at 9:02:57 a.m., which meant I needed to wait until 9:07:57 to make the call. Time is a fascinating thing, kid. You're going to find this out.

When you're little, you feel like it takes forever for some days to go by. I remember waiting for Christmas during my holiday break from school. We'd get done with classes on December 18th or December 19th (or sometimes December 20th or December 21st—one of the holes in my bookkeeping is that I didn't write down data in my notebooks until I became an adult). That week (or less) before Christmas seemed like it would never end. Of course, it always did end; it's just that my anticipation created the illusion of slowed-down time. On the flip side (idiom), when you're an adult, you have so many things to do that it seems like you never have enough time. The truth is, time—and even time is just a human construction—moves at the same speed for anticipatory children and stressed-out adults. Only our perception of it differs.

At 9:04:14, your mother came into the kitchen, where I sat.

"I have a brother," I said.

"I know."

"No, I mean it's official now."

Your mother was still bleary-eyed—I've told you she isn't sleeping well—but she put her arms around my neck and she hugged me. I turned in the seat to give her a bigger hug, and she pushed me away.

"My boobs hurt," she said.

I blame you for that, kid.

While your mother made breakfast, I went back to staring at my watch. When the time I was waiting for showed itself, I dialed your Uncle Hugo on my bitchin' iPhone.

The phone rang five times and then went to voicemail. Your uncle's message was terse: "It's Hugo. Spill it." I thought that was funny.

"It's your brother, Edward. Call me back."

I hung up. This perplexed me. Surely five minutes was long enough for the woman at St. Vincent Healthcare to explain everything to your Uncle Hugo. Maybe he had more questions than I did. Maybe I should have asked more questions than I did. I began to get anxious, and I realized that the only way I could calm down was to rely on structure. I made this realization at 9:08:49, and so I resolved to wait until 9:13:49 before I called him again.

I again fixated on my watch.

"What are you doing?" your mother asked.

"Waiting until I can call Hugo again."

"Don't be silly," she said. She passed a plate with some toast across the table to me. "Have breakfast and wait for him to call. He will."

"Nine-ten-thirteen."

"Edward."

"Nine-ten-fourteen."

"Edward!"

I looked up at her, and she frowned at me. "You're out of control," she said. "Do you feel out of control?"

"A little bit."

"OK. Take a deep breath, eat your breakfast, and just wait, OK?"

"OK."

I had a piece of wheat toast and a cup of marionberry yogurt. I took my fluoxetine and my diabetic medicine. I also kept stealing glances at my watch.

At 9:13:49, I picked up the phone again.

"Edward!"

"I have to," I said.

I called your Uncle Hugo again. And, again, five rings led to voicemail.

"It's Edward. Call me."

I hung up.

"This doesn't make any sense," I said.

"Maybe he had somewhere to be," your mother said, a sensible thought that I didn't want to believe.

"I need to go over there," I said.

"What? No." Your mother was adamant (nice word). "Look, I know you're excited, but there is no reason for you to go over there and bother him. What's changed, really? You already knew he was your brother."

"Everything's changed!"

"No," she said, slowly and soothingly as she could considering my state of agitation. "You need to calm down."

"I'm going over there."

"I wish you wouldn't."

"I am."

My bitchin' iPhone began buzzing and moving across our dining-room table. I looked at the display: Hugo Hunter. I answered it.

"Hi," I said. My voice cracked like that of a pubescent (excellent word) boy. Your mother giggled.

"Hey, Edward, sorry about that. I was in the shower. Sounds like we got some good news, huh?"

"You haven't heard?"

"No, there were voicemails from you and the doctor. I figured I'd just cut to the chase." Your Uncle Hugo knows his idioms, too.

"We're brothers," I said. "Officially."

"That's great. Never had a doubt."

"Neither did I."

"I guess we can start telling people," he said. "If you want to."

"I want to."

"Do you feel any different? You know, now that it's confirmed and everything?"

I looked at your mother. "No, I don't feel different."

Your mother burst out laughing.

I called Scott Shamwell at the shop and reminded him that I had an appointment this morning. I also told him I had some interesting news for him that I would reveal later. That was not a nice thing to do, because Scott Shamwell pressed me to tell him now.

"I can't," I said.

"Is it about the business?"

"No."

"Is it bad news?"

"No."

"So it's good news?"

"Yes."

"Just tell me."

"No."

"Go to your stupid meeting, then." Scott Shamwell laughed after he said this, but I think he was covering up exasperation (love that word). He's not good at disguising how he really feels.

"I'll be in by 11:08, if there's no problem with traffic," I said.

"That's fine. I cleared out the backlog, but there's two more jobs that came through the door this morning." Since the night I found him getting drunk after seeing his father and brother in court, Scott Shamwell has been focused on his work. Long after we close up the shop at night, he keeps repairing engines. He says it keeps his mind off "the shitty-ass situation up in Musselshell County." The federal government seized his family's farm and all of the belongings on it, all of which will go to auction. I asked Scott Shamwell if he wanted to try to get some of it back—you can pick up some good bargains at government auctions—and he said, "Lesbian unicorns will fly out of my ass before I pay good money for my own stuff." I wasn't entirely sure what that meant. If lesbian unicorns flew out of Scott Shamwell's ass, he could sell tickets and never have to work again.

I knocked on Dr. Bryan Thomsen's door promptly at 10 a.m., and he summoned me to enter.

"Let's forget the perfunctory greetings, Dr. Bryan Thomsen," I told him. "We have a lot to talk about."

He put his reading glasses on the desk and asked me to sit. I settled into my usual spot.

"Go ahead," he said.

"Have you heard of Hugo Hunter?" I asked him.

Dr. Bryan Thomsen leaned forward. "Sure, yeah. Boxer, right? Billings guy. He was in the paper recently."

"Yes," I said. "Also, my brother."

"Really?"

"Yes."

He leaned back in his chair again. Dr. Bryan Thomsen does a lot of leaning forward and leaning backward. I'm not sure why I didn't notice until today.

"How did you find this out?" he asked.

So I told him the abbreviated version of the story, because I didn't want to lose precious portions of my hour to something I already knew. Dr. Bryan Thomsen did me the courtesy of not interrupting my story, except for the part where he said, "Yes, I remember your telling me about your father's affair," which he shouldn't have done. I don't want to have to worry about what Dr. Bryan Thomsen does and doesn't remember at crucial times like these.

When I finished, he said, "I take it you have some concerns?"

"Two."

"Let's talk about them."

Now I leaned forward. "OK, first, I've never been a brother or had a brother before. What do I do differently?"

"I'm not sure you do anything differently. What you're doing is forming a relationship. You've done that before. I'd dare say you've become quite good at it."

"But this is different."

"How?"

"I don't know. But it is. This is a blood relationship. St. Vincent Healthcare confirmed that."

Here came Dr. Bryan Thomsen, leaning toward me again. "Have you ever heard the phrase 'You can't choose your family, but you can choose your friends'?"

"Yes."

"Well, let's think about this. The blood says you and Hugo are family, but you've never lived that way. You didn't grow up in the same house. You didn't identify as brothers. So, in this case, you have a chance at both of those things. You want to have a close relationship with him, I take it?"

"Yes."

"That relationship, I'd say, is going to look a lot like a new friendship, because you don't know much about each other yet. That's the basis from which you two can work. The brotherly bond, at least in a traditional sense, isn't there. This is actually a wonderful opportunity, Edward, because as you become closer friends, the brotherly bond will kick in, too. Do you understand?"

"I think so."

"Think of your friend Scott Shamwell," he said. "How do you feel about him?"

"He's my good friend."

"Is there anything you wouldn't do for him, if you could?"

I thought about that for a few seconds. "I don't think so."

"So, in a sense, you could say you feel brotherly to Scott. Like he's part of your family."

I saw now what Dr. Bryan Thomsen was driving at (idiom) (also, a sentence-ending preposition).

"This makes sense to me," I said.

Dr. Bryan Thomsen leaned back. I think I am going to start to keep a running tally of his leaning forward and leaning back and add it to my data sheets.

"You said you have another concern," he said.

"My mother."

"I figured. You say she doesn't know?"

"That's correct."

"And you think you should tell her?"

"I have to. I can't say, 'Here's Hugo Hunter, my brother,' and just expect her to accept that. She will have some questions."

That made Dr. Bryan Thomsen laugh.

"Right. Of course." He was still giggling a little bit, and then he leaned forward. I took a pen from my shirt pocket and made a mark on my left hand.

"I suppose the best approach is to be direct," Dr. Bryan Thomsen said. "Tell her the facts, tell her you like this man and want to get to know him better, and don't linger on the part of it that is unpleasant for her. Remember that she'll have some complicated feelings about this. He's a newfound brother to you, but to her, he's a fresh manifestation of an old wound. Be sensitive to her."

"I understand."

He leaned back. I made another mark on my left hand.

"One other thing, Edward," he said. "You'll probably want to have this conversation with her in person. You and your mother do a lot better in person than you do over the phone."

Dr. Bryan Thomsen again closed the space between us. I again marked on my palm, which had seven slashes on it from my pen.

"How's the pregnancy going?"

"Good."

"It's the seventeenth week now?"

"Eighteenth." This is one of the things that bother me about Dr. Bryan Thomsen. He sees me every two weeks, so he should know by now that every time he asks me about the pregnancy— and he has, every time we have met since I told him—it will be an even-numbered week. This is basic mathematics.

"Second trimester," he said.

"Yes." He knows this, too. Dr. Buckley never wasted my time this way.

"Is Sheila having back trouble?"

"Not that I know of."

"Have you asked?"

"No. Why are you interrogating me, Dr. Bryan Thomsen?"

"I didn't mean to. I'm just curious. I've been through three of these things."

"She's fine."

"OK, then. Anything else you want to talk about?"

I looked at my watch. If I wanted them, I had twenty-seven seconds more of Dr. Bryan Thomsen's time.

"Hold on," I said. I looked at my watch, and I waited for the seconds to tick off so I could leave right on the minute. Do you remember what I told you before about perception and the passage of time? When you're waiting for twenty-seven seconds to go by, and you're not talking because you want to concentrate on your watch, you might as well be waiting for the next ice age.

Did you catch that, kid? That's hyperbole. Some people think I'm boring and repetitive—they've said so and your mother has said so—but I'm capable of being hyperbolic. I'm capable of many things.

The seconds display morphed from a :59 to a :00.

"Goodbye," I said, and I shook Dr. Bryan Thomsen's hand.

Scott Shamwell was agog (beautiful word), as I suspected he would be. Suspicions are sometimes the least trustworthy of feelings, so it's always good to see one confirmed.

"Hugo Hunter is your brother?" he said.

"Yes."

"*The* Hugo Hunter?"

"Yes."

"Hugo Hunter, Badass?"

"Yes."

"Hugo Motherfucking Hunter?"

"Scott Shamwell, these are all the same person."

He put down the magneto ignition system he was working on and looked at me. "That's incredible, man. I love that guy."

"You know him?"

"No. I mean, yes, but only by reputation. I loved watching him fight. That's what I mean. Dude owes me fifty bucks, though."

This was a strange thing for Scott Shamwell to say. I couldn't tell if he was being serious or just engaging in his usual blowhard tendencies (I love the phrase "blowhard tendencies"—your mother came up with that in regard to Scott Shamwell).

"Does he know this?" I asked.

Scott Shamwell started laughing so hard that he coughed. "You're a funny dude, Ed buddy. I bet half a Benjy on him when he fought Mozi Qwai. Bastard lost." Almost immediately, Scott Shamwell looked crestfallen. "Oh, Jesus, I didn't mean to say 'bastard.'"

"What's half a Benjy?" I asked.

"Fifty bucks."

"I don't get it."

"Half a Benjamin Franklin."

"I still don't get it."

"Benjamin Franklin is on the hundred-dollar bill."

"I get it now."

"It's funnier when I have to explain it," Scott Shamwell said.

"Did you make half a Benjy up?" I asked.

"Probably."

"Nice job."

When I got home tonight, I found your mother napping on the couch. I knelt down to her and placed eight kisses on her lips. She woke up midway through them.

"Hello, Sheila Bear," I said.

She threw her arms around my neck.

"I'm tired," she said.

"Does your back hurt?"

"A little."

"Why didn't you tell me?"

"It's no big deal."

"Dr. Bryan Thomsen said you would say that."

She kissed me again. I like it when she does that.

"He's a very smart man," she said.

"Sometimes," I said, and she laughed.

She sat up. It was a bit of a struggle. You are now about the size of a cantaloupe.

"This kid kicked all the live long day," she said.

I shook my finger at you from in front of your mother's tummy and scolded you. "Stop kicking, kid!" I'm pretty funny sometimes. I hope you understood that it was a joke.

"Don't be silly," your mother said. "I like it. It reminds me of what's important."

"I'm sorry."

"It's OK. You're pretty funny sometimes."

"Please tell me when you're hurting."

"I will."

I helped your mother to her feet and into the dining room. I helped her sit down, and then I said I would make dinner.

"That's means we're having spaghetti," your mother said. She's a very smart woman.

While I got the water boiling and began browning hamburger for the sauce, your mother talked to me.

"We need to do something," she said.

"What?"

"We need to start talking about names for this kid."

"Unisex names?" I didn't see how this naming business was possible when we didn't know whether you're a boy or a girl.

"No, just possibilities. Haven't you been thinking about this?"

At once, I felt stupid. I've been content to call you "kid," after I realized "C.S." wouldn't continue to work and "B.S." would be an abomination (good word).

"A little bit," I lied.

"We can start making some lists, so we'll at least have some options when the baby arrives. OK?"

I stirred the spaghetti and then added the Newman's Own sauce to the browned hamburger. I don't make homemade sauce the way your mother does.

"OK."

Holy shit, kid.

Finding a name for you makes this seem even more real. That's just an illusion, of course. The fact is, it's been real since the moment we found out your mother was pregnant. But naming you brings a whole new set of challenges.

I hope we don't mess this up.

CLOSING THOUGHT

I've given more thought to your name than I let on with your mother. When I told your grandmother about you, she put immediate pressure on me to name you after my father if you're a boy (which means you'd also be named after me) or after her mother, whose name was Dahlia, if you're a girl. "Your father's name means something in Billings," she said. "Your child will be inheriting a legacy. And if it's a girl, well, Dahlia is just a beautiful name." She confuses me sometimes, kid. In many ways, she couldn't wait to be free of my father after he died. She sold their house and married someone else. And now she'd like to put his name on you. People will confound you. Please know this.

You don't have to worry about either of those names. I object to the first one because I know what it's like to deal with the expectations of having someone else's name. Your grandfather, my father, used to call me "Teddy" because it was a diminutive (good word) of the name he went by, Ted. He clearly wanted me to be a miniature version of him, and I ended up being quite unlike him. That was hard on him and hard on me. I see no reason to put that kind of burden on you.

I don't like "Dahlia" because I think my mother has forgotten how much she actually disliked her mother. My Grandma Dahlia died when I was quite young, so I don't remember her well, but I do know how much your grandmother has complained about her in the forty-one years she has been dead. A lot. I'd rather name you after someone your mother and I both admire.

I didn't tell your mother about your grandmother's heavy-handed thoughts about your name. It would have only aggravated her. This is called managing a situation. I learned about this from Dr. Buckley originally, and I have refined my technique with help from Dr. Bryan Thomsen. One of the things I've learned is that it isn't necessarily a lie to leave out information that will only upset someone else. So when I got off the phone with your grandmother, I told your mother the pleasant things she said and left out the uncomfortable parts. This is also called "editing." I'm a good editor.

It's saved my bacon more than once. That's an idiom, kid.

My child ...

You'll pardon me if I fudged the truth with your father. I'm feeling more and more weary as this goes on, and here, maybe not even at the midpoint, I catch myself looking ahead to what might be in store.

In the 19th week, your sensory systems will be developing—which means you may be able to hear my voice. I've been talking to you straight along, but now I'll be doing it even more. This will also mark the acceleration of my getting bigger as I carry you. Not looking forward to that, I have to say.

In the 20th week, you'll be the length of a banana, and you'll be accumulating stuff in your bowels that could be your first poop. I find myself strangely fascinated by this.

In the 21st week, if you're a girl, your vagina will be forming. (If you're a boy and you're reading this, please disregard this information.) Oh, how we'll have talks about that. Count on it. My mom didn't talk to me nearly enough about this, and I had to learn some things in a very difficult way. I won't let that happen to you. I also understand that I may be getting some acne around this time, due to increased oil production. Can't say I'm thrilled about that, either.

I love you,
Your mother

Here are a few of the names we've considered for you, but I think we're just going set these aside and wait for your arrival. I think we'll know the proper name when the time comes. Maybe when you read this someday you'll be surprised:

BOY	GIRL
Raymond	Christina
Jared	Dina
Christopher	Errin
Matthew	Mary
Elliott	Skyler
Paul	Elisa
Flint	Cassandra
Joseph	Tipitina

DEBACLE (GOOD WORD, BAD THING)

Well, kid, before I tell you why your Uncle Hugo left our house tonight and may never come back, and how I came to punch Scott Shamwell in the face, and how your mother is angry with me that I cost her a friendship, I should tell you that the evening started out wonderfully.

I did what I promised your mother I would: I hired a caterer to bring food and drinks to the house. We had a taco bar and lots of different kinds of wine and beer, and everybody showed up on time at seven p.m.—your Uncle Hugo and his son, Raj; Scott Shamwell; and Mark Westerly and his wife, Lainie.

I've never thrown a party before. I never had friends the way I seem to have now—or at least had before tonight—and so there was never any reason. So much has happened, though, that getting everyone together seemed like the right thing to do. Your mother wanted to meet Hugo. I wanted to meet Raj. I wanted Mark Westerly and his wife to meet Scott Shamwell. I wanted us all to be together and become friends, and we were on our way, kid.

Then my mother showed up, and maybe I'll never have these friends again.

This sucks elephant ass, as Scott Shamwell would say. I wish he were here now. I would apologize for punching him in the face.

Your Uncle Hugo was so kind to your mother. He gave her a big
hug when they met, and she accepted it, which was no small
thing. Your mother is a warm and loving person, but she is not an
immediate hugger. You have to earn it from her. Your Uncle Hugo
asked if he could rub her belly, and she said yes. He rubbed
gently and said, "Here's bringing the kid good luck," and that
made me feel good because he calls you "the kid," too.

Raj looks just like his father, only younger (which makes sense,
as he is eighteen years younger), but he has an entirely different
personality. Your Uncle Hugo is outgoing and talkative—the
last time I was at his house, he said being stopped on the street
and asked for an autograph is what he misses the most about his
boxing days. He loves being around people. Raj, while a nice
young man, is much more quiet and circumspect (a good word for
you to learn). He had the least to say of anybody at the party, and
that includes me. And I usually hate being in a crowd. I think
Raj and I have much in common.

Scott Shamwell and Mark Westerly holed up in the dining
room, next to the big bowl of guacamole, and they talked about
sports. Scott Shamwell, when he was in high school twenty-one
years ago, was a good running back, apparently. Mark Westerly
remembered him, even though he mostly covered your Uncle
Hugo, and they talked about those old teams and old players.

Your mother and Mark Westerly's wife sat on the couch and
chatted. I kept trying to veer over and listen in, but every time I
got close, your mother would look up and say, "Edward, go see
if Raj wants something else to drink" or "Edward, show Hugo
the backyard" or "Edward, will you get me some chips?" It was
frustrating, because I wanted to listen, not do all of that stuff. I did
hear them talking one time about knitting, and your mother was
giving Lainie Westerly some tips for something called "intarsia"
knitting, which I guess is complicated. I don't know anything
about knitting. I bet the people at Purl Jam miss your mother,
though. Or would if she hadn't been arrested.

I moved from place to place, replacing drinks, offering food, answering questions when I was asked. I tried to stick close to your Uncle Hugo, to make sure he was having fun, and we smiled at each other a lot. The only two people in the room who knew what it was like to be brothers were us. Scott Shamwell has a brother, but he's in prison now, Being Hugo Hunter's brother is more fun than that.

About an hour into the party, your mother sidled (good verb) up to me, slipped her arm around my back, and said, "How are you?"

"A little overwhelmed."

"You OK?"

"Never better." This is a tossed-off phrase, kid. I've been alive for 16,519 days, so any contention that I was doing better at that moment than in any other would be highly suspect. What I meant, of course, is that I was doing fine.

"Lainie says she can probably get me a job at Billings Clinic after the baby comes, if I want to go back to work."

"We're a St. Vincent Healthcare family."

"Yeah, but it's just a job."

I bent down and kissed her forehead. "OK."

"I'm just saying, it's nice to meet someone who's helpful like that. These are good people."

"Yes, they are."

Your Uncle Hugo came over and put his arm around your mother. We had the beginnings of a decent chorus line. (That's a joke, kid. I'm pretty funny sometimes.)

"Good party, bro," he said.

"Thanks, bro," I said.

Bro!

Your grandmother knocked on the door at 8:51 p.m. I didn't know it was her until I opened the door, but I know the time because I looked at my watch when I heard the knock. When I opened the door, I saw her and Jay L. Lamb standing there.

"Mother," I said. "I didn't know—"

"I thought I would surprise you. There are a lot of cars in the street." She peeked in the living room and saw the gathering.

"Oh," she said.

Jay L. Lamb shook my hand. "Good to see you, Edward."

"You, too, Jay. Come in."

Everybody at the party gradually became aware that others had entered the room, and they turned to look.

"I guess we should have called," your grandmother said.

"No, I'm glad you're here." This, too, was a case of my saying what I think someone wanted to hear. Internally, I was wigging out. I like situations I can control. My mother, your grandmother, does not usually create such situations.

I handled the introductions. Mark and Lainie Westerly first, followed by Scott Shamwell. When I got to your Uncle Hugo, my mother cut me off.

"I know who you are."

"Hugo Hunter, ma'am."

She turned to me. "What's he doing here?"

"Mother—"

Your mother stepped in between us. "We invited him here."

"Do you know who this is?" my mother said.

"Yes."

"Then I ask again: What's he doing here?"

Your Uncle Hugo started for the door, Raj in tow. "We'll go, Edward. Thank you." As he passed my mother, he said, "Ma'am."

The Westerlys were next out the door. Your mother mouthed "I'm sorry" to them.

"Maybe you should be going, too," my mother said to Scott Shamwell.

"No," he said. "I think I'll stick around."

My mother looked exasperated.

I couldn't say anything.

I hate it when that happens.

The rest of it, you can probably figure out. My mother, your grandmother, has known since your Uncle Hugo came to prominence that we share a father. Neither she nor my father shared that with me. I wish that surprised me, but it doesn't.

"I mean, all you had to do was look at him and know who his mother was, that tramp," my mother said. "The single most painful thing in my life was your father cavorting with her, and you bring that man into this house? I'm appalled."

Your mother was none too happy with that, and she let your grandmother know.

"The only thing that's appalling is your behavior," she said to my mother. "How dare you come here and behave this way."

"This is my house," my mother said, a contention that is not true. We both owned it once. But when I married your mother, your grandmother let us put the house entirely in our names.

"It's our house," your mother said.

Jay L. Lamb stood by my mother and tugged at her arm, trying to get her to go. I tried to find words. Scott Shamwell drank a beer and watched everything.

"They are brothers," your mother said to your grandmother. "You might not like that, and I can even understand why you wouldn't, but this is not your decision to make. Edward wants to know him. I want to know him. What you want has no place in this."

"He's trash," my mother said.

I finally found something to say. "Now, Mother, you don't know anything about him."

Scott Shamwell stepped into the middle of things.

"Lady," he said to my mother, "you're a piece of work. Why don't you just get the hell out of here."

"Who is this person?" my mother said.

I turned on Scott Shamwell. "Please don't talk to my mother that—"

"Fuck her, Ed. She has no right."

That's when I punched him.

Now, I should tell you that I don't think I hurt him. I hurt me, though. My hand is not as strong as Scott Shamwell's jaw.

Scott Shamwell just looked at me for a few moments after I hit him. He touched his jaw. His eyes were wider than usual, but I couldn't tell if he was scared or angry or sad. He just looked at me. And then he said one word: "OK." And then he walked out.

Your mother went right back at your grandmother. "Get out now or I'm calling the cops."

Jay L. Lamb at last succeeded in pulling my mother away. The door closed, and a few moments later, I heard one engine start (Scott Shamwell's, I imagine, based on the order in which people left the house) and then another. As the sounds faded out, I went to the dining room and began picking up glasses and plates.

"What are you doing?" your mother asked.

"I'm cleaning up."

"No, I mean about this. You cannot let her behave that way. I made friends tonight, and I want to keep them. Now, what are you going to do?"

I stopped and I looked at her. I think she wanted an answer I couldn't give to her.

"I'm cleaning up."

CLOSING THOUGHT

This sucks.

THIS STILL SUCKS

Ordinarily, I am asleep by now, but my brain is addled and so I will tell you more about what happened.

Your mother followed me around for a few minutes, telling me what I ought to do about my mother. And finally I yelled at her and told her she's just as bad as my mother sometimes, always telling me what to do. She said, "If that's your attitude, I'm just going to bed." I said, "Fine." She said, "Fine." And then she left. Now she's asleep and I'm the one who can't find rest.

I received a text message from your Uncle Hugo on my bitchin' iPhone. He wrote: *Gonna lay low for a while. Don't want to cause u any trouble with ur mom.* I hate that your Uncle Hugo uses texting shorthand. I hate more that he's apparently going to avoid me.

I called the shop, but Scott Shamwell didn't answer. I hope he's not mad at me, although I can't imagine why he wouldn't be. I did punch him, even though it hurt me more than it did him.

Your mother wants me to tell your grandmother that this is my life and I can do whatever I want and she doesn't get a say. I think it's easy for your mother to say that. She doesn't have a long history with my mother, and her own parents are dead. Do you think she would say that to them if they were still alive? Maybe she would. I don't know.

What I do know is my mother is the only parent I have left. Yes, she is controlling, and yes, she was out of line tonight. But she has also done many fine things for me. I love her. I can't just tell her to get lost (another idiom; I wouldn't be telling my mother to end up in a place where she doesn't know where she is).

Soon, you're going to meet your own mother. You will come to rely on her for many things. And maybe then you'll be able to consider what it would mean to tell her to get lost. Maybe then you'll know that such a thing is just not possible.

I wish tonight had never happened. But time never stops moving, whether it seems fast or slow, and so tonight was inevitable.

Well, now I feel dumb.

I should have held you and talked rationally to you last night, Edward. But dang it, nothing about that woman is rational— except, maybe, for her sense of hurt about being betrayed by your father, but even that, something I could sympathize with on any number of levels (I WILL hunt you down if you ever cheat on me), is diminished because she's just so CONDESCENDING to people.

I woke up tonight because I didn't feel you sleeping next to me, and I missed you. And you were out here on the couch, which is going to mess up your back, and I read your note to our child, and I feel really stupid for being on your case. I'm on your team. Always your team. It really hurt me what you said about how I'm like your mom. But it also made me think.

In answer to your question, though, YES I would tell my parents to get their big fat noses out of my business. That's all I'm saying. You don't have to tell her to get lost. You just have to tell her to butt out. This is your decision to make, whether you want to know Hugo or not, and she has NO STANDING.

I'm sorry. I'm getting overheated again. Your child is, too. He/ she has kicked me three times since I started writing this.

I support you, my love. Now, let's talk about this and decide what we're going to do. OK? I love you. I'm going to wake you now and take you back to bed, and I'll show you this when you wake up again in the morning.

Love,
Sheila

SUCKY SATURDAY (ALLITERATION)

I woke up at 6:54 a.m., the only time this year I've done so and only the third time in all my years of recordkeeping that I've been awake at that time. I found your mother's note on the dresser and read it, and then I woke her up.

One of the reasons we do well as a married couple is we let calmer heads prevail. This is a strange phrase, so I'll explain what I mean. Both of us tend to react in the moment that we're agitated. In your mother's case, you need only look at how she stood up to my mother last night. In my case, you need only look at how I couldn't respond. The point is, neither of us was in position to talk calmly about the situation. Instead, I wrote down how I felt and she wrote down how she felt, and this morning we were able to talk about it. We've recognized that this approach works for us.

I'm glad your mother doesn't want me to tell your grandmother to get lost. That would not fly (a figure of speech; nothing actually gets airborne). We agreed that I need to visit my mother at her downtown condominium and explain to her how I came to know your Uncle Hugo and why I want to have a relationship with him. Our hope is that your grandmother, given a night to think about things and the opportunity to talk directly with me, will have a more considered reaction to the situation.

If she doesn't, your mother said we could explore the "nuclear option." I don't even know what that is. From the way she giggled, your mother may have been kidding. I don't know. Your mother is pretty funny sometimes.

After I had my breakfast (oatmeal), my fluoxetine, and my diabetic medicine, I first stopped at the shop. I don't mind telling you that I was nervous. As much as I love my mother, my relationship with Scott Shamwell is more crucial in a practical sense. We're business partners, and we see each other nearly every day. I hoped he wasn't mad at me.

I found him sitting in a circle of weed-trimmer parts. He looked up at me.

"You're not dressed for work."

"I have an appointment," I said.

"A lot of that lately."

"I know."

"The deal was you'd be here, helping to do the work."

"I have been. I will be."

Scott Shamwell fitted the casing on the motor. "Do you want me to leave?"

I moved toward him. "No. Do you want to?"

Scott Shamwell threw his wrench down, and it clattered across the concrete floor. I jumped.

"Where would I go, huh? This is what I have, this right here. I don't have anything else. OK?"

"OK."

Scott Shamwell put his hands over his eyes and slowly moved them down, turning his face into something grotesque. After he had done so, I saw that he was crying.

"I've been waiting all morning for you to come in here and fire me," he said.

"I came to apologize."

"Why? I'm the dick."

"You are not a dick, Scott Shamwell."

"I'm sorry for cussing out your mom."

"I'm sorry for punching you in the face."

Scott Shamwell jutted out his lower lip. "Is that what it was? A punch? I thought a stiff breeze blew into the room." He laughed, and then he blew his nose, and then he rubbed his eyes again.

I recognized that he was making a joke, so I drew back into a fighting stance, but I had a big grin on my face to let him know I was in on the game, which, now that I write it down, is a really weird phrase that I won't even attempt to explain. Let's just say that I knew he was making a joke and I made a joke right back. I'm pretty funny sometimes.

"Watch it, boy," he said. "I'll have to lay a whipping on you."

"I'll tell my little brother Hugo Hunter if you do."

At this, Scott Shamwell threw up his hands in surrender, and we both laughed again.

He's my good friend.

I told Scott Shamwell that I would come back in the afternoon to help with the backlog of work. Something neat is happening with our business. People who've already come in are starting to tell their friends about us, and we're getting referrals and some repeat business. We're paying our bills and we've started being able to pay ourselves a small salary. It's not enough to live on yet, but that's OK, because I'm fucking loaded and Scott Shamwell doesn't have a lot of expenses living at the shop.

I went to the South Side to your Uncle Hugo's house. I'd responded to his text message last night, even though I wasn't sure what to say. I wrote: *I'm sorry about what happened.* He didn't write back.

I tried to call him before I got to his house, but he didn't answer. I was beginning to think that your mother was right, that I should give him some space. "He didn't sign up for this," she said, in reference to the deplorable (good word) way my mother treated him. Once in front of your Uncle Hugo's house, I sat in the Cadillac DTS and I dealt with two competing urges:

1. I wanted to shut off the car, walk up to his front door, ring the bell and tell him that we're brothers (St. Vincent Healthcare has confirmed this) and we would figure out how to deal with my mother and her objections. This option would have an element of chance attached to it, because I hadn't yet spoken with my mother again.

2. I wanted to drive away and respect your Uncle Hugo's decision to "lay low" for a while. This option meant letting someone else control the situation. I don't like to do that.

I drove away.

I'm not sure why.

I'm not sure it was the right decision.

Here's a thought, kid: Sometimes, there are no right decisions. Sometimes, there is only the less wrong decision.

I'm not sure this was the less wrong decision, either.

My mother buzzed me into her condominium building. I always get nervous when I'm there. I have to make this long walk down a hallway, then ride the elevator up to her floor, then another long walk to her front door. Since March 13, 2009, when she moved out of the house she shared with my father and into this condominium, she has spent less time here with each passing year. She lives predominately (excellent word) in North Richland Hills, Texas, where she has a house with Jay L. Lamb. They come to Billings for several weeks each spring and summer, mostly for some of the big fundraisers she supports. My mother is big on making appearances at fundraisers and other gala events. That kind of life would make me anxious, but it seems to work for her.

Jay L. Lamb stood at the front door, opening it for me as I approached. "Good to see you, Edward," he said, and I replied, "You, too, Jay." This, again, is something you say to someone out of nicety (another fine word), regardless of whether it's the truth. I don't really care if I never see Jay L. Lamb again, but my mother loves him, so I probably will.

My mother was in the living room, and she was wearing a yellow dress and shoes (pumps, I think they are called), with jewelry, and her face had already been made up. Kid, I've told you a lot about the differences between your mother and your grandmother, and here's one that is superficial: Your grandmother will not allow anyone to see her until her face has been made up. Your mother couldn't give a good goddamn (my father used to say that) and often goes for days at a time without putting on makeup. She's lovely without it.

"Sit down, son," my mother said, and so I chose the loveseat across from where she stood.

"You've come to talk about last night, I guess," she said.

"Yes."

Jay L. Lamb stood next to my mother, who sat down on the couch facing me. "Would you like something to drink, Edward?" he said.

"No, thank you."

"Darling?" he said to my mother.

"Ice water," my mother said.

I fiddled with the drink coaster on the table next to me. "Fiddled" is a verb that can be taken literally, as in playing the fiddle (a countrified term for violin), or as a synonym for "played with." I meant it in the latter way. You cannot play the violin with a drink coaster. As I've said many times before, American English is strange.

"Now," my mother said, "before we get too far into this, I want to apologize for last night. I should have called before we showed up like—"

"Mother, surprising me wasn't a problem."

"Now, please, don't interrupt me. I'm not finished. I should have called. We might have been able to discuss this alone instead of in front of your friends. It didn't need to be such a scene, and I'm sorry for that."

"Thank you, Mother. That's why I'm here."

"Good," she said. She took a swig of water. "Are you sure you don't want something to drink?"

"No, thank you."

She stood. "I've been arguing with myself this morning about whether we should have told you about this Hugo Hunter person. I don't even know why I say 'we.' Your father was absolutely unreachable on this matter, and he never believed—or at least never acknowledged—that he had paternity. He'd say, 'She would have come to me and told me.' He thought that woman had integrity. Your father was a fool in many ways, Edward. I'm sorry to say it so bluntly, but he was."

My mother's back was to me, so I looked at Jay L. Lamb. He had this thin smile that looked like it required a great effort.

"I have to say, I was surprised we never heard from that woman or her family, that they never made an effort to extort something from us," she said. "That's what baffles me about why he's shown up now—and that's why I'm suspicious."

I waited for her to turn around and face me before I spoke. "He says he didn't know until recently."

"I don't believe that."

"That's what he said."

"Edward," she said, "these people aren't to be trusted. There's an angle."

"It's not 'these people.' It's just him. He wants to know me."

"I'll bet."

"He does."

Jay L. Lamb cleared his throat and started in. "You see, Edward, there's a lot at stake here. Your father's reputation, for one—"

"There's no threat to my father or his reputation," I said. "In any case, he's gone. It wouldn't matter now."

My mother took two quick strides toward me, moving aggressively enough that I rose from my chair.

"It's a threat to me," she said. "It's an embarrassment to me. It always has been. The way your father and that woman carried on, it was humiliating to me. For there to be a child...I cannot have that. I swallowed the humiliation in an effort to keep my marriage intact. And now here he is, a grown man, trying to insinuate himself into my life."

"My life," I said.

"If he's connected to you, he's connected to me," she said. I'm not being melodramatic when I say that she almost hissed it at me. It was that terse and ugly. "If he's in your life, he's in my life. And listen to me: I will not have that. Not for a single second will I have that."

"He is my brother."

"Don't you say that."

"He is. He wants to know me. I want to know him."

I tried to move away from my mother, but she reached out and grabbed my arm. "What possible reason does he have to want to know you?"

Jay L. Lamb stepped between us and removed her hand from me. "Don't say that, Maureen."

"It's true," my mother said. "Edward, you're a sweet man, but you're being played for something here. I know what it is. Jay knows what it is. This piece of trash wants something, and it's not a relationship with you. He's taking advantage of you."

"He's not," I said.

"He is. I'm warning you. Stay away from him. You'll regret it."

"I'm leaving."

That's what I did. I walked out her door, down the hallway, onto the elevator and rode down to the ground floor. My Cadillac DTS was parked in front of the building. I got in, backed out of the parking space and made a right turn onto First Avenue North, then rode that out to where the street jogs left, then right onto Broadwater Avenue.

Waiting for the light, I beat the shit out of my steering wheel with my fists. That's hyperbole. There is no shit in the steering wheel. Just a horn. When it went off, the driver in the car ahead of me showed me his middle finger.

I called Scott Shamwell from the house. I had intended to go from my mother's condominium to the shop—I'd mistakenly assumed that we would resolve our differences, and there you have a good indication of why you should never assume, kid. After I left my mother's place, I wanted only to come home and see your mother's sweet face and find out what she thought. So I called

Scott Shamwell and said I wouldn't be in, and I apologized again for not doing enough to help our business.

"Dude, do what you gotta do," he said. "I'm kicking ass and rebuilding fuel-intake systems."

Scott Shamwell is pretty funny sometimes.

As for your mother, I could have guessed what she would think. But I told you just a minute ago that I don't like to assume.

"The woman is certifiable," she said. That is an indirect way of calling your grandmother crazy, which isn't nice but may well be accurate. "Edward, you're a grown man. You can talk to anybody you want. You can have any friend you want to have. She doesn't get a vote."

"I know."

I don't think your grandmother is crazy, OK, kid? I don't think I have a cogent idea of why she is acting this way. I know that she often chafed at being in my father's shadow when he was alive, of standing behind him instead of beside him. I'm speaking figuratively here, kid, something that makes me uncomfortable. I know that she views her life since his death as being more free than it was before. I also know that she hasn't always trampled my freedom to do what I please. She stood up for me against my father's controlling ways. It confuses and pains me now that she's the one trying to control me.

"Did you tell her that?" your mother asked.

"What?"

"That you can do what you please?"

"Not in those words, exactly."

"In exactly what words, then?" Your mother stood in the living room with her fists balled up and on her hips. This is one of the ways she reveals she is angry.

"I said 'I'm leaving.'"

"That's not enough."

"That's all I have right now."

"You have to tell her. You have to be unmistakable in what you say to her."

I lost it, kid. This is an idiom that means my temper flared.

"Just leave me alone," I said to your mother. "She criticizes everything I do. You criticize everything I don't do, or how I do it. Just leave me alone."

Your mother set her jaw. "Fine. I will."

"Fine," I said. "I'm glad." I wasn't glad. I'm not sure why I said I was. You might as well prepare yourself now, kid. You're going to say a lot of things in your life that are directly the opposite of what you mean, and you're going to wonder why you did, and you probably won't know. Life is stupid sometimes.

Your mother walked away from me. I went into the computer room and I closed the door and I waited for my heart to stop beating so hard.

I waited a long time. Twenty-two minutes and fourteen seconds, and then I left the house again.

I shouldn't have bragged earlier about how good your mother and I are about resolving debates. Clearly, we have much room for improvement.

I'm going to tell you a story about your grandfather.

He died on Thursday, October 30th, 2008. He was in the parking lot of a golf course on the West End of town, preparing to go to the driving range to work on his swing, and he collapsed. He was taken to St. Vincent Healthcare, and doctors there tried to revive him, but it was too late. He was dead.

This inspires many feelings in me, and I have spent much time since then thinking about him. When I was a little boy, he was a good father to me. As I grew older, we had sharp disagreements, and when he died our relationship was in bad shape. The day before he died, he backhanded me in Jay L. Lamb's office when I resisted his attempt to make me stop being friends with Donna Middleton (now Donna Hays). That was my last interaction with him, being hit in the face. It took a long time to get over it, and you can be sure of that because I'm lying: I'm still not over it.

I was in the right about Donna Middleton (now Donna Hays), just as I'm in the right about your Uncle Hugo. Your mother thinks being in the right is enough, but I know from my own experience that it's of little comfort when you lose someone important to you.

How can I choose your Uncle Hugo if it means I lose my mother? How can I choose my mother if it means I lose your Uncle Hugo? Why do I have to choose? I didn't ask for this decision.

I told you about how there's sometimes not a better choice, just a less-bad one. Sometimes, there's not even a less-bad one. Sometimes, every choice is terrible.

I miss Dr. Buckley. Dr. Bryan Thomsen is not deficient in any significant way, but Dr. Buckley had a talent for seeing the logical, sensible path for me to take in moments of confusion. I don't know that I've ever been more confused than I am right now. I need help, kid. How can I help you with the problems you'll inevitably have (sorry, but you will) if I can't find the way out of my own?

That's a rhetorical question, by the way. You don't have to answer it. That would be far too much to ask of you at this juncture. But think about it if you can, OK?

I'll tell you another story about your grandfather. For more than three years after he died, I couldn't bring myself to drive past the golf course where he collapsed. It wasn't difficult for me to avoid that place; it's on the far West End of town, a long way from any of the places I regularly go. Just the same, I knew I was purposely avoiding it. That's superstitious behavior, and it's out of character for me. Superstitions are vastly inferior to facts.

Today, after I left the house angry at your mother, I felt like I had to see that golf course. We still have much snow on the ground because this winter has been a pain in the fucking tuckus, as Scott Shamwell likes to say, so no one was playing. Still, I drove into the parking lot and made a few circles in my Cadillac DTS, and then I rode out to the Terrace Gardens cemetery, just a few blocks away, where my father—your grandfather—was laid to rest.

I visit the cemetery a couple of times a year to look at his gravestone and to put fresh flowers in the vase. Oddly, I don't make regular pilgrimages that are strictly scheduled, like I do with so many other things in my life. I just go when I feel compelled to, and today was one of those days.

We put my father into the ground on November 1st, 2008. The newspaper had a big write-up, and many well-known people, including the governor, came to pay their respects to him and our family. I remember walking around at a reception at my parents' house and listening to the conversations. People talked about how my father's influence would live on, that he would never be forgotten, that his imprint on Billings, Montana, would be celebrated long after he was gone.

I feel like I can tell you the truth about this, kid. It's a bunch of bullshit. (This has nothing to do with cattle. Or feces.)

Nobody talks about him anymore, it seems. My mother sure doesn't want to, and while your mother is patient with me when I wish to talk about my father, she didn't know him and thus can't offer much to the conversation. For a time after he died, there was talk among the county commission about funding a scholarship in his name or even putting up a statue on the courthouse lawn. Neither of those things happened, and at this point, it would be foolish to think they will.

He went into the ground, people promptly forgot about him, and life went on for everybody else. That's the truth of the matter, kid. You can be as rich and well-known as my father was, but when you're dead, you're dead.

The only people feeling his legacy are me, my mother, and the brother I didn't know I had.

CLOSING THOUGHT

I've said it all, haven't I? I'm tired. I'm going home.

From: imsheilastanton@gmail.com
To: imedwardstanton@gmail.com
Re: Just come home

It's raining, and you're out there somewhere mad at me, and I just want you home. Please look at your bitchin' iPhone and see this and come back.

I'm sorry I got on your case. You're right, I push too hard sometimes. I feel like we're being pushed by your mother, and all I want to do is push her back. I pushed you instead. I forgot whose team I was on.

Your mother called here looking for you. It took everything I had to keep from answering the phone and telling her off. Maybe I should. What do you think? Maybe I could say the things that are harder for you to say.

Anyway, she left a message. She says she wants to try again with the conversation, and that's some story. I don't think she'll be satisfied until you agree to everything she wants. That's what I think. But the message is there, so you can listen to it. That reminds me: Why do we have a land line? And an answering machine? It doesn't make any sense.

Sorry. I zoned out for a minute there.

Come home. Please, come home.

BUCK UP, BUCKAROO*

*—my father—your grandfather—used to say this

I went to work today, Monday, determined to make things as normal as possible. Let's face it, kid: Things have been far from normal for a while now, dating to the moment we found out about you. Your mother and I agreed that I needed to just go to work, then come home at the regular time (I'm usually home by 5:06 p.m., unless a traffic problem binds me up), eat my dinner, watch TV with her, and then go to bed. We agreed that a bit of normalcy would help settle me down. We also agreed that your grandmother, my mother, is trying to manipulate me by suggesting another meeting. I'm not going to return that phone call.

The problem with fixating on normalcy is that you can't necessarily control the things other people do, things that might be out of the ordinary. This became clear when Mark Westerly came into the shop at 9:13 a.m. and asked if he could talk with me.

"Would that be OK?" I asked Scott Shamwell, who had been happy to see me back at work and had several jobs set aside for me. I didn't want to disappoint him.

"Have at it," he said, and then he gave a wave of the hand to

165

Mark Westerly. I'd forgotten that those guys became friends at my debacle of a party.

Mark Westerly and I went into my office so we could have some privacy.

"Hugo doesn't know I'm here," he said as he sat down.

"OK."

"I'm just saying so you don't think I'm his intermediary. I don't want you to think you have to go through me to talk to him."

"OK," I said again.

He leaned forward and put his hands on my desk. I leaned forward, too.

"That said, I have spoken to Hugo, and I think I know him about as well as anyone. I'd like to give you a little insight, if I'm not intruding."

"You're not intruding at all, Mark Westerly."

"OK, good." He settled back into his chair. "Here's what I think you have to understand: Because of the way he was raised by his mother and then his grandmother, and the fact that he doesn't have either of them anymore, he's never going to allow himself to get close to anybody he thinks may leave him. I'm talking friend, brother, girlfriend, whatever. It doesn't matter. He can't handle abandonment."

"OK," I said.

Mark Westerly maintained eye contact with me. It was intimidating. He wanted to make sure I understood everything I was being told. "Now, this thing works both ways," he said. "He also doesn't want you to lose anything by knowing him. That's what he said to me, in exactly those words. He doesn't want to be a problem for you and your mother."

"Does he like me?" I asked. I surprised myself with the question. I've never particularly cared whether anyone likes me, other than your mother and Donna Middleton (now Donna Hays) and Kyle Middleton and Scott Shamwell.

"Absolutely, he does," Mark Westerly said. "He likes you very much."

"I like him, too. We're brothers."

Mark Westerly smiled. "You are at that."

I fiddled with papers on my desk as I tried to formulate my next question. I ended up just being blunt. "So what are you telling me to do?"

"I can't tell you what to do," Mark Westerly said. "I'm telling you what I think you need to know about Hugo. If you tell him you want him around, that you want to be close to him, he'll probably do it. He cares that much about you. I'm telling you, as someone who knows him and cares about him, don't tell him that if you can't commit to it. Don't say, 'I want to be your friend,' then turn around and cut him loose. You get what I'm saying?"

"Yes."

"And by the same token, if you feel like you can't know him without damaging your relationship with your mother, he'll get it. He'll understand. Just be honest with him. That's what I'm saying."

"Yes."

Mark Westerly stood up and offered a handshake, which I accepted. "Thanks," he said. "I hope I didn't overstep. I wrestled with the idea of coming to see you, but I've been around the block with Hugo a few times, and I know where the fault lines are, if that's a description that makes sense. He values loyalty above all else. I'll let him tell you the stories if you choose to hang in there with him. I'll just say that he's come by this the hard way."

"I wish I knew him as well as you do," I said.

Mark Westerly winked at me. "You know what?" he said. "It's a pain in the ass sometimes. It's also worth it."

He went back into the shop and said a few words to Scott Shamwell that I couldn't hear, and then I remembered something.

"Mark?" I said.

He turned around. "Yeah?"

"Sheila really enjoyed getting to know your wife."

"It was a good time," he said, and then he had a halfway smile on his face. "You know, until it wasn't."

"Sheila hopes she hasn't lost a new friend."

Mark Westerly finished his smile when I said that. "You don't know Lainie very well if you think she gives up that easily."

It's obvious I don't know Lainie Westerly very well. I've met her only once. But from the way Mark Westerly and Scott Shamwell were smiling, I could infer that he meant they could still be friends.

Your mother will be happy to hear that.

I told Scott Shamwell what Mark Westerly had said to me.

"Dude's a straight shooter," he said. "You gotta give him that." (By the way, kid, this has nothing to do with the way Mark Westerly handles a firearm.)

"Yes."

"So what are you going to do?"

I stood up and pulled the start cord on the lawnmower I'd been repairing. It fired up on the first tug. Another $59 for us.

"I don't know," I said.

Scott Shamwell took the mower from me and moved it into the holding room where it would wait for its owner to retrieve it.

"I don't get it," he yelled from the holding room. "I'd hang out with him. Who cares what your mother thinks? She has some weird loyalties, man."

When he came back into the main part of the shop, I said, "You go see your mother in Havre every other weekend, even though she's staying loyal to your dad."

"That's different."

"No, it isn't."

"She needs me," Scott Shamwell said.

"Maybe my mother needs me, too. Maybe I need her."

Scott Shamwell looked away from me and got back to work.

Scott Shamwell and I usually go to a restaurant in the Heights for lunch, but today I came home to tell your mother about Mark Westerly's visit. She met me in the driveway.

"Your mom was here," she said.

"When?"

"About twenty minutes ago. I was going to call. I was trying to settle myself down before I picked up the phone and yelled."

"What did she say?" I had a pretty good idea, but it's best not to assume, especially in emotional matters.

"Just that she wanted to talk to you. She asked where you were. I wouldn't tell her. I said, 'You're not going to go down there and make him upset.' I said it just like that."

"This is getting dumb." I started walking toward the door, with your mother following me.

"I said more than just that," she said.

I went into the living room. "What?"

"I told her that she was the most selfish person I know."

"OK."

"And that she's a bad mother."

I didn't feel well. It was like sludge was moving through my stomach, which is of course impossible.

"What did she say?"

"She said I'd know soon what it's like to be a mother and that until then I should shut up. That's when I told her to leave."

"OK." I sat down on the couch.

"Are you mad at me?"

"No."

Your mother sat down and took my hand. "I guess I let her get to me."

"She's good at that."

"I think I might have hurt her feelings."

I squeezed your mother's hand. "She'll get over it."

She set her head against my shoulder, and we just sat there. Nobody had lunch. I can probably afford to skip it, but your mother is eating for two. I should have insisted that she have something to eat.

I told your mother about my meeting with Mark Westerly. She immediately called Lainie Westerly and proposed a girls' outing. That's what she said, "let's go on a girls' outing." This is silly nomenclature (another excellent word). By the way, this is precisely why we still have a land line. Your mother doesn't have her own cellular phone, and if we didn't have a land line,

I could not read the *Billings Herald-Gleaner* online while your mother was using my bitchin' iPhone to talk to Lainie Westerly. It always amuses me when your mother assumes I haven't thought something out. I think out everything.

After she got off the phone, I told her I would go see my mother, your grandmother.

"This needs to be resolved," I said. I resolved to resolve it. I had the resolve to resolve it and achieve my resolution. If you ever wonder why language is so difficult, kid, there's your demonstration. I just used the same word in three different ways.

"OK," your mother said. "Tell her I'm sorry."

"Are you?"

"No, not really."

"Then I will not tell her that."

I left, but not before I kissed your mother eight times on the lips. That's what we do, and amid all this uncertainty and lack of normalcy, I think it's important to maintain our standards.

I STAND UP FOR MYSELF

I said, "It's Edward," and my mother buzzed me into her building. I took the long walk to the elevator, then the ride up, then the long walk to her door. It's strange, because I would have predicted that I'd feel anxious about going to my mother's condominium, but I didn't. I felt like I was doing exactly what I needed to do. That goes to show you how unreliable predictions can be, kid.

Jay L. Lamb again opened the door. He was dressed in a charcoal-colored button-front shirt and black slacks, and I felt self-conscious in my work overalls. My mother was waiting for me, sitting pretty in the chair I had occupied on my previous visit.

"You're hard to find," she said.

"Not really. I was at work. Sheila said you were looking for me."

My mother shuffled some papers on the living-room table. "Sheila has a tart little mouth on her. She always has."

"She got angry. She does that sometimes. So do you."

"And you as well," your grandmother said. "I'm not the one who stormed out of here the other day."

"Yes," I said. "I get angry, too."

She picked up one of the sheets of paper.

"I need to ask you something," she said. "Who is Scott Shamwell?"

I hadn't expected that question. "He's my friend."

"This is the man who cussed at me at your house."

"Yes."

She pushed the paper across the table. "You should sit down. This is going to take a while. Read that."

I sat on the couch. Jay L. Lamb lingered behind me. I picked up the paper, and I recognized it. It was a photocopy of a canceled paycheck for Scott Shamwell. I set it down.

"He's also your employee," my mother said.

"Business partner."

"Business partner! Wonderful!" She said this in a mocking way, a way that suggested the exact opposite of wonderful.

"I thought we were going to talk about my brother," I said.

"I wish to never speak of him again, and don't call him that," she said. "But I do want to talk about this Scott Shamwell. Have you seen this before?" She pushed another paper toward me. This was a printout of a *Billings Herald-Gleaner* story about the sentencing of Scott Shamwell's father and brother.

"Yes, I've seen this."

"Your business partner is a drug dealer."

"No," I said. "He's not. His father and brother were."

She stood up. "I don't know what's gotten into you. These are not the type of people we do business with. I looked at your bank account, and you've done quite well with this venture of yours. Why would you jeopardize that by dealing with this man of low character?"

"Why were you looking at my bank account?"

Jay L. Lamb came up behind me. "Your mother is a co-owner of the account. You know that. It's what your father intended. It was never supposed to be your money to spend willy-nilly."

My mother cut back in. "And I've been extremely tolerant, I'd say. I didn't flinch when you took a bath on that silly motel in Colorado. But this is going too far." (Just so you're not confused, kid, your grandmother used "a bath" in the idiomatic sense that I lost a lot of money. There was no hot water or shampoo involved.)

"What is?"

"Edward, please don't be obstinate. This Shamwell person has to go."

I stood up. "No."

"This isn't a request. You have exposed this family to great risk these past several weeks. Now, get rid of him."

"No." I said it louder this time.

My mother's voice cracked and softened. "Please, sit down. Don't make this harder than it has to be."

I sat. I was dubious (good word) about the rest of her assessment. Harder for whom?

I got my answer in my mother's next breath. "Here's what's going to happen. I'm suspending your access to this money. Your father and I didn't fight and claw for what we gave you just so you could squander it on people of low of character."

The money. Kid, I'm not the sort of person who likes to make predictions—I've made myself clear on that—but I knew on the drive over that the money was going to come up. I knew it, and I prepared myself for it. And now I sat and listened, and I formulated. I wanted my mother to have her say so I could have mine. I wasn't sure either of us would want to say anything more after that. I knew I surely didn't want to hear anything else.

"I'm not taking it away from you," my mother said. "I'm putting it in trust. When I'm dead and gone, I won't care what you do with it, and I won't be able to stop you from ruining your life if that's what you want to do. Or maybe your own child—my grandchild—will be more sensible than you've turned out to be."

"You're wrong about me, Mother. You couldn't be more wrong," I said. I'd wanted to stay silent until she was done, but I couldn't help it.

"I take no pleasure in this. But I'm doing what I think is right."

I stood again. "You're done, then? May I speak?"

My mother waved her hand.

"I'm going to keep my shop going, and Scott Shamwell is

going to keep being my partner," I said. "I'm going from here to my brother's house, and I'm going to hang out with him. I'm going to invite him to my house for dinner, if he wants to come. Tomorrow, I'm going to take my wife to see Dr. Arlene Haworth for her checkup. We're going to find out how our baby—your grandchild—is doing. We're going to be thankful for our friends, and grateful for the good times we're having together. And Mother, I never thought I would say this to you, because I love you, but you're not invited to any of these things. I do not want to see you again for the entire time you're here. I may not want to see you again ever, but I'm not prepared to say that just yet. So when you're sure you've done the right thing, you also need to be sure of what it's going to cost you."

My legs quivered, just a little, as I turned and walked toward the door.

By the time I reached the street, my cheeks were wet.

Your Uncle Hugo doesn't drink beer, non-alcoholic or otherwise, so we clinked together our diet cola bottles as we sat on his patio and watched the sun hang low in the sky. I was glad he'd opened the door when I knocked. I had much to tell him, starting with a pledge that I wouldn't abandon him. Why would I do that? Look how long it took me to find him.

Your Uncle Hugo took a semester off from his classes at Montana State University Billings to do promotional work for his book, but that has begun to wind down. When I knocked on the door, he was busy making his course selections for summer school. Your uncle is a remarkable guy. He dropped out of high school in 1993 to start his boxing career, but until that time, he had been an excellent student at Billings Senior High School— better than I was six years earlier at Billings West High School. He showed me his report cards, which his grandmother had kept stashed away in a box. Nothing but A's and B's, a solid grade-point average, and good marks for attendance and conduct.

Last year, he received his general equivalency diploma, and then his son, Raj, paid for him to go to college, using money your

Uncle Hugo had set aside for Raj after a title fight ten years ago. He's studying English and elementary education, and he wants to be a schoolteacher.

"You want another one?" Your Uncle Hugo sucked down his cola. Most of mine was still left.

"No," I said. "I just want to watch the sky."

I didn't mind the cold. It was worth sitting out there to see everything lit up in orange and purple and streaks of red. Trouble, in the form of thinking about your grandmother, still tugged at me (idiom), but I felt like I had managed to let things slow down enough for me to appreciate a sunset.

Hugo came back out, sliding the door shut with his foot, and sat down next to me.

"You OK?" he said.

"Yes."

"You're sure about this?"

"Yes."

I could see him eyeing me, looking me over, trying to figure out if I was being honest with him. I made sure not to mention that Mark Westerly had come to see me; Mark had asked me not to.

"You know," he said, "my old trainer let me down the way your mom did tonight. It's not the same thing, of course, but he was like a dad to me, so it hurt in a similar way."

"No," I said. "I didn't know that."

"Still haven't read my book, huh?"

Damn. Your Uncle Hugo got me with that one.

"Sorry."

"It's OK. I'm patient," he said.

"What happened?"

"Oh, I was about to fight this guy, and he put a large bet down in Vegas against me. Unethical as hell, but it came through for him. It didn't come out till a year or so ago. Haven't talked to him since."

"That sucks elephant balls," I said. Scott Shamwell would have been proud of me.

"Elephant-size elephant balls," he said. I had to laugh. What other size could there be?

"Elephant balls so big they have their own gravitational field," I said.

"Interplanetary elephant balls," he said.

We're pretty funny sometimes.

I came home alone. Your Uncle Hugo had already told Mark and Lainie Westerly that he'd have dinner with them, but we agreed to get together again soon. I like him. Even if he wasn't my brother, I'd want to be his friend. I wanted to be his friend when he was famous and I didn't even know he was my brother. He just seemed really cool, and I liked that.

I told your mother what happened. I told her I had what Dr. Bryan Thomsen likes to call "clarity." What that means is that although I did not choose the circumstances, and would not have chosen them if my mother hadn't forced the issue, I could see clearly what I needed to do. Having your Uncle Hugo in my life, and maintaining my friendship and partnership with Scott Shamwell, is the proper choice. Putting my attention on you, my child, is my top priority. We're halfway to the point where we'll be seeing you, and there's so much left to do to prepare for your arrival.

Your mother asked me if I was sad. How could I not be? That's a rhetorical question, kid. You don't have to answer it.

I wonder if I worry too much about whether I'm happy or sad anyway. It seems like both of those things show up and leave on their own schedule. Maybe I should just worry about whether I'm doing the appropriate thing or making the appropriate choice.

In this case, I think I am.

Finally, I told your mother about the money.

"We're broke," I said.

"We are not broke," she said.

"We are."

"No, we're not."

We didn't come to an agreement on this issue. I think it's a matter of perspective. I've never been without either my father's money or my father's implicit (good word) financial backing. I'm scared. I don't mind telling you that.

Your mother gave me some dinner, a pork chop and asparagus, but I didn't finish it. I couldn't concentrate. I told her I'd just like to write to you and then go to bed. I'm nearly done with the first part, and now I feel sleepy. Thanks for reading, kid. You're my hope for the future, because the present looks rotten.

CLOSING THOUGHT

I think I'm out of closing thoughts, kid. From now on, if it's worth noting, I'm just going to write it down. If it's not, I won't. Here's something you might as well consider now, before you get a harder lesson later: You can start out with a great idea about what you're going to do and how you're going to do it. Maybe that will happen. Maybe it won't. The thing is, you can't see the circumstances that might change things until they've already happened.

I don't like maybes. I like yes or no, black or white, right or wrong.

Not that it does me much good.

We're not broke.

Setting aside the rest of your father's message, because he's a wonderful, sensitive man and he's feeling so hurt, this stuff about being broke is just the biggest wad of nonsense I've ever heard.

Great, yeah, so the $5 million and whatever is gone. That's a lot of money. It's so much money that it was hard to even contemplate that it existed. I don't know when you'll read this or what your sense of numbers will be, but trust me: In 2014, $5 million is a crazy amount of money. Maybe when you're all grown up, it won't be anything. But it's something now.

Your father would do well to look around at our neighbors. I've gotten to know the woman next door. Her husband left last year, and she's raising two kids on 30-grand a year, no savings, no nothing. If she loses that job, they're in a lot of trouble. The guy on the other side, he retired about 15 years ago. He lives on Social Security and a small pension from his time in the bakers' union. Your father knows this. He mows the guy's grass, because that old man can't afford a lawnmower or to pay someone to do it.

That's broke. Not what we are. It really annoys me that he'd say that to me. It's so unaware. Your father isn't like the people he came from, thank God—he's not a big, loud philanderer like your grandfather, and he's not an elitist like your grandmother. But he comes from privilege, and he just doesn't know about struggle. It's irritating.

Let me tell you something about my mother and father. My daddy got a nice little inheritance when his own father died and the family farm was sold. Nothing extravagant—we might have had some decent savings if he'd held on to it—but a nice sum of money. He and Mom put it into building a motel, because they wanted to run a family business and they wanted to have a big family. Medically, that didn't work out—there was only me—but this is what they wanted.

I grew up seeing my folks fight and scrape to make the ledger balance every month. I saw my Daddy learn to repair his old Suburban because he couldn't afford to buy a new one. Your father asked me last year if we should get a new Cadillac. Not because there's anything wrong with the one we have. Because the new Cadillac had better features, he said. "We're fucking loaded," he said, and I hate it when he talks like that. Who cares? THE CAR WE HAVE NOW IS FINE.

I'll tell you something else: Your father has apparently forgotten that I sold that motel and have nearly $250,000 put away from the sale. That's not in the $5 million or whatever that your grandmother took back from him. That's our money, and it's in my account in Colorado, and if I need to spend it to keep this family going, that's what I'll do. I won't even care.

The woman next door would like to have that cushion, let me tell you. So would the nice old man on the other side of us. We're not broke. We're not remotely broke.

Now, that's not to say that I don't care what your grandmother did. I can't say I'm surprised, as I've always found her to be too materialistic, but this was beyond the pale (your father can explain that phrase to you). I shouldn't even say this to you, but it will be a long time before you read this and by then maybe you'll know this about your grandmother and love her despite it: She is a sad, petty person. She is self-centered, and the worst part is she has no idea. Your father loves her, as he should because she's his mom, and I know it took a lot for him to stand up to her the way he did.

She's lucky I wasn't there. I would have been much harder on her. I might have tried to fight her, that's how angry I am. Your father loves her. I tolerate her, because I love your father. But I couldn't have tolerated this.

There is sadness in my house right now, and she's to blame. I'm extremely angry at her.

I love you.

Goodnight.

I NEED HELP

I woke up at 5:41 a.m., a most unusual time for me. Never in my record-keeping have I awoken at this time. Your mother lay in the bed next to me, and she seemed to be sleeping peacefully. I was glad to see that. She needs it. You need it.

I stepped out onto the porch and gathered up the *Billings Herald-Gleaner*. With my new job, I don't get to read the newspaper much anymore. Here, I'm referring to the printed newspaper, on actual paper; by the time you read this, there may be no more printed newspapers anywhere. By the time you read this, there may be no more paper anywhere. It seems preposterous, another fine word, to suggest this as a possibility, but technology is not to be underestimated.

Anyway, today was a rare morning when I had time to read the newspaper and eat my breakfast without being in a hurry. I wanted to let your mother sleep, and I needed to think about some things.

Do you remember what I said about being happy and being sad, and how those feelings come and go? Today, I am happy and sad at the same time. Logically, this does not seem possible, but emotions are not logical. There is a complexity to emotion that sometimes leaves people confused. Oh, yeah. I'm also confused today.

I always wanted a brother. Or a sister. A sibling. As I grew up in my father and mother's house, I was lonely. This wasn't just because I didn't have many friends, although I certainly didn't. I didn't have anyone I could relate to. My father and mother could relate to each other. I spent my time inside my own head. (Let's be clear: I don't mean this in a literal sense—that is physically impossible. What I mean is that I would entertain myself with my own thoughts. I'm an entertaining person, I think, but that doesn't mean I wasn't lonely.)

One time, when my father was drunk, he told me that he and my mother didn't have any more children because of how I turned out. That made me cry. It made my mother cry, too, but it also made her angry at my father. Maybe he didn't mean it only he knows for sure, and he's dead now—but I disliked myself because I thought I had precluded the one thing I really wanted.

So here I am. I'm forty-five years old, and I've discovered I have a brother. There's a feeling that comes with this. I think it's love. It's a feeling like your heart is going to fill up and then overflow and maybe even explode. Usually, when your heart feels that way, you should go to the doctor and make sure you're not having a cardiac event, but in this case, it's a feeling you want. Other than finding out that your mother loved me, and finding out about you, it's the best feeling I've ever had.

This feeling exists side by side with one of the worst feelings I've ever had, and that's the fear that I won't see or talk to my mother again. She has behaved so deplorably (good adverb, but not a good quality) toward me, and in some ways it's worse than anything my father ever did to me. She knows what he did. And she knows better. And yet, here we are, in conflict. I hate it.

I was thinking last night about my father and what he would say about your Uncle Hugo. We used to watch him box together. I've told you that. My mother says he was willfully ignorant of his relationship with Hugo. I wonder if that's true, or if he really didn't know. I wonder, if my father were here, whether he would accept your Uncle Hugo into our family. Could he make my mother accept that? I have my doubts. Mostly, I just don't know. I hate not knowing. If you have a fact-loving brain like mine, not knowing is like torture.

If there's anything I've learned that is worthwhile, it's this, kid: Life is a lot more interesting, and a lot more fun, when you fill it with people you love. It took me a long time to learn this, and I sometimes have to remind myself of it when people aggravate me.

I've been alone. But then I met Donna Middleton (now Donna Hays) and her son Kyle. I met her husband, Victor. I met Scott Shamwell and your mother. I met my brother, your Uncle Hugo, and his son (your cousin!), Raj.

I've also lost people. I lost my father. I lost Mister Withers, my shop teacher in high school who later hired me to work at the *Billings Herald-Gleaner*. He died last September, and I went to his funeral, and I saw him lying in his coffin. That was strange; it was disconcerting, because I could plainly see that it was him, but nothing about him seemed real. The Mister Withers I knew had open eyes and a smiling mouth, and he called me "my boy." The Mister Withers they put into the ground looked like a wax figure. I didn't like it.

I also lost Dr. Buckley to retirement, and now I've lost my mother, even though she's still alive.

I'm so sad, and I don't know how to fix it. I don't know if it's something fixable. It might be something I just have to endure.

For what it's worth, Dr. Bryan Thomsen says it may be something I just have to endure. That's not the answer I wanted to hear, but Dr. Bryan Thomsen is a smart man. He may be correct. He often is.

I don't ordinarily see Dr. Bryan Thomsen on Mondays, but I called him after breakfast and asked if he could find room in his schedule for me. He didn't even ask me what was going on. The request itself was so unusual that he simply said, "I have an opening at 10:30, if that works for you," which is a weird way to say it, because it suggests that if I'd said, "No, sorry, Dr. Bryan Thomsen, 10:30 will not work for me," he would have said, "Good, because I don't have an opening then." Language is strange.

As it turned out, 10:30 did work for me, and I was even able to go to the shop and get a power rake running again before I left for Dr. Bryan Thomsen's office. That gave me a chance to fill Scott Shamwell in. I left out the part about my mother wanting me to fire Scott Shamwell. I think it would have made him sad. I concentrated instead on my decision to keep your Uncle Hugo in my life.

The words Scott Shamwell used made it clear that he thought I'd made the correct decision. "Ultimatums are for weak sisters and pussies," he said, and I giggled at the latter word even though I don't think there's a word that makes your mother angrier (except, maybe, the C-word, which I will not explain— you'll have to learn it from someone else).

"I'm serious," he said, and it seemed like he was revving up toward one of his rants where he strings together curse words in odd and interesting combinations. I was looking forward to that, actually. Instead, Scott Shamwell's tone softened and he said, "I'm sorry, Ed buddy. It's a shame you had to choose."

He gathered up a wrench and went to work on a motor mount. Scott Shamwell knows a thing or two about selfishness. His father put the entire family in jeopardy by making and selling methamphetamine. What my mother did wasn't as widely destructive as that, but she still forced me into a choice I didn't want to make. I remember what Dr. Buckley said about that, years ago: "People who force such decisions do so to get confirmation of their own importance to you. The irony is, it erodes the love and trust you've worked so hard to build."

Dr. Bryan Thomsen said pretty much the same thing today. He wasn't as eloquent as Dr. Buckley—few people are—but I understood what he meant.

"I hate hearing about this," he said. "You know, I work with a lot of people who have contentious relationships, and I've seen and heard a lot of ultimatums. They never work. Ever. And the person who presents one is rarely prepared for having to face the choice she didn't want. That's your mother now. She's going to have to deal with what you decided."

"So what do I do?" I asked.

"You let her."

He must have been able to see in my face that I didn't care for his answer. "What I'm saying is, you've been clear. You were forced into a choice, and you made it. Now she has to be clear in deciding whether she can live with that choice. There's really not a role for you here. You have people relying on you—your wife, Scott, your brother, your child—so you just have to go on with things. Unless..."

"Unless?"

"Well, unless you want to change your choice. Do you want to do that?"

"No. I mean, I don't think so."

"You're wise to avoid it," Dr. Bryan Thomsen said. I like it when he calls me wise. "It would change the entire dynamic of your relationship with your mother, and in a way that wouldn't be good for you. This is an important boundary for you to hold with her."

I smiled. Truly, I did. "Well, Dr. Bryan Thomsen, it's not like the dynamic is very good right now."

He smiled back at me. "Well, you know what they say. Things can always get worse."

I like Dr. Bryan Thomsen. He has a pessimism that appeals to me.

Dr. Bryan Thomsen gave me one last bit of advice before I left at 11 a.m. He said he didn't want to rush me out of the office but that someone else needed him at that time. I told him I understood.

"Edward," he said, "we've talked before about grace. I want to urge you to hold that in reserve if you can. I feel like I've gotten to know your mother over these past few years, and I don't think she's a cold or cruel woman. Some parents are. Some children are. I don't think she is. Do you?"

"No."

"She may come to understand how wrong she's been."

"Yes."

"But she's a proud person. It may be difficult for her to acknowledge this."

"Yes."

"Grace is your way of leaving a door open so she can find her way back outside your boundaries. Do you understand?"

"I think so."

"Do you think you can do that?"

I considered the question for a moment. I was very angry when he asked it. I'm very angry now, as I write this. I don't want to punish my mother, but I also don't want to talk to her right now. I may never want to. That's the reality of how I feel.

"I don't know," I said. "I can try."

JUNE

TWENTY-SIX WEEKS

It's been a while since I wrote to you, kid, and for that I'm sorry. If you could see day-to-day life around here—and you can't because your eyes aren't open yet, and even if they were you're inside your mother's womb and there's no way to see us—you would know that we haven't forgotten about you. You're big enough now that there's no mistaking your mother is pregnant, which leads otherwise normal people to say all sorts of strange things to her when we're out in public. We've even had people come up to us and ask to touch your mother's stomach. That's a weird and off-putting request, kid. Your mother always says no, which is her right and her boundary. Some people look like they're offended when she says this. *They're offended.* I fear I'm not going to be able to explain much about this world and the people in it when you start asking questions.

At this point, kid, you're about the length of a zucchini. I found that out on the Internet, which has any number of places that will compare the size of a gestating child to a fruit or vegetable. And there's also this: If you're a boy, your testicles are descending into your scrotum. That is exciting. If you're anything like Scott Shamwell, you're going to touch and talk about your testicles a lot.

We also don't forget about you because you kick a lot, and it amuses your mother every time you do. She will start to giggle and then say "Edward, come feel the baby kicking," and I'll come over and put my hand on her belly because I'm allowed to. Sometimes I will feel you kick, but other times I don't, as if you become aware of the presence of my hand and stop kicking. Your mother says that's because I have a calming influence on you. I don't know if that's true. Maybe you're just having some fun at my expense.

We also don't forget about you because your mother is throwing up even more now. It's called "morning sickness," which is a strange name for something that happens at midday and nighttime, too. It's awful when she throws up, and her face turns red and her eyes water, but every time she says it's a blessing that she gets to experience this. I don't know, kid. I don't see the blessing, but I think you're pretty lucky that your mother looks at it that way.

Finally, we don't forget about you because we love you. We love you completely. This is not something I would have predicted. I remember how, when we first found out about you, you were little more than a concept to me. I didn't see how I could love you without meeting you. But I do. I love a little zucchini that may or may not have descending testicles. Who knew?

That's just a joke, kid. I'm pretty funny sometimes.

I wanted to assure you of our attention to you, kid, because things have otherwise been chaotic around here. Scott Shamwell and I have settled into long hours at the shop, and that's paying off well for us. We have a steady stream of repeat customers and new referrals, and they seem to be happy with the work we're doing for them. I come home in the evening tired, and your mother and I have dinner, and then we talk about you—we always talk about you—and then we go to bed. Or, sometimes, I have to leave work early because we have an appointment to see Dr. Arlene Haworth, who assures us that you're doing just fine. Sometimes, your mother and Lainie Westerly go to lunch or shopping, and they have bought so many clothes for you that we've run out of places to store them. I said this to your mother about three weeks ago after I noted how many clothes we had: "We're not having triplets, are we?" I thought I was being pretty funny, but your mother did not talk to me for about an hour. And then she threw up. I blame you for that, kid.

Anyway, get ready to wear a lot of clothes. That's what I'm trying to tell you. I like the ones with funny sayings on them, like a onesie your Uncle Hugo got you that says If You Think I'm Cute You Should See My Uncle. Scott Shamwell asked your mother if he could get you a shirt that said Eat Poopy and Die, and your mother said, "Shut up, Scott." I laughed at him. That was pretty funny.

One thing that hasn't changed is the situation with your grandmother. Dr. Bryan Thomsen has urged me to hold my boundaries with her but to leave her room to come back to me if she decides to. I'm holding my boundaries, and she hasn't come back. I see her downtown sometimes, when I'm driving through or walking to the bank, but neither of us says anything. She and Jay L. Lamb are doing their regular springtime activities, and I have my routine, too. I guess this is what happens when you drift apart from someone. Life goes on. That's a saying. It always struck me as too obvious to be useful, but I see it in a different way now.

I'm glad I can talk to you about these things. It's not really a dialogue, per se (that's Latin). It's me spouting off with the expectation that perhaps one day you'll read these words. If you do, perhaps I will be far enough away from what's going on now that I'll be able to speak of it with more clarity. Not much is clear now. I work. You grow. Your mother takes care of both of us. Days begin and end. We wait.

For what? You, mostly. The rest is a mystery.

I have to go now, kid. Your Uncle Hugo is coming over for dinner, and he's bringing his son, Raj (your cousin). It's been eleven days since I've seen Hugo, and thirty-two since I've seen Raj. I've missed them.

Isn't that funny? A few months ago, I didn't even know them.

Oh, kiddo, you are a load. If the numbers are right, we're two-thirds of the way through this, maybe a little more. My back, my hips, my boobs. You're doing exactly what everybody said you would.

You should see your father. This partnership with Scott has transformed things around here—not always for the best, I'd have to say, because the late nights and erratic schedules are a burden on him because of the way he is and on me because I'm holding down everything else. But the tradeoff, on the whole, is in the plus column. Your father has purpose in his working life, and that's important no matter how much or how little you have. A man needs that, I think. A woman, too, for that matter. I have to watch myself. I don't want to be casting you into any hard gender roles. I think that's not good.

I think purpose is what I'm missing. Don't get me wrong: Right now, the job is all about you. Carrying you. Giving birth to you. Being the best mother I can be. There's no higher purpose.

But would I be too selfish if I wanted something more, too? Something just for me? It doesn't feel selfish when I say it to myself, but I haven't dared yet say it to anyone else. Not even Lainie, who's turning into the best girlfriend I've ever had. I don't know how to say exactly what I mean, so for now, let's just keep it between the two of us, what do you say?

Love,
Your mother

GUESS WHO'S COMING TO DINNER?*

*—*This is the title of a really good movie that came out in 1967, before I was born. It's about a black man and a white woman who want to get married and their parents, who are scared of all the opposition they'll face. I think you would like it, and I'll probably show it to you someday. The movie seems to suggest that things are tough but getting better. They certainly are tough, whether in 1967 or now. I'm not sure they're getting better, though.*

Another week has gone by and I haven't written you, kid, and there's a good reason for that. Your mother has decided that we don't have enough going on with a new business and a baby on the way and an ongoing shitburger of a problem with your grandmother. She thinks we ought to move to a new house. No, wait, let me put that more precisely, as precision seems the one thing left that I have some say over: She says we're going to move to a new house.

I had a lot to say about that, but nothing I had to say has changed what she says. This sucks.

But let me back up (not literally; I'm sitting at my desk, typing on a keyboard, and cannot walk) and tell you what happened.

Your Uncle Hugo and cousin Raj came to dinner. I told you about that. It was a nice meal of broiled salmon and roasted vegetables. Your mother is a talented cook, and she puts salt and pepper and onion powder and garlic salt in food at just the right proportions to make even broccoli taste good. Your Uncle Hugo and cousin Raj seemed to enjoy the meal, and we talked about what was new in our lives. Your Uncle Hugo is now working at the YMCA and teaching stay-at-home moms how to box. He said a couple of them are really good and that their husbands ought to be careful about what they say around the house. I'm not sure it matters. I'm a husband, and nothing I say is even listened to.

I told your Uncle Hugo about a rototiller I had repaired that day, and he said he envied my talent for fixing things. That made me feel good.

Your mother, she talked about how big and active you're getting, and how the Internet said you were starting to get hair and that your eyebrows were coming in. That was a nice thing to talk about, and your Uncle Hugo said he wished he'd paid more attention to those things when Raj's mother was pregnant.

That's when Raj spoke up.

"Well, I wasn't going to say anything yet, but since we're talking about babies…"

Kid, let me tell you this: your mother was standing up and heading over to hug Raj before I had any idea of what was going on. I must have looked as confused as I was, because Hugo reached over and slugged me in the shoulder (it hurt; don't tell anyone) and said, "Raj and Kimberly are having a baby, man!"

"Who's Kimberly?"

"My girlfriend," Raj said. He said it like I should have known, but I've never seen or met this person, so acting as if I would just know that assumes a lot. I don't like assumptions. I prefer facts.

"It's probably good that she's your girlfriend, then," I said.

Your mother laughed as she sat back down. "Of course it's a good thing."

And then I finally put everything together.

"You're having a baby," I said.

"Well, Kimberly is, but yes," Raj said.

"So I'm going to be a great uncle," I said.

"That's about the size of it," your Uncle Hugo said.

I'm pretty smart sometimes. Also, that kicks multiplicities of ass, as Scott Shamwell says. If the evening had ended there, it would have been better.

The evening did not end there. Later, after dinner, we were having coffee in the living room and I told Raj that he ought to bring Kimberly to meet us. Kid, that may not seem like a remarkable statement to you—for all I know, you're going to come into the world eager to meet people, which will certainly make life easier for you than it has been for me—but believe me when I tell you I wouldn't have said such a thing four or five years ago. I wouldn't have wanted anybody to come over here. You know what I said earlier about things not getting better? Forget it. I had a bad attitude. Some things get better, some things get worse. It's hard to make everything line up the way you want it.

"Please do bring her," your mother said.

"Yeah, I will," Raj said. "She wanted to come tonight, but she got called into work."

"Where does she work?" your mother asked.

"Kohl's, out on the West End."

"I like that place," your mother said.

"It's something," Raj said. "We're both just trying to get as many hours as we can. Been talking about getting a bigger place. Now, with the baby…"

"A one-bedroom apartment isn't going to cut it," your Uncle Hugo said.

Your mother stood up and gathered a couple of cups and carried them to the kitchen. I heard them clatter into the sink, and then she came back to the living room.

"What if you lived here?"

I stood up. "Sheila."

Your mother held up her hand, her palm facing me. I know what that means. You'll learn soon enough.

"Here?" Raj said.

"Yes," your mother said. "Two bedrooms. A full, finished basement. Plenty of room."

"Sheila," I said. Again she held up her hand.

"But what about you guys?" Hugo asked.

"We'll move."

"We will?" I asked.

"Yes," your mother said.

"I don't know," Raj said. "I don't know if we can afford it."

"How much do you think is fair?" Your mother threw the question at Raj as soon as he was done speaking. (This is not literal. She said it. She did not pick up the words and throw them. That would be absurd.)

"I don't know," he said again. "It'd probably get eight-fifty as a rental. Maybe more."

"Fine," your mother said. "How about six-fifty a month?"

"Sheila," I said.

"Edward doesn't look so good," Hugo said.

"Six-fifty," Raj said. You could tell the wheels were turning. This is a common American idiom that means he was thinking about it. Idioms are so prevalent in speech and so potentially confusing that I think maybe you ought to just stay in there as long as you can, kid.

"Sheila," I said.

"Just wait a minute," she said to me.

"I don't want to cause any trouble," Raj said. "But, man, six-fifty. That could work."

"No trouble," your mother said. "We've been thinking about moving."

"We have?" I asked. I tell you, kid, I was beginning to think your mother had been living in some dimension other than the one I'm in.

"Yes," she said. "And now we will. And you and Kimberly will move in here, Raj. It'll be perfect."

"OK," Raj said.

"OK!" Hugo said.

Everybody looked at me.

"Sheila," I said.

"We'll talk later," she said.

"Sheila," I said.

"Later," she said. She said it with her teeth clenched, almost as if she was growling, and that, too, is a signal that you'll no doubt come to know well. It means that if you say one more word you're probably going to regret it. So I didn't say anything else.

Your Uncle Hugo and cousin Raj finished their coffee, and they left. Your mother said, "We'll be in touch soon, Raj. This is going to work out great."

I waved goodbye. I didn't feel as though there was anything I could add.

Anyway, kid, that's what happened.

Yes, Edward, that's what happened, but you also left a lot out.

You didn't tell our child what we talked about later that night. You didn't say how the idea came to me in a flash, that we could do something big for our (OUR, Edward!) nephew and solve something that I've been feeling more and more and haven't had a way to articulate.

You didn't say that I've found it difficult living in this house—and it's YOUR house with YOUR history, even though you've welcomed me in as your wife, just as the motel in Colorado was MINE with MY history. You didn't say that I've been longing for a place that starts out as ours, together, no baggage, no histories that predate you and me, together. You didn't say that you understood this after I explained it to you. You said you did understand, and I believed you. What am I to believe now?

You didn't say that you also acknowledged this place is probably too small for us. For Raj and Kimberly, it'll be just right. It's bigger than the apartment they live in now, and they're young kids just starting out. But you and me, we have years on them, and we have possessions, and I am getting tired of half my stuff being in boxes in the basement, with no indication that it's ever going to get unpacked. I don't feel settled here. I told you that.

More than that, this doesn't feel like home to me, Edward, not the way it should, and not the way I want it to as we're preparing to welcome a new life into this world.

You didn't say any of that in your note to our child. It makes me wonder if you heard me. It makes me wonder if you care about how I'm feeling.

Now, before I go too far down that road, there is something else I should say.

I know I sprang this on you before we even talked about it. I am sorry. I truly am. I just got so excited when the idea came to me, and I knew Raj would be excited, too. And he was! Did you see his face as he and Hugo were leaving? This is going to be so special for him and for Kimberly, and we get to do this for them.

I know this means change, and you don't like change. But I think if you take a long look at everything that has happened—

and I'm talking clear back to the time we first met each other when you and Kyle came and stayed at my motel in Colorado—you'll see that the only thing you can really count on is that things change. Sometimes for good. Sometimes for bad. But always things change, whether you want it or not. We've both seen that. Do you know how difficult it was for me to come here with you, especially after we tried so hard in Colorado? It was a change I almost couldn't imagine. But I came. Because I'm with you no matter what.

This will be a good change, Edward. A necessary change.

We will have a home of our own. We will be able to find a place that suits us perfectly, and in doing so we will clear the way for someone important to us to improve his situation.

And there's one more thing, Edward: I just got us $650 per month for a house that's already paid for, which means we can roll that payment toward our living expenses. We can pay cash for the new house. I have it in the bank in Denver. I'm not F-word loaded, but I have money. We have money.

You're not the only one who's pretty smart sometimes.

I love you,
Sheila

NUMBERS

At this stage, kid, while it's interesting to think of you as a fruit or vegetable with eyelashes and maybe even testicles, you're an abstraction (love this word) in other ways. I have no idea what your voice is going to sound like, whether you're a boy or a girl, whether your nose will be small like mine or more angular like your mother's, whether you will be quiet and thoughtful or loud and rambunctious (I love the word "rambunctious"), what subjects will interest you in school, and so on. We are eager to find out these things, of course. I would say the questions of who and what and how you will be consume most of the conversations your mother and I have about you. We like to talk about those things. But it's hard to project too far out. Right now, we're just tending to regular appointments with Dr. Arlene Haworth and hoping for a healthy birth when you arrive.

However, on the off-chance that you grow up to be a real-estate agent, here are some figures you might find interesting:

In Billings, Montana, where we live and where you will be born, barring some unforeseen circumstance, there are, today—Wednesday, June 18th, 2014—537 homes for sale. You'll be further interested to know that in the past twelve months, 2,009 homes have sold in Billings, which means those 537 currently available homes represent an inventory of 3.207 months' worth of houses. If you were to go deeper into these numbers, you would know that an inventory of six months or more represents a healthy market for buyers. Anything less than that is a healthy market for sellers.

What that means, kid, is this: Not only are we leaving this comfortable house on Clark Avenue but we're also at the mercy of the seller of whatever house we buy, because there's a lot of demand for houses in Billings and not much supply.

My father—your grandfather—was a smart businessman. I don't like to engage in conjecture, because facts are superior, but I do think your grandfather would look at these facts and conclude one of two things:

1. We should stay in the house we are in.

2. We should sell the house we are in, because the market favors sellers, and use the proceeds of that sale to buy our new house.

Your mother is undeterred (a good word I should use more often) by the sellers' market and unconvinced by my conjecture about what your grandfather would do if he were here and this were his decision to make.

"Edward," she said, and I could tell she was exasperated (an excellent word) because the second syllable of my name came out elongated, like this: "EdWAAAARD." "This isn't about making money. If it was, we'd be getting every dollar out of Raj that we could. Now just let me look at these houses."

Your mother has taken over my computer. She was at it this morning while I had breakfast, poring over online listings of homes for sale. She was at it this evening at 5:06 p.m. when I got home from work. I made spaghetti for dinner, and I took it in to her because she said she couldn't come out and eat at the table. At this rate, when you're ready to show up she's just going to crawl up on the computer table and poop you out onto the keyboard.

Finally, at 6:46 p.m., she came into the living room.

"I've found eight houses I want to look at," she said.

"Out of five hundred and thirty-seven, you found only eight?"

"Yes, Edward." ("EdWAAAARD.") "Out of five hundred and thirty-seven, I found eight that are the right size, with the right amenities, at the right price, in the right neighborhoods. Now, I want you to do something for me before we start arranging to look at these."

"What?"

"Don't cower."

(I didn't realize I was, kid. Also, your mother used a very good word.)

"I'm sorry."

"This will be fun."

"Yes. OK." Fun sounded like something I would want to have.

"I want you to make a scorecard for these houses. Write

HOUSE SCORECARD

By Edward Stanton for Edward Stanton and Sheila Stanton

Category	Edward	Sheila
Outside appearance (curb appeal)		
Ease of leaving the driveway		
Ease of lawn maintenance		
Paint quality on the garage		
House number		
Perceived niceness of neighbors (facts better than perception)		
Distance from shop where I work with Scott Shamwell		
Distance from my Albertsons for shopping		
Master bedroom		
Spare bedroom 1		
Spare bedroom 2		
Spare bedroom 3 (if applicable)		
Coat closet		
Living room		

down every category you can think of—bedrooms, condition of yard, whatever—and leave a place for you and I both to give the category a score of one to ten. We'll mark up these cards as we go along. This will help us decide which one is best."

"OK," I said. Then I giggled. I won't lie to you, kid. I was excited. I always need a new project. "Can I have the computer now?"

"Yes."

I got up off the couch and ran past your mother into the spare bedroom. At 10:12 p.m., she asked me if I was coming to bed, and I said no, not yet. At 11:17 p.m., I finished my work, and then I wrote this to you.

It's 12:04 a.m. now. Tomorrow's going to be a shitburger because I'm tired. But for the first time, I'm excited about looking for a house. This scorecard is going to be great.

Dining room
Kitchen
Bathroom 1
Bathroom 2
Bathroom 3 (if applicable)
Storage areas
Basement (if applicable)
Places where I can put tools and stuff
Backyard
Front yard
Side yards
Landscaping
Structural integrity of driveway
Structural integrity of foundation
Structural integrity of fencing
Hot-water heater
Cooling method
Heating method
Exterior paint color(s)
Interior paint color(s)
Miscellaneous

I woke up just after 2 a.m. (oh, I'm sorry, Mister Precision: it was 2:08) because my back hurt and you were snoring next to me. I'm glad you wrote to our child again, but seriously, Edward, POOPING out the baby? Do you know how any of this works? I'm going to tell Dr. Haworth you said that. Also, please stop cursing in your notes to the baby. You know I don't like that.

I found your scorecard. Very nice, dear. A few minor critiques:

First, the distance from our current Albertsons is a non-issue. There are Albertsons stores all over this town.

Second, "structural integrity" of things like driveways and foundations are assessed by home inspectors, which we will hire if we find a home we'd like to buy. WHEN we find a home we'd like to buy. You can still score these categories if you want, but listen to me, EdWAAAARD: You will not be bringing tools to the home viewings. I know you. I will do a thorough inspection of the car before we leave. Don't mess with me on this.

Third, I love you. (That's not a critique. That's a fact.)

Oh, Edward, this baby is starting to be a load. My back and my hips, they ache all the time. It's hard to find a comfortable position sometimes. I'm going to sit in your recliner for just a bit and see if I can get some sleep.

I'm going to eat a bowl of double fudge ice cream first.

And maybe some Vienna sausages.

Goodnight, sweet boy.

ONE DAY, ONE HOUSE

It's Saturday, and your mother wasn't kidding about finding a house. I mean, I never thought she was, but at 9:16 a.m. today a man named Hart Keithley knocked on our door and introduced himself—"I'm Hart Keithley," he said when I opened the door—and your mother edged me aside and welcomed him in and said, "Edward, this is Hart Keithley, our real estate agent. He's going to take us to look at a house."

Hart Keithley extended a hand, and I shook it. I looked at your mother. "Why aren't we using Lacy Scott? She helped my father buy this house, and she helped my mother buy her condo downtown."

"I wanted to use Hart."

I looked at your mother. I looked at Hart Keithley. Hart Keithley smiled at me. "It's going to be great," he said.

Well. OK.

Your mother and I rode in the backseat of Hart Keithley's Buick LaCrosse. It was a nice enough car, although I have no idea why Buick thought a small city in Wisconsin would make a good car name. It had leather seats and rode comfortably.

"Do you like this car?" I asked Hart Keithley.

"Sure do."

"I have a Cadillac DTS. It's a better car than this one, I think." Hart Keithley laughed. "Maybe so."

"I'd need to read articles and get under the hood of each car to know for sure," I said.

"I hear you."

"Maybe later today, after we look at the house."

"Edward, no," your mother said.

"Some other time," Hart Keithley said.

I looked out the window. We were crossing Shiloh Road, far on the west end of Billings.

"This is a long way from where I work," I said.

"Great house, though," Hart Keithley said.

HOUSE SCORECARD

By Edward Stanton for Edward Stanton and Sheila Stanton

Category	Edward	Sheila
Outside appearance (curb appeal)	5	8
Ease of leaving the driveway	1	Dumb
Ease of lawn maintenance	2	5
Paint quality on the garage	1	Dumb
House number	-16	Stupid
Perceived niceness of neighbors (facts better than perception)	0	N/A
Distance from shop where I work with Scott Shamwell	-106	!!!!
Distance from my Albertsons for shopping	-107	!!!!
Master bedroom	8	1,816
Spare bedroom 1	7	7
Spare bedroom 2	8	9
Spare bedroom 3 (if applicable)	9	9
Coat closet	3	10!
Living room	8	9

"That's what you say, anyway," I said, and Hart Keithley looked at me in the rearview mirror and didn't look pleased.

"I want to see it," your mother said.

I looked out the window again. Then I used the button to roll down the window. Then I raised the window halfway. Then I raised it all the way up. Then I reached for the button again and your mother put her hand on mine and stopped me.

Hart Keithley looked at me in the rearview mirror, smiled with his lips closed, and kept driving.

We saw the house, kid. It's not worth the effort of describing it to you, for two reasons.

First, we're not buying it, so it's a moot point. Second, we have scorecards.

Dining room	6	6
Kitchen	1	5,817
Bathroom 1	4	8
Bathroom 2	8	16
Bathroom 3 (if applicable)	N/A	N/A
Storage areas	10	10
Basement (if applicable)	7	8
Places where I can put tools and stuff	11	10
Backyard	1	5
Front yard	1	8
Side yards	1	8!
Landscaping	1	0!!
Structural integrity of driveway	8	?
Structural integrity of foundation	10	?
Structural integrity of fencing	10	Fine! 10!
Hot-water heater	10	10
Cooling method	9	10!
Heating method	1	10!
Exterior paint color(s)	3	10!
Interior paint color(s)	1	10!
Miscellaneous	N/A	Shit!

The grand total: I scored the house a -74. Your mother scored the house a 7,837 and did not speak to me the rest of the day.

Hart Keithley tried to smile but found it difficult to do so, and then he dropped us off at our soon-to-be-former home on Clark Avenue and drove away.

The Buick LaCrosse has pretty good speed on the takeaway, but I still think my Cadillac DTS is better.

Edward, I am going to say all of this to you when we wake up, but I'm putting it here as a test run and so our child can see, if he or she someday reads this, that while disputes are part of life, how you handle them is what marks you as immature or mature.

I don't think you were mature today while we were looking at the house. And while it may not have been mature of me to respond with silence, I want you to know it wasn't to punish you. I said nothing for the rest of the day because I was scared of what might come out of my mouth if I did speak, and how much it might hurt you, and how much that might hurt me and us.

Yes, Edward, we are not going to buy that house. Even if you had taken the scorecard seriously, which you most certainly did not, I wouldn't have wanted it. You're right: It's too far away from where we'd want to live. You're also right: the yard is too big and too much to handle. You work plenty hard for our family already. You don't need that much yard to manage on top of it, and I can't guarantee you I'd be able to help once the baby comes.

But Edward, listen: The house was fine. The house was very, very close to what we want: more bedrooms, more space, a bigger kitchen, more storage. If we could find that house on a smaller lot closer to town, we would be in business.

That's what I want to look for. Please don't sandbag this. Please be my partner. I've already explained why I think this is important. I will explain it again if I have to.

I could tell on the way out there that something was agitating you. Please talk to me about what it is, so we can deal with it together. Once you started writing down those ridiculous numbers on your scorecard, I knew you were upset, and I got upset, and things got worse. I'm sorry for my part in that.

I don't think Hart will be back. We're going to have to find someone else to help us with this. Please cooperate and put forth the effort. We need this.

I love you.

Also, we're out of Vienna sausages. Please get some more this week. And some dill pickles. The crunchy ones with the jalapenos. I like those.

MY BROTHER

Your mother and I talked this morning and agreed to cooperate with each other while we look for a new house. We also agreed that we should call Hart Keithley and ask him to try again with us, that we would be better behaved the next time. When you're as old as I am, kid, it's a shameful feeling to admit to another human being that you've been acting like a child. So here's a bit of advice for you: While you are a child, live it up. You won't get to act like that forever without making a fool out of yourself.

Your mother was just about to call Hart Keithley when my bitchin' iPhone rang. Your Uncle Hugo's number and face came up on my screen, so I knew it was him. Or someone who had his phone. I don't suppose you can know anything just on the basis of a number and a face on your phone screen. You need a voice, too. Anyway, it was your Uncle Hugo.

"Edward, I'm lost," he said.

"Do you mean you don't know where you are, or you're in emotional turmoil and have lost your bearings in a spiritual sense?"

"I mean I can't fucking find my fucking way home. Don't fuck with me."

I'd never heard your Uncle Hugo speak that way.

"OK."

"I called Mark's phone, but he's not picking up. Raj is at work. Help me."

"Where are you?" The words felt thick on my tongue. This is just a way of describing them. Words don't have physical weight. What I'm saying is that I felt scared.

"I don't fucking know."

"I mean, where were you trying to go?"

"I was at the Y, teaching my class. I tried to go home."

"So you drove south?"

"Yes. Fuck!"

"Hugo, please." Your mother moved up against me, and all three of us—you, me, her—were touching each other. "What's around you?"

"I see the river."

"Which direction is it flowing?"

"How the fuck..." Your Uncle Hugo started weeping. Don't judge him for this, kid.

"Is it going to your left or your right?"

"Right. I think."

"OK, you're on the other side of the river. Look behind you. Does a road go up into the hills?"

"Just a second." He was still crying. "Yes."

"I think I know where you are. Stay there, OK? I'm coming."

"Hurry."

"I will."

"Don't hang up."

"I won't."

I found your Uncle Hugo on South Billings Boulevard, across the river near the city dump. His car was in the parking lot of a convenience store, and he sat on the hood watching the road. "There you are," he'd said as I approached in my Cadillac DTS. He climbed down as I drove into the parking lot. His hair was mussed and his eyes were red and watery. I rolled down the window.

"Thank you," he said.

"Yes."

"I know where I am now. But I wanted to wait for you."

"OK."

"I should have asked them." He hiked his thumb toward the store. "I was afraid they'd recognize me."

"I understand."

"Will you follow me?" he asked. "Make sure I get home?"

"Yes, Hugo."

He walked back to his car, got in, and started it. It's a nice car, a 2014 Toyota Camry that he bought with his book money. It's black and sleek. I like it.

Your Uncle Hugo drove back mostly the way I would if I were (subjunctive mood—we'll talk about this a lot) going to his house from South Billings Boulevard. He drove north to the frontage road, then got onto State Avenue by turning right and went southeast and then east to South 30th Street, turned left, then turned right on 8th Avenue South, then left on South Broadway and right into his driveway. The only thing I would have done differently is avoided the left turns. I thought it best not to critique your Uncle Hugo on that. His day was hard enough. And, anyway, I was proud of him for finding his way home. And scared for him that he had to.

We stood by your Uncle Hugo's garage and talked. Your Uncle Hugo talked. I listened, and prompted him.

"It's starting," he said.

"The CTE?"

"Yeah. Headaches, always had those. But this is something different."

I wanted to touch your Uncle Hugo's arm, but I didn't. I don't know if I did the right thing by doing nothing.

"I missed a turn somewhere," he said. He was looking past me, it seemed. "And then I turned where I thought I should turn, and that was wrong, and I kept driving, and then I turned again. And then…"

"You didn't know where you were?"

"Yeah."

"I'm sorry. Maybe it was a glitch."

"Maybe."

"Maybe," I repeated.

"But maybe this is where it gets worse."

"Maybe," I said.

Your Uncle Hugo reared back his right hand and punched the aluminum garage door, faster than I could register what he'd done. The sound of it made me jump.

"I'm not ready for this," he said. He punched the garage door again. A big dent cratered in.

"Hugo, stop."

He punched it again. And a fourth time. And a fifth.

"Hugo!"

Rusty red streaks marked the spot in the garage door where your Uncle Hugo hit it. I looked at his right hand, and blood streamed out of his knuckles, forming rivulets in the tiny wrinkles of his hand.

"Hugo," I said.

He held his hands out to me, palms down.

He looked like he wanted to cry again.

I finally got the bleeding to stop, and I put ointment on your Uncle Hugo's right hand, and I wrapped it in gauze according to his directions.

"Do you know why I waited for you?" he asked.

"So I could make sure you were OK?"

"Yeah," he said. "But also because the first thing I wanted to do, before I called you, was drive into the river. That scared me."

"You want to die?"

"Hell, no. I was chickening out. No, I don't want to die. I want to live, and I'm goddamned scared."

"I know. I'm sorry."

He used his free hand and wiped his eyes and under his nose with his index finger.

"I got so much to see. My kid's kid. Your kid. I got school. I feel like I'm losing it all."

"You aren't."

"No," he said. "Not today. But what happens tomorrow? Or next week?"

"I don't know." Your Uncle Hugo was asking about hypotheticals. I don't like them. I prefer facts.

"What if I get lost again?" he asked.

"I'll come get you."

He looked at me. "You would, wouldn't you?"

"Of course," I said. "I'm your brother."

Sorry, kid, I have to add to this. I just woke up at 2:28 a.m. and was thinking about your Uncle Hugo, same as I have been since I left him at his house, after Raj came over.

I'm scared. I don't mind telling you that. Because it seems like something has changed, only we don't know what it has become. Maybe your Uncle Hugo never gets lost again, and we always wonder what happened today. But I don't think he thinks this was the end of it, and neither do I, even though I despise engaging in conjecture.

Think about this, kid. Your Uncle Hugo started boxing as a kid, and he became one of the best in the world when he was only seventeen years old. And now, it's twenty-two years later—which may sound like a lot of time, but it seems to go by fast, as I've told you before. And now all of those things he did when he was just a boy are having a terrible effect on his life.

This is a question for when you're older, but I'll ask it now: Would you be willing to have the consequences of your actions in your youth be delayed until you were in the middle of your life?

I wouldn't.

I don't think your Uncle Hugo had any idea it would be this way.

I think it's why he's scared now.

I think it's why I'm scared, too.

My heart breaks for Hugo.

I want to add something to what your father said about not judging Hugo for crying. I hope we raise you in a way that you won't judge anyone who cries. I can tell you with no reservation that your father came home and cried, and I held him on the couch and let him do it. I think he's asking you not to judge because he's a man, and men get this signal in our society that they shouldn't allow themselves to feel their emotions. And I think that's led to a lot of fucked-up things, if you don't mind me being a little crass like Scott Shamwell.

That's all I'm going to say. Your father cried, and I'm glad he did, not because of his pain but because he allowed himself to feel that. Your father is a special man.

That's all for tonight. Your father just went back to bed after writing to you again. I hope he sleeps. I hope I do, too.

Love,
Your mom

TIME

It has been a while since I wrote to you about your grandmother. There's a reason for that. Several reasons, actually, the most important one being that we've continued not talking. As you know by now, I'm not the sort of person who regularly engages in conjecture, so I'm not going to say I expected anything different. Just the same, I probably wouldn't have believed you had you told me, say, a year ago that your grandmother and I would no longer speak with each other. Of course, that whole scenario is laughable, since there wasn't a you a year ago, and you cannot yet speak. Maybe I should just forget about trying to make this point.

Here's the funny thing, though, kid, and I don't mean "ha-ha" funny: Even though it hurts my feelings that I'm not on speaking terms with my own mother (your grandmother), so much is going on in my life I haven't had time to dwell on it. There's this house business with your mother and the work at the shop with Scott Shamwell and getting to know your uncle and his son and your mother becoming friends with Lainie Westerly and meals and TV and everything else (which is a lot of stuff). For your mother and me, being ourselves is a full-time job. I suspect this will be how it is for you, too. We'll let the facts bear that out one way or another.

I guess what I'm saying is this: Days begin and end, and sometimes what you have to do takes up so much of your time that you don't notice other things, like the hurt of not being able to talk to your own mother. The episode with your Uncle Hugo scared me in two ways. First, and most important, because it scared him and made him lash out, and I want my brother to be happy. Second, because if he's going to be my brother—and I promised him and Mark Westerly that he would be—I'm going to have to watch over him. That's what big brothers do.

Two days ago, right after dinner, I got a phone call from my good friend Donna Hays (who used to be Donna Middleton). She called to congratulate me about you. Can you imagine that, kid? You already have people, besides your mother and me, who care about you.

"How did you know?" I asked Donna.

"I got the card."

"What card?" I looked over at your mother, and her face had this big grin on it.

"The one Sheila sent," Donna Hays said. "Were you ever going to tell me?"

"Probably," I said. "I've been busy."

Donna Hays laughed, and then she told me all about what's going on with her life in Idaho and how her son, my good friend Kyle, is playing sports and getting big. "He's discovered girls now," she said, "and so I'm pretty much invisible to him." I think she didn't mean that literally.

"Is Kyle there?"

"No," she said. "He's over at a friend's house playing some video game. It may be days before I see him."

"Days?"

She laughed again. "I'm just kidding. He'll get hungry soon. That always brings him home."

I laughed, too, because I felt like that was the right thing to do. I'm sorry I didn't get to talk to Kyle. I realized, in that moment, how much I missed him. When he was a little boy and lived across the street from me, we used to stand him up against the edge of the garage door and mark off his height. But we haven't done that in years, and this spring I finally painted over the old markings. I knew what I was doing, but the fact that the garage needed to be painted seemed more important than a bunch of old pencil scratchings. Now, I'm not so sure about that.

Do you understand what I'm saying, kid? Days begin and end and I miss my friends, although I didn't think about that until I was reminded of it. Time is a strange thing.

This evening, your Uncle Hugo called and asked me if I'd read the *Billings Herald-Gleaner*. I glanced over at the front door and saw the newspaper still with a rubber band around it, and I felt bad about that. I don't read the newspaper the way I used to, when it was just me in this house and I didn't have a wife and a job I had to go to. Now, I'm able to go on the Internet to get my daily statistics about the temperature and precipitation, and I keep those numbers in a spreadsheet now rather than in my old notebooks. The newspaper doesn't have much use to me anymore, but I haven't been able to bring myself to cancel it.

"No, Hugo, I haven't."

"So you don't know about this thing tomorrow?"

"What thing?"

"They're putting up a statue of your father at the courthouse." His voice made a gurgling sound, like he was clearing his throat. "Our father, I guess. Is it OK to say that?"

"It's the truth," I said.

"You didn't know?" he asked.

"No." I wrote to you about this sometime back, kid, and told you I didn't think it was going to happen now that my father has been dead for so many years. This is what makes conjecture such a foolish thing to engage in.

"I think I want to go," your Uncle Hugo said. "Just to see it. Just to hear what people have to say about him. Do you want to go with me?"

I do want to go, kid. I want to go badly. But...

"My mother will be there," I said.

"I know. The newspaper said she's supposed to talk. I was thinking I could hang back. It's going to be on the courthouse lawn. Maybe I could just stand back by a tree and see it and not bother anybody."

"You probably could. I'm not sure I can. People who knew my father will know I'm there."

"Yeah." Your Uncle Hugo cleared his throat again.

"Our father," I corrected.

"Thanks."

"It's the truth," I said.

"So you don't want to go?"

"I don't know if I should," I said.

"OK."

"I'm sorry, Hugo."

"No, really, I get it."

"How are you feeling, Hugo?"

"Fine," he said.

"Really?"

"Yes. Fine. Stupid. I got a bicycle. I'm not sure I should be driving anymore."

"What did you do with your Toyota?"

"I'm going to sell it. College money for my grandkid, I guess."

"Yes."

"Thanks for asking after me," he said. "And for the other day. Thanks for that, too."

"You're welcome."

We said goodbye and hung up. Without warning, I felt sad. But, then, I suppose that sadness doesn't really warn anybody it's coming. That's why it can be such a difficult emotion. You'll learn this eventually. I wish I could keep sadness away from you, kid, but life doesn't work that way.

I hate this.

You know all of this, Edward, because we talked about it after you hung up the phone with Hugo. But I'm writing it down so the kid can someday read it. Or maybe we can, somewhere down the road, and we can remember that what seemed such a problem really wasn't.

So for your benefit and the kid's, let me say it again: I think you should go with Hugo tomorrow. I think I should go, too, but I'm just so weary sometimes that I don't think I want to stand up longer than necessary.

The reason I think you should go is the event is meant to honor YOUR father, and I don't see where your mother gets to influence your decision. Maybe she would like for you to come. Maybe that would help things between the two of you. I don't know. What I do know is that you shouldn't be giving her control over your decisions.

Yes, yes, you said she'd be upset about Hugo, and you're right about that, but again: IT'S A PUBLIC EVENT, EDWARD! You can't have a public event and then get mad about the public who shows up.

When you wake up, I think you should call Dr. Thomsen and discuss this with him. I think he'll tell you that you're taking responsibility for what your mother might think and that's not your job. I think he'll tell you to do what you want to do.

That's all I'm going to say.

Oh, Edward, I'm awake again. You're finally sleeping. You were tossing around and talking—it was all nonsense that I couldn't make out—and I know you do that when you try to go to sleep with too much on your brain. I'm glad you finally fell into deep sleep. I'm envious.

I've been re-reading all of your notes to our child, and I'm just so in love with you, Edward. You've gone from talking about him/her as a poppyseed to saying things you don't even say to me (which we need to work on, but I've known you long enough now that I'm just happy you're saying them to someone). I realize our child remains just a concept in some ways, but take it from me as the mother, who's connected body and soul: Our child is very much real, and very much on the way to us.

Promise me, Edward, that you'll always stay this focused on our child, that you'll always show the love you've already given. My parents surely loved me, and even though they've been gone a long time, I can still draw on that every day. Think of how much your daddy means to you now—in some ways, more than he ever did while he was alive. Your mother loves you, too. It's just so frustrating that she's so far absorbed in herself that she can't see past it.

My hope for you, for me, for us, is that our own child never has to bargain out the love. That he/she always knows. It's important.

I love you.

SHITBURGER

I didn't decide to go until ten minutes before the ceremony was supposed to start. I put down my crescent wrench, and Scott Shamwell looked over at me and asked what was going on.

"I need to go," I said.

He looked at his left wrist, as if there were a watch there. Scott Shamwell never wears a watch, and yet he always does this when time of day is at issue. I always point out that he isn't wearing a watch, and he always says "So? I can see that it's half a hair past a freckle." This makes me laugh, so we do it every time. We're pretty funny sometimes.

This time, I didn't laugh.

"What, Ed buddy?"

"They're putting a statue of my father up at the county courthouse."

"Oh."

"I think I should go. I want to, anyway. Sheila thinks I should."

"OK. Well, go. I can finish up here."

I stood up, but I didn't leave.

"Ed?"

"Yes?"

"Your face is all twisted up, like you're taking the biggest dump of your life."

"OK."

Scott Shamwell stood up, too.

"Ed?"

"Yes?"

"Do you want me to come with you?"

"Yes."

Thom Hemphill, the Billings mayor, was already talking into the microphone when we got to the courthouse in my Cadillac. His words diffused (love that word) into the air and were hard to make out, but I gathered that he was saying nice things about my father, who used to be mayor before he was elected to the county commission. I was surprised at the turnout; maybe a hundred and fifty people stood on the expanse of lawn, listening to Mayor Hemphill. I don't know why, exactly, I was surprised. I had no reasonable basis to predict how many people would come, and predictions aren't my bailiwick (superb word) anyway. I prefer facts. It's just that my father— your grandfather—has been dead for nearly six years, and that's a long time. It made me feel good that so many people seemed to still care about him.

Scott Shamwell and I found your Uncle Hugo where he said he would be, far across the lawn from the podium where the mayor, some members of the city council, the county commissioners and my mother sat. He had his arms looped around a tree branch, and he waved as he saw us coming.

"Didn't expect to see you," he said to me.

"Didn't expect to be seen," I said. I'm pretty clever sometimes.

Scott Shamwell wore wraparound sunglasses and a tank top T-shirt with these words on it: IF WANKING GAVE YOU KILLER ABS, MINE WOULD BE IN JAIL. I'm not sure what that means. Scott Shamwell shook hands with your Uncle Hugo and then threw a couple of half-speed jabs at Hugo's midsection, which your uncle parried (great word) with ease.

I stood next to your Uncle Hugo while Scott Shamwell sat at

the base of the tree. Mayor Hemphill finished his remarks, and everybody applauded politely, including us.

Mayor Hemphill then said, "Now, I'd like to introduce the woman who has carried on Ted Stanton's legacy of good works here in Billings and Yellowstone County: his widow, Maureen Stanton Lamb."

My mother—your grandmother—stood up.

"She really is beautiful," your Uncle Hugo said.

"I guess."

She did look nice. She had on a deep red dress and a white hat and I could tell even from a distance that she had been meticulous with her makeup and nail polish. I was looking at the people seated on the podium, trying to see if I recognized anyone, when I was certain that my mother located me at the back of the crowd. I held up my right hand and waved. She turned away from the microphone and said something to Jay L. Lamb, who sat next to her empty chair. He stood up, and she returned to the microphone.

"Uh oh," I said. Your Uncle Hugo gave me a sideways glance, but I didn't say anything else. He looked at the podium again.

My mother—your grandmother—began talking, but it was as if the words were just white noise. I couldn't make out what she said. My attention fixated on Jay L. Lamb, who made his way down the podium stairs to the lawn, then veered along the periphery (excellent word) of the crowd, made a hard right turn once he was clear of the gathering and headed toward us.

"Hi, Jay," I said when he reached us.

"Edward, I think you should go."

Scott Shamwell rose from his spot in front of the tree, using the trunk of it to hold him up. "I think you should eat a dick," he said to Jay L. Lamb.

"Scott, I..." I said.

"Scott Shamwell," Jay L. Lamb said.

"The one and only," Scott said.

"Jay," I said.

"We're just watching, sir," your Uncle Hugo said. "We're not bothering anybody."

"You're bothering her," Jay L. Lamb said, pointing to my mother, whose words were incidental to what was happening.

"Jay," I said.

"OK, fine," your Uncle Hugo said, "we'll go." He turned to leave, and Scott Shamwell grabbed him by the wrist.

"The hell, you say. We're not going. We've got a right to be here."

"I'm trying to be nice," Jay L. Lamb said.

"Obviously," Scott Shamwell said.

"Jay," I said.

Your Uncle Hugo tried again. "Just let us stick around for the unveiling. We'll go quietly after that."

Jay L. Lamb diverted his attention to my mother, who continued to speak. He shrugged and held the palms of his hands straight up. My mother didn't break stride in her remarks (kind of a dumb way to put it, now that I think about it) but nodded.

A few minutes later, she stopped talking and stepped to the side of the podium, where a big black sheet covered the statue of my father. The mayor and the three county commissioners joined her, and they pulled the sheet off together. And sure enough, underneath was a bronze statue approximating my father. It was tall, like him. The mouth was open, as his often was. The chest was puffed out. The hair was slicked back.

I missed him, despite everything mean he ever said to me.

And the four of us—Scott Shamwell, me, your Uncle Hugo and Jay L. Lamb, my father's lawyer and now my mother's husband—stood there and clapped politely.

When it was done, Jay L. Lamb looked at me and your Uncle Hugo. "Your end of the bargain, please."

We turned toward the street and began walking away, Scott Shamwell a few steps behind.

"Hey, Lamb!" Your Uncle Hugo and I turned around. Scott Shamwell had cupped his hands to his mouth. Jay L. Lamb, about fifteen yards away, turned back toward us.

"Better make it two dicks, old boy."

225

To: whambamshammysham@gmail.com
From: imsheilastanton@gmail.com
Re: today

Scott, you're such a good friend to Edward. Thank you. Now listen: You need to stop doing things like telling Jay L. Lamb to eat two dicks. It's pretty funny, I'll grant you that, but it's not as funny as you think it is. And it's a bad influence on Edward, who's sitting on the floor right now with his brother and giggling and saying "Better make it two dicks, old boy." He's going to be a father soon. Please don't help him be a teenager. Help him be the best man he can be. I know you have it in you.

Edward loves you. I love you, which seems amazing. Our child is going to love you.

But, seriously, you need to stop.

Love, Sheila

PHOTOGRAPHS AND MEMORIES*

"—this is the title of an old song by a man named Jim Croce, who died in a plane crash in 1973. It's from the perspective of someone who has lost love and is bemoaning (I love the word "bemoaning") her absence by going through the tangible evidence that she was once in his life. I like Jim Croce's music a lot, much more than I like music that is being played today. I don't know, kid. There may not be any good music left when you grow up. I'll make sure to save you some Jim Croce and R.E.M. and Stevie Wonder and Matthew Sweet and anything else I can think of. You'll need it.

After we dropped Scott Shamwell off at the shop, your Uncle Hugo and I came back to the house on Clark Avenue—if your mother has her way, the house you'll never live in. I went down into the basement and hauled up some photo albums that my mother—your grandmother—gave me after my father died. I'd been promising your Uncle Hugo we could look at them, and today, after the ceremony in the park, seemed like the right time.

I hadn't opened the albums in a long time. Some of the pictures are forty or more years old, and the adhesive on the album pages has grown brittle. Some of the pictures slid out onto the floor.

CRAIG LANCASTER

Your Uncle Hugo picked one up and looked at it. "This is you and him?" He showed it to me. My father and I were standing on the sidewalk. I had on shorts, no T-shirt, and knee-high tube socks. My father wore an aqua Western-style shirt, jeans with a big belt buckle, and cowboy boots. His left hand was on my left shoulder.

"Yes," I said. "That's in front of our first house. It's also on Clark, but farther up."

"Do you remember this?"

"No. But we moved out of that house on April 19, 1974, so it would have been before then."

"You remember the date?"

"Of course."

"That's amazing."

Your Uncle Hugo held the picture out and regarded it some more. "He was a big man," he said. "Like you."

"Yes."

"It's funny how I'm so small."

"What's funny about it?"

"I don't know. Strange."

"I suppose."

We thumbed through more pages and more photographs. I saw myself in yearly school photos. I saw my mother, young and pretty, and then older and still pretty as the pages kept going. I saw my father and his smile, and the way other people in the photographs looked at him, like they were in the presence of a force of nature. I guess they were. I saw my Grandpa Sid and my Grandma Mabel—my father's parents, and your great-grandparents—at our house for Thanksgiving. I'd forgotten what they looked like, exactly. I've been without them for so long.

"This is making me sad," I said.

Your Uncle Hugo closed the book. "I'm sorry."

"It's not your fault. I'm glad we looked."

"Me, too."

"Do you hate him?" I asked your Uncle Hugo.

He thought for a couple of seconds. "No. I didn't know him. I

228

mean, I met him. That's what's kind of weird. But I didn't know, and I didn't know him. And my mom, she didn't hate him. I guess it's hard for me to find hate. I just wish I'd known, you know?"

"Yes. I hated him. Sometimes."

"I hear you. How do you feel now?"

"I miss him. I wish you'd known, too."

Your Uncle Hugo play-punched me in the shoulder. I play-punched him back.

"But this is OK, right?" he said.

"Yes."

Your Uncle Hugo stayed for dinner with your mother and me. We had pizza delivered—"Sorry, guys, but I'm just not up to cooking," your mother said—and ate out on the back porch. Late spring and early summer around here can be really nice, kid. I hope you like it.

I didn't get to talk much. Your mother and your Uncle Hugo were going a mile a minute (not literally, and it really has nothing to do with distance) about his mother and grandmother. I think I've told you that his mother, who would have been your great-aunt, died very young of pancreatic cancer. His grandmother, Aurelia, raised him and took care of him. She's dead, too, though. I think that's one of the trade-offs of getting to be alive. If you live long enough, you're going to lose people close to you. And one day you, too, will die, and other people will miss you.

"I wish I could have met Aurelia," your mother said.

"I wish you could have, too," your Uncle Hugo said. "She was amazing."

"But tell me this: How did she tolerate the boxing?" your mother asked. "I just can't imagine being able to handle that."

Your Uncle Hugo tossed a piece of pizza crust into the box. "She was practical," he said.

"How so?" I asked.

"I started boxing because I was getting beat up a lot at school and in the neighborhood," he said. "She just wanted that to stop. By the time I found out I was good, there was no stopping me."

Your mother lay back in her chair. "Sorry," she said. "Baby's kicking."

"Or punching," your Uncle Hugo said, and we all laughed.

"How good were you?" your mother asked him.

"He was an Olympic silver medalist," I said.

"Should have been gold," your Uncle Hugo said.

"Right," she said. "But how good, really?" She bore in on your Uncle Hugo with that question.

"Do you remember the Tommy Hearns-Marvin Hagler fight?" he asked. "Happened around 1985?"

"Yes," I said.

"No," your mother said.

Your Uncle Hugo rested his elbows on his knees and intertwined his fingers. I caught your mother looking at the wrap on his damaged hand. "It lasted eight minutes. Eight minutes of hell, they called it. Both guys just throwing the hardest punches they could. Two champions, bombing away at each other. Hagler won by knockout. It could have gone the other way, though. He was in big trouble. Hearns was pounding him. Unbelievable fight."

"I remember," I said.

"Anyway," your Uncle Hugo said, grabbing another slice of pizza, "I wasn't that good."

I had trouble sleeping again, Edward. Woke up. Ate a pint of ice cream. Please buy more tomorrow—well, later today, I guess.

I got on the computer and found that boxing match Hugo was talking about. It was on YouTube. I turned the volume low and I watched it. I still can't believe what I saw.

I've never seen anything like it. It was raw and barbaric. Those men were trying to kill each other, I think.

I turned off the computer and I wept. I'm not even sure why.

That's not true. I wept for Hugo and the life he's had.

I wept for our child and this world that awaits.

I'm so scared sometimes.

I love you.

S

ANOTHER DAY, ANOTHER HOUSE

It's also the last house, apparently. Because your mother is the boss of everything now.

Hart Keithley came back to the house on Clark earlier today and picked your mother and me up. I was surprised to see him after the debacle a week earlier, but your mother told me that she had called him and apologized for our behavior. "Please be nice this time," she said. "I'll be nice, too."

That sounded good. But it just got worse.

This time, we didn't drive all the way to the west side of town. Hart Keithley took us to a ranch-style house just four blocks from the place on Clark. It was half-brick and half-wood, on a big corner lot with a beautiful green lawn. Inside were hardwood floors and new kitchen appliances, a living room with a fireplace, and three bedrooms upstairs. In back was a covered patio. The landscaping was immaculate (a rare quality and a wonderful word). It even had a hot tub.

"It's everything I want," your mother said, "and everything we need."

I could not disagree. I couldn't find anything to fault in this house, except that it wasn't the one on Clark Avenue.

"It's a great house," I agreed. "But I don't want it."

"So this is the one?" Hart Keithley said. He said it as if I hadn't said the words I just said.

"Yes," your mother said.

"Hey," I said.

"It's listed at $219,000," Hart Keithley said. "Do you want to make an offer?"

"Yes," your mother said.

"No," I said.

"Yes, we do," your mother said.

Hart Keithley looked at her. Then he looked at me. I looked back to your mother.

"I want to talk."

"This is the house," your mother said. "We're getting this house."

Hart Keithley looked at me.

I looked at him and didn't say anything.

"We'll give them $210,000 cash," your mother said. "The only contingency will be the inspection. And we'll close in thirty days."

Holy shit. "Wait," I said.

"Are you sure?" Hart Keithley asked your mother. He looked at me.

"I'm sure," your mother said. "Edward, this is the house. We're putting in this offer."

I looked at Hart Keithley and I shrugged.

We had been home less than an hour when Hart Keithley called and told us that our offer had been accepted by the owners of the house. I was in the computer room when the call came. I am being steamrolled here, kid. As Spencer Tracy said in *Guess Who's Coming to Dinner*, I'm being pressurized.

Your mother hung up the phone, and then she came into the computer room, threw her arms around my shoulders and gave me a big kiss.

"Our own house," she said.

"Ours?"

She stepped back from me. "Don't be that way."

"Oh," I said. "Would you prefer that I just go buy a car and bring it here and tell you it's ours? I bet you wouldn't. Because you have to be the boss of everything."

"As a matter of fact, Mr. Nasty, you would do that. You control plenty around here."

"I don't have any say in where we live."

"You had every say in where we live since we got here. I need a place that's just as much mine as it yours. I told you that." Your mother started crying.

"So you just picked the house and everything."

"I did because you wouldn't."

"You didn't give me a chance!"

Your mother turned and left the room and she slammed the door on her way out. I yelled after her, "Don't slam the doors in my house!"

I couldn't make out what she said in response because she was crying and because there was a door between us, but I think she might have told me to engage in sexual congress with myself, which is anatomically impossible and probably painful even if it were possible. Earlier this year, that would have cost her a dollar.

I stayed in the computer room for more than three hours. Even when I had to urinate badly, I stayed in there. I could hear your mother moving through the rest of the house.

Finally, when I thought she'd gone to bed, I left the computer room and slipped into the bathroom. As I held my tallywhacker and aimed it at the toilet, I thought of all of Scott Shamwell's euphemisms (a great word) for urination.

"Letting go the yellow flow."

"Draining my main vein to make my bladder gladder."

"Juicing the lizard."

"Shaking the dew off my lily."

I laughed.

Your mother's voice came from the other side of the door. "What's funny?"

I finished my business and zipped up.

"Nothing," I said.

"Will you come into the bedroom and talk to me?" she asked.

I started washing my hands. "I'll be there in a second."

I thought of another. *"Releasing the Krakken."*

I laughed again.

"I'm sorry for what I said," your mother told me.

"I'm sorry for being mean, too."

"I was out of control today at the house," she said.

"Yes."

"I'm sorry."

"OK."

"What is it?" she asked. "What's the problem?"

I didn't think I could put it into words. This is a difficult situation, kid, because as I've told you over and over, I like things that clearly fall into one category or another. When I'm happy about something, I just want to enjoy being happy. When I'm sad, even though that's a difficult emotion, I can at least allow myself to feel that and wait for happiness to come back to me.

But what could I do with this? I was happy your mother was happy with the house, I understood what she wanted from it, but I could not lie to her and say I was happy. I wasn't.

"I like living at 639 Clark," I said.

"I know you do."

"I don't know how I'll feel about living on Avenue B. I don't even like the name of that street. It has no character."

"But the house does."

"Yes. I know."

Your mother shifted in her seat. "So what's the problem? My behavior aside, what's the problem?"

"I don't know."

"It's only a few blocks away."

"I know."

"You can keep going to the same Albertsons."

"I know."

235

"You can make all right turns."

"I know."

"Edward," she said, "I don't know what to say. Is it just that I did this too fast?"

"No. But that's a big part."

"I'm sorry."

"I know. Me, too."

"It's just that, well, we are in a hurry. The baby's coming soon."

"I like this house," I said.

"I know," your mother said. "But we're outgrowing it."

"I know." I stared down at the patch of floor between my shoes.

"And we can do something nice for Raj. Remember that. Hugo is very appreciative. This is a good thing."

"I know."

"Edward," your mother said. "Look at me." I bit my lip. "Look at me."

I looked up at her. Her eyes had turned red and watery.

"A house is only as good as what's in it, who's in it, and what goes on there. That place on Avenue B will be a happy house, because I'll be there and you'll be there and our child will be there. And this place will still be happy, because someone we care about will be living here and making his own memories."

She leaned against me and snuggled her head in under my chin, and I wrapped my hands around her shoulders and pulled her in, and I began to think of everything we had to do to get ready to leave this place and get ready for you. I began making lists in my mind, and I began to feel overwhelmed, and I held on to your mother, and I hoped for the best. I'm happy that we'll be going to bed not so angry with each other; that's a good marriage skill, I think. A better skill would be to cooperate better in the first place. I still can't say that I'm happy about what we're going to do. We're going to move. I'll just have to hope everything works out all right.

I don't like to rely on hope. You never know how that's going to go.

JULY

THIRTY DAYS

That's how long it took, from the time we said yes to the new house to now.

You became the size of a head of cauliflower, and we came to an understanding that this move was best for us and for you. Your mother and I packed the Clark Avenue house together.

Your brain became stronger, and your mother developed worsening heartburn, and I arranged for movers to come and load up all of our belongings.

Your senses became more developed, you grew to the size of a butternut squash, and your mother had to stop helping stack our belongings in the front room and take to bed for a few days.

You swallowed, and sucked, and prepared to breathe. I took your Uncle Hugo to the phone store and got him his own bitchin' iPhone. I'm the backup on his account. If he ever gets lost again and has his phone, I will be able to find him. Technology is slicker than cat shit in the rain, as Scott Shamwell sometimes says.

You needed lots of Vitamin C and folic acid and iron and calcium, so your mother increased her consumption of juices, milk, and yogurt, and we went to the title company and signed the papers and became owners of a new house. Your mother came home from that and went straight to bed. Dr. Arlene Haworth says this is normal. We're coming down to it, with this move and with you.

At 7 a.m. sharp the day after tomorrow, the movers will show up and put all of these things—everything we own—in the back of a big truck and drive it four blocks to Avenue B.

After they're gone, your Uncle Hugo and cousin Raj will show up with a U-Haul truck and start putting Raj and Kimberly's belongings in this house.

It won't even be empty for a day.

We'll be gone, they'll be here, and that will be that.

Change is gradual. Change is sudden. Change is constant.

I feel so silly for having ever resisted it. That was futile (a good word, and a helpless feeling). And I think your mother and I have ironed out our differences. It wasn't easy. I had to rely on Dr. Bryan Thomsen in ways I haven't in a few years. But we got there.

We're ready to move and ready for you, kid. Ready as we're going to be, I suspect, though suspicion is so much inferior to knowledge.

When you arrive, we'll see if I was correct.

Little one, I want to tell you about my mother. Her name was Ruby. It was the name her parents gave her, but it didn't really fit. She wasn't small and sparkly and perfect. She had hard edges to her, and she looked a little bit like she was made out of spare parts. One leg was an inch shorter than the other. Her arms were scrawny, but her hands were big and tough. She could chop wood and change a tire, better than Daddy could. I'd sometimes look at her and wonder what he saw in her physically, but I know now that was a superficial assessment. She was sturdy and strong and a bit plain, but she was also his best friend. No, no, it was more than that. She was the person he trusted most, the person who knew him best, and the person who loved him most fiercely.

I wish you'd gotten to meet her. I know she would have wanted to meet you.

Here's the thing, though, and I've never told anybody this, not even your father. I bonded hardest with my Daddy, not with her. I liked the things he liked. He showed me how to throw a baseball and fix the chain on my bike. He helped me catch june bugs and snakes. He read me books and played records for me. I was his little girl. I was her daughter. There's a difference.

When they died, of course I was devastated at losing both of them, but it was like his being gone was, I don't know, 75 percent of the pain and hers was just the 25 percent on top. Does that make sense? It seems awful to write it in actual words, much less think it, but that's how I felt at the time. It took me a long time to swallow that guilt. Maybe I never did.

I want you to know that I shortchanged my mother and never fully appreciated what she did for us. The best thing she did for our family was loving Daddy and supporting him, and part of that was letting him be my teacher and friend while she took on the tasks of making sure I was fed, clothed and sent off to school. It was easy to love Daddy for taking such an interest in me. It was harder to love her for making sure I did what I was supposed to do.

I've been thinking about this a lot these past few days as I've watched your Daddy take care of us. I haven't felt well. You're big, and you're taking up all the room in there, and I'm finding it hard to stand up for long or even breathe sometimes. I've read all the books. I know this is normal. But it's hard. Harder than I ever imagined it would be.

Your daddy is doing all the things I can't do, making sure everything happens when it's supposed to. My mother used to do that, too. I see the parallels.

It's funny. The last two nights, in those slim hours when I'm actually getting some sleep, I've been seeing her. She comes to me in a room and she sits and talks with me, and I can smell her the way I could when I was a little girl. I never remember what she's said when I wake up, but it seems real, and the scent of her lingers in the room even when the sun has come in. It's unsettling and comforting at the same time, and I'm caught between wondering why she's come now and hoping she comes again.

I've missed her.

SO MUCH FOR HARMONY

Kid, I'm writing to you from Scott Shamwell's cot at our place of business. Scott Shamwell isn't here. I don't know where he's gone or when he's coming back. I told him I was going to be busy tomorrow moving into our new house, so perhaps he decided to take a day off and drive up to Havre to see his mother. I don't know. It doesn't even matter.

What matters is it's 9:03 p.m. and movers are scheduled to be on the doorstep of the Clark Avenue house in nine hours and fifty-seven minutes, and I can't tell you, at this moment, whether I will be there to meet them. I can't imagine not showing up; what's the use of an imagination anyway, when the facts will bear out in time and fall where they may? I also can't imagine what I'm going to say if I do show up.

Dammit, kid. I should start at the beginning.

We had Raj and Kimberly over for pizza tonight. We couldn't cook for them, because everything was already packed up, but we wanted a chance to get together and go over the idiosyncrasies (excellent word) of the house on Clark Avenue, so they'll know how to handle it. The house was built in 1937 and thus is very

243

old, and it shows its age in some ways. For example, the back door sticks, but if you push in just the right way and use your foot to goose it along (this has nothing to do with large birds), you can close it nicely. And the pipes in the basement sink have a tendency to freeze in sub-zero weather, so it's best to keep the faucet dripping on those days unless you want burst pipes and water damage. (That's dramatic overstatement, kid; nobody wants water damage.)

In short, we wanted to introduce them to their new house, and I wanted to be able to talk to Raj privately and tell him two things: First, that I really am proud to be able to give him the keys to this house where I learned to live alone and with somebody else. Dr. Bryan Thomsen helped me see that part of my resistance to moving lay in my emotional attachment to the Clark house. He told me that I didn't have to let go of that connection, that if I could expand my thinking perhaps I would see that the house could do for someone else what it did for me. Frankly, kid, I found that wording to be imprecise, as the house is inanimate and didn't actually do anything, but I could see the point he was trying to make nonetheless and didn't argue with him.

We were saying our goodbyes to Raj and Kimberly when we heard a knock on the door. I was standing there anyway, about to open it for the kids (it's funny to call them "kids," as they're grown adults, but that's what your Uncle Hugo calls them), and so I didn't even look to see who was knocking. It was my mother— your grandmother—and Jay L. Lamb. It's too bad I didn't look. Maybe we could have pretended we weren't home and none of the rest of this bullshit would have happened.

(I'm sorry I cussed. Your mother won't like that. I'm not sure your mother likes me, or whether I like her. I'm getting to that part.)

Everything happened fast, kid. I'll reconstruct it as best I can.

My mother, your grandmother: "We'd like to come in and talk."

Me: "I have company, Mother."

Your mother, pushing her way in front of me: "Maureen, you can't just barge in here whenever you want."

Me, putting my arm in front of your mother and moving her back: "Goddammit, Sheila. Just hold on."

Your mother: "You did NOT just push me."

My mother: "See? See how she is?"

Jay L. Lamb: "Come on, everybody, let's—"

Me: "Eat a dick, Jay."

My mother: "You did NOT just say that."

Raj: "Holy shit, dude."

You can imagine the rest.

Wait, no, you can't. Remember what I just said about imagination. Facts are the coin of this realm. (This has nothing to do with pocket change. It's a dumb phrase, kid. Forgive me.)

Fact: Your grandmother, once she found out who Raj and Kimberly were and why they were there, said she would take the house away from me.

Fact: She cannot. I own the house on Clark, and while it's true that her name was once on the deed, I asked her to remove it when your mother and I moved here. It's my house and your mother's house. If I die before your mother, it's her house. My mother, your grandmother, has no say.

Fact: I was about to tell your grandmother this when your mother told me that it was high time (altitude has nothing to do with it) that I put your grandmother "in her place."

Fact: I told your mother to shut up. When your grandmother said "finally," I told your grandmother to shut up. And I told Jay L. Lamb that if he said one word I would poke out his eyes and piss in the empty sockets. I actually said that. I'm not even sure how to go about such a thing.

Fact: Everybody—your mother, your grandmother, and Jay L. Lamb—is angry at me now.

Fact: Raj and Kimberly left. They were the only ones in the whole house who acted sensibly.

Fact: Your grandmother and Jay L. Lamb left. Your mother

told me I was way out of line to say what I did to her, and I told
her to shut up again, and then I left, too.

Fact: I'm sitting on Scott Shamwell's cot, writing to you.

Are those enough facts for you? I hope so.

I'm sick to my stomach.

To: imedwardstanton@gmail.com
From: imsheilastanton@gmail.com
Re: tonight
I don't want to see you again until you're ready to be respectful.
But I need to know where you are. Answer this and tell me. And
then come back when you can act your age.

To: imsheilastanton@gmail.com
From: imedwardstanton@gmail.com
Re: re: tonight
I'm at the shop. You might consider your own lack of respect
toward me. I know you love me, but do you like me? Do you respect
me? You don't act as though you do. I'm sick of you ordering me
around. Be my partner, not my mother. I already have one of those,
and she's trouble enough.

To: imedwardstanton@gmail.com
From: therealhugohunter@gmail.com
Re: tomorrow
Is everything still on? The kids said there was a blowout with
ur mom. All cool? We can figure something out if we need to.

To: therealhugohunter@gmail.com
From: imedwardstanton@gmail.com
Re: re: tomorrow
No need. It's their house. Proceed with the plan. We'll be out by
11, the movers said. I'll leave the keys in the mailbox. Or Sheila
will.
Also, it's "your."

GUYS' NIGHT IN

OK, kid, it's like this: I'm drunk. I'm drunky wunky. Scott Shamwell says I'm Drunky McDrunkerson. That's because I had eight beers. Alcohol beers. Not that wussy stuff I usually drink, Scott Shamwell says.

Oh! Scott Shamwell came back. He had a bunch of beer. I drank some.

But the funniest thing is that Jay L. Lamb came by, too. I'm serious as a room full of owls, kid. I don't know what that means. Scott Shamwell said to say it. He's drunk, too.

But, no, listen: Jay L. Lamb came by. He saw Scott Shamwell and he got scared, but I told him to come in. He said your mother told him where I was because he went back to the house on Clark. So he came to the shop. I told him to come in and that Scott Shamwell wouldn't bite him. That made me laugh.

Jay L. Lamb says he and my mother, your grandmother, are going back to Texas tomorrow—technically, I guess, later today. He said he wouldn't feel right about leaving if he didn't talk to me one last time. He said everything that happened tonight was a horrible mess, and he wants to try to help smooth it over.

Do you know what I said? Do you? I said: "Jay, tonight was a total shitburger." And he agreed with me.

Then Jay L. Lamb asked if he could have a beer. I said that he probably ought to so he didn't feel out of place, and I know something about feeling out of place. He said OK, could he have a beer. And I said, "Shit, Jay, why don't you ask Scott Shamwell?" So he asked Scott Shamwell.

Do you know what Scott Shamwell said? Huh? Do you?

He said: "Here you go, white bread." And he tossed Jay L. Lamb a beer. Wasn't that nice? Jay L. Lamb drank it, too.

Jay L. Lamb told me that he and I have a lot in common. I said, "Well, Jay, I don't eat dicks." Scott Shamwell laughed so hard that beer came out of his nose. And then Jay L. Lamb said, "No, listen, I'm serious."

So I listened. And he was serious. And he's right.

We do have a lot in common.

We both married bossy women.

We both give in too easily when the bossy women we married want something. Jay L. Lamb said, "I told her tonight, I said, 'Maureen, you're going to regret this if you don't find some common ground with your son.' I said, 'Maureen, I'm going to go talk to him.' And, well, she didn't stop me. But I have to tell you something, Edward."

"You like eating dicks?" I asked. Scott Shamwell laughed so hard he had to get up and go to the bathroom.

"Edward, listen to me."

So I listened again.

"She's intractable on this Hugo Hunter," he said. "I think she's wrong. I told her she's wrong. But right now, that's where she is. She can't accept that you're letting him into your life. If he's in, then she's out. For now. I hope she reconsiders."

"She's said as much," I said. "That she's out, I mean."

"I know."

"So what's different?" I asked.

"I don't know. Maybe nothing. I thought maybe if you knew I was sympathetic..."

"Well, thank you for that."

"Is there anything you'd like me to relay to your mother?"

"Yes," I said. "Hugo Hunter is in."

"I understand."

"Why do you put up with her, Jay?" I asked.

"Because I love her." He looked at me hard, like he was going to scold me, and then his voice softened. "And because she puts up with me. I have my own issues. I'm sure you and Sheila do, too."

He said a mouthful there, kid, and that's not a phrase to take literally.

We shook hands, and Jay L. Lamb left.

Scott Shamwell came out of the bathroom. "I hung back there at the end," he said. "Guy turned out to be pretty decent after all."

"Yes," I said.

"You feel OK?"

"I feel sober," I said. "That's weird."

"You're not sober, hoss."

"I know."

"And neither am I."

"I know."

"And I'm cool with that." He stretched his arms, and then he lay down in his cot. And he's snoozing now.

I have nowhere to sleep, and I don't want to drive, and I need to talk to your mother.

Oh, kid.

Oh, kid, I need to lie down.

I need to throw up first.

He'll be here tomorrow. He told Raj he'll be here tomorrow. It was nice of Raj to check in with me and make sure I was OK. Sure, he was also worried about his own situation, but your father told him and Hugo to proceed with the plan, and so that means he'll be here tomorrow.

I know your father is cataloging all of this stuff. All these things we've written to you, he's kept in archives. He wants you to see it, all of it, when you're ready. And while I understand that, I just... well, tonight. Do we want to relive this? Do you?

Nobody's proudest hour happened tonight. Nobody's. Maybe Jay L. Lamb's; I have to say I was surprised to see him, and even more surprised at his kind words. But even he's playing an angle.

I hope your father is here tomorrow. Everything we have is in boxes in the living room, waiting. And he's twenty-some blocks away, with his best buddy.

I told him to stay away, and he's staying away.

Oh, I wish I'd reconsidered that. I wish I'd reconsidered many things.

Love you.

MOVING DAY

I woke up yelling and wet. Scott Shamwell stood over me and waggled (neat word) an empty bucket at me in a menacing way.

"What was that for?" I asked. I flung my hands toward him and tried to hit him in the eyes with the excess water, but he dodged it and laughed at me. My shirt was soaked. So was the concrete floor around me.

"I just wanted to see if that looks like it does in the movies," Scott Shamwell said. "It does."

"But why did you do it?" I looked at the clock on the wall beyond Scott Shamwell. 7:26 a.m. Holy shit.

"You gotta go, man," Scott Shamwell said.

"The movers are already there," I said.

"Yeah, and you're gonna go meet them, and you're gonna work it out with Sheila, and you're not coming over here and staying with me anymore when you and your old lady fight."

Scott Shamwell had been smiling when he first hit me with the water, but he wasn't smiling now. He had that serious face he sometimes wears, the one I'd seen when he left the family farm and when he asked me if I was going to fire him after I punched him in the jaw. Scott Shamwell can be surprisingly serious.

"I don't know what to say to her," I said. "Nothing's resolved."
"Yeah?" Scott Shamwell said. "Nothing's going to get resolved here. Get out and don't come back until after you're moved." He set the bucket down and walked past me to the workbench and he sat down with his back to me.

I walked to the door, wringing out my shirt.

I drove in circles among the morning traffic in downtown Billings, up Sixth Avenue and across to Fourth and then back down and back across to Sixth. I did this three times, until the clock in my Cadillac DTS and on my bitchin' iPhone both read 7:57 a.m. and I realized I couldn't avoid it anymore. The movers would be nearly an hour into their work of loading up everything your mother and I own. I'd have to face them, and her.

When I pulled up on Clark Avenue, parking in front of the house that Donna Middleton (now Donna Hays) used to live in, the movers—two of them—were carrying out our bedroom bureau. It was wrapped in blankets to keep the sharp edges from being broken off, and wide strips of cellophane wrapping material held the blankets in place. Your mother stood on the front porch, her hands on her hips, watching them. She glanced at me, then back to the movers. I turned off the ignition and got out of the car.

It was the longest walk of my life, kid. I don't mean that literally. I've made much longer walks, in both time and distance, although I couldn't give you any hard data on those because they're not something I track. (Maybe I should.) What I'm saying is that I approached your mother without knowing what to say, and knowing that I would have to say something, or that she would have to.

It may be a long time before you know the feeling I'm about to describe. It's something that will happen to you when you deeply care for another human being and find yourself in conflict with that person. I walked to your mother, and I wasn't ashamed of myself exactly—I knew I should not have stayed out all night and that I should have been here when the movers arrived, but I wasn't sorry for confronting your mother on the way she's been treating me. I was sorry I had told her to shut up; that wasn't "constructive," as Dr. Bryan Thomsen might say.

What I wanted was some sort of reset button for married living, so your mother and I could go back to a time when we weren't treating each other poorly and saying mean words. But how do you do that? (I'm not asking you, kid. I don't expect you to have the answers, at least not yet.)

"Sheila," I said.

"Can you follow the short guy?" She pointed at the smaller of the two movers, a man who looked to be in his twenties. He had a wide body and short legs. He looked powerful. "Answer his questions. I can't keep up with both of them." She said all of this while fixating her eyes away from me.

"Sheila, listen," I said.

Your mother at last looked at me. Her eyes were watery. "No, not now. Later." She tried to smile, but it didn't take. "Let's finish this. OK?"

"OK, Sheila."

Other than a break for water, the two movers worked straight through the early morning, with your mother trailing the tall one, the leader, and with me following the short, muscular guy. I found out his name was Nestor, a name I like very much. He didn't need any help from me. Your mother and I had taken great care in labeling the boxes we packed, and Nestor could move three and four of them at a time by employing a dolly, which is like a lever with wheels. I was impressed by Nestor's strength and industriousness.

Three times, your mother and I arrived at a doorway at the same time, and I stood aside to let her go through first. She quietly said "thank you" each time, and the last time, I reached for her hand. She let her thumb brush my forefinger and then let go. She then walked into the living room and out the front door, following the mover to whom she'd assigned herself. (Jimmy. Frankly, kid, my mover had a better name.)

At 11:07, the last box went into the moving truck. I walked over to Jimmy and made sure he had the address of the house on Avenue B, and I said we would meet him and Nestor there in a few minutes.

Your mother already sat in the passenger seat of the Cadillac DTS when I opened the driver's side door and climbed in.

"I left the keys in the mailbox for Raj and Hugo," I said. I started the ignition.

"OK," your mother said.

"They worked fast," I said.

"Yes, they did."

"Are you hungry?"

"A little."

"Do you want to stop and get something?" I checked the mirrors to make sure the way was clear, and then I pulled out onto the street.

"No, I packed a little cooler with a couple of sandwiches. It's on the truck."

I followed Clark to 4th Street West, then turned right and right again on Yellowstone Avenue and on 6th Street West, making a loop of statistically safer driving maneuvers.

"We need to work this out," I said at last.

"I know we do. Let's get through this."

We crossed over Grand Avenue to Avenue B and I made one last right turn. Jimmy and Nestor were already at the house with the truck, and they had stacked boxes on the front lawn.

I pulled up in front of our new neighbor's house and wondered if I would like whoever lived there, and if whoever lived there would like us, in whatever incarnation (a nice word) of us we were going to be after today.

MOVING NIGHT

Jimmy and Nestor finished moving everything into the house on Avenue B at 4:05 p.m. The first thing they did was bring the bedframe and the mattress and box springs into the house and set them up in the master bedroom, giving your mother a place to lie down. That's why all the boxes were sitting in the yard when we drove up. They were clearing the truck to get at the bed. I appreciated their consideration for your mother, and I told them so.

While your mother slept, I told Jimmy and Nestor where to put everything else. I had to make an executive decision about the placement of the couch and entertainment center in the living room, because I didn't want to disturb your mother. Everything for all three bedrooms went in the guest room, again so your mother could get her rest. Jimmy and Nestor and two dollies cranked through the work easily and efficiently, and I resolved to write a letter to their employer commending their fine work. That's the polite thing to do, kid, and it's the kind of thing that is greatly appreciated by someone who gives you superior customer service. There will be more on this topic as you grow up.

At 12:30 on the dot (there is no dot; this is an idiom), Jimmy and Nestor took a lunch break. I found the cooler your mother

256

packed and took out two cheese sandwiches, one for her and one for me, and a bottle of Diet Dr. Pepper for us to share. I took this into the bedroom.

I found your mother sitting up in the bed, her back propped up by pillow she'd stacked against the wall.

"I brought you lunch."

She opened her eyes and looked at me. "Thank you," she said.

"Are you OK?"

"Yes. Why?"

"Your eyes were closed."

"Oh," she said. "Baby's kicking."

That's you, kid.

I sat down on the floor beside the bed and set the sandwiches between us.

"I'm sorry," she said. "I couldn't stand up anymore."

"It's OK."

"How are they doing?"

"About halfway done," I said. "They're hard workers."

"That's good."

"Do you want to talk now?" I asked.

"No. I'm too tired."

"Sheila, this hurts."

"I know. I'm hurt, too."

"We have to talk about this. We have to."

She set her hand on mine. "Edward, I'm not mad anymore. I don't think I'm mad. I'm raw. I'm exhausted. My feelings are hurt—"

"My feelings are hurt, too," I began.

"—just as I know yours are. We're going to work this out. I know we are. But we have to talk about a lot of things, and I'm just—"

"Tired," I said. I put my hand on top of hers.

"Yes."

"OK," I said. "Eat your sandwich." I patted her hand and then picked up my cheese sandwich, and I took a big bite out of it and I growled like a tiger and your mother laughed. And for the first time today, I felt like things would be OK. Eventually. Eventually is not a concrete time, kid. It's an estimate, and a lacking one at that. It's also relative, because everybody has a different idea about when "eventually" will be. I don't like estimates and I don't like relativity, but sometimes you have to take what you can get.

The installer from the cable company arrived fifty-three minutes after I'd signed the paperwork and paid Jimmy and Nestor ($642, kid—even when I was fucking loaded, that was no small amount of money).

She connected the TV in the living room and set up the modem for the Internet while I unpacked boxes and placed books on the shelves. When she was done, I signed the paperwork she handed me while also good-naturedly haranguing (good word) her about the price of the cable service.

"I got the silver package?" I asked.

"Yes, sir."

"And that's $68 a month?"

"That's correct, sir."

"And the Internet is $53?"

"That's correct, sir."

"So $121 a month, total?"

"I guess that's what it adds up to, yes. It's the same as what you had at the other address."

"Tell me, does the cable service also wash windows? Will it take out the trash?"

"I don't follow."

"I'm teasing you about how much it costs. I'm deliberately overstating matters to make a point."

"I'm just the installer, sir."

She gave me my copy of the paperwork and then she left.

Some people have no sense of humor.

Your mother slept through the early evening, as I unpacked kitchen boxes and bedroom boxes and organized my tools in the garage.

A pizza delivery came—we've been lazy lately as far as cooking, and our pizza intake is far too high—and still your mother slept. I set a timer on my bitchin' iPhone to go off every thirty minutes, and when it did I would put down whatever I was working on and go check on her. Every time, her body was turned toward the east wall of the bedroom, and the covers were pulled up over her chin and mouth, and all I could see was the mop of hair on the pillows. I'd stop, and I'd hold my breath, and I'd listen, and finally your mother would snore and I'd smile and leave again, back to the business of unpacking and moving into this house.

At 9:07 p.m. your Uncle Hugo called and said Raj and Kimberly had finished moving their stuff into the Clark Avenue house. It's their home now, not your mother's and mine anymore. We live here on Avenue B. The layout here is completely different, with bedrooms upstairs and a kitchen, living room and den downstairs. The house on Clark Avenue has old hardwood and carpet, while this one is polished hardwood everywhere. Neither has the radiant floor heating that I would prefer, and I'm used to the cramped kitchen on Clark, not the wide-open one here.

But I see the possibilities here that your mother saw, and while she was wrong to commit to buying this house without talking it over with me, I must admit that she chose well.

It's all going to work out, kid. That's a prediction. It's not as good as a fact, but I'm feeling confident.

Goodnight.

HI.

I don't know what to call you.

You can call me Uncle Hugo. Your dad has been telling you about me, so I'm that guy. I just left him at his house. Poor guy. He's had a hell of a hard day, and it's not gonna get any easier for a while, I don't think. The last thing your dad said to me, he says, "Hugo, write down what happened for the kid, would you, please?" He's formal and polite, even when he's exhausted. Said he's keeping a scrapbook for you or something and needs help.

So, anyway, I'm doing what he asked, only I'm recording it on this old cassette recorder I have in the house. I hope that's OK and stuff. He's a good guy, your dad. I don't know him super-well yet, but he's my brother, so if he wants something that I can give him, he's got it. That's the way I roll. I don't want to let him down.

So here's the deal, as best I understand it. I wasn't there for much of it.

Your mom, she woke up sometime in the night, I don't know, 2 or 3 in the morning, and she went into the bathroom and then came back out and woke up your dad, because she was bleeding...shit, kid, I don't know if I want to tell you too much about this. Also, sorry I said "shit." OK, look, your mom, she was bleeding from her vagina, and that's all I'm going to say, because somebody else can explain that to you.

Anyway…

That's a bad deal, bleeding like that when you're pregnant, and your dad said it was really heavy, too, so he drove your mom to the hospital as fast as he could and got her to the OB wing or whatever, and the doctors got on it. And, anyway, they thought they had some time, but you had to be born. So you were. Today, July 30th.

Oh, shit. I should have started there. Welcome to the world, little girl. You're a tiny thing, just a little more than three pounds, so you're going to be in something they call the "Nick You" for a while as you gain strength. But the doctor, he was real reassuring to your dad. Babies at thirty-three weeks do remarkably well, he said. He called you a little fighter and said your outlook is really good, and that's great. It's just really, really great to know that.

Your mom, though, it's a tougher situation. She lost a lot of blood, and the doctor said it was a fight to keep her alive, but they did. By the time you hear this, or read it or whatever, you'll know the story, but I'm telling you: Your mom's hanging in there. The thing is, though, she had a few strokes—small ones, little ones, her blood pressure had dropped so low, you see, and, well, I don't know all the medical stuff. They think you were putting pressure on a blood vessel, and it burst. That's what they think. And listen, that's not your fault. This kind of stuff happens. Your mom, she lost a lot of blood and she had these strokes, that's what they told your dad, and they just have to see how things go. But she's stabilized and she has good care, and the doctor said your dad has got to be hopeful, and that's what I said, too.

Your dad, he's got a team. He's got me and my kid, Raj. He's got Mark and Lainie, my good friends and his. And he's got that Shamwell guy, and a friend of his who's flying in tomorrow.

We're going to keep him focused and fed and stuff. I finally made him come home tonight, after he called me and asked me to come to the hospital and I sat there with him for, I don't know, ten hours? Fifteen? It all runs together. But I said, "Look, man, you gotta go sleep." He didn't want to. I said, "You ain't gonna do anybody any good on a couch in a hospital, man. Go home." I rode in his car with him and saw him off to bed. And then I walked home. My bike is back at the hospital and stuff. I didn't even think about it.

I don't know what else to say. Hang in there, sweetheart.

Bye now.

JULY 31ST

Goddammit, kid. What have you done?

I know it's not your fault. I know this rationally, and the doctors have satisfactorily explained what happened and why your mother bled so heavily and why she had these strokes—"isthemic" strokes, they're called—and why we'll just have to wait to see what her long-term outlook is. I've known for months, ever since we found out you would be coming, that childbirth carries risks, and that childbirth for a woman your mother's age (she's been alive for 14,293 days, or 39 years) has even more risks. But your gestation was completely ordinary right up to the moment it wasn't, and now we have this problem.

If there had been no you, there wouldn't be any of the rest of it. Maybe something else would have happened, something even more devastating. This is the problem with conditional statements and conjecture; I can't control the other details. I can't control how angry I am at you, how scared I am for you, how scared I am for your mother, and how alone I feel out here.

Hugo comes and sits with me. Mark Westerly does, too. Lainie Westerly. Scott Shamwell. Even Donna Hays came and hugged me and kissed me on the cheek, and now she's sitting next to me, reading a magazine while I write this. She's a good friend.

But I'm still alone.

I haven't met you, and I haven't seen your mother yet today. The medical people say I will. They said time is your mother's ally. I'm not sure what that means. When I ask when she'll come home, they're noncommittal. When I ask when you'll come home and if you'll come home with your mother, they say it won't be long and they don't know. They are masters of imprecision. None of this is very reassuring.

Your mother was born on June 15, 1975.

I want you to know I love her. More than I ever imagined I would love anyone. And in the face of this uncertainty, I also have to say this: I don't want to be here without her.

And then I think of you, and how whatever happens I have to be here for you and with you.

I hate you for what you did to your mother. You might not have known what you were doing, but if there's no you, there's no need for a new house, there's no reason for your mother to push herself so hard, there's no ruptured blood vessel, there are no strokes. That's the truth. I'm sorry if this hurts you. The truth doesn't care about your feelings.

This is also the truth: Maybe something else would have happened. Maybe something sooner. Or maybe your mother and I would have lived into old age together with no children and no reason to leave the house on Clark Avenue.

I just don't know. I have no facts here.

They let me sit with your mother for an hour. I held her hand and stroked her thumb with my forefinger, and I swept her hair behind her ear. The medical people are keeping her sedated because of her internal injuries. They haven't yet been able to assess her strength. One of the things that sometimes happens with a stroke is the victim loses strength on one side of the body. Your mother may have some of that loss of strength. She'll almost certainly have to do physical therapy, Dr. Arlene Haworth says. She says this, and I can tell she's leaving something out, and while I'm not one for conjecture, I can guess what it is: "if."

I talked to your mother and told her that you're doing fine, that you're a little girl and I'm waiting for her before we see you. I told her that your Uncle Hugo and Donna Hays are helping with the house, that she should just concentrate on getting better, that we have friends and people who love us.

I told her I love her, and that I love you, and that I'm sorry for saying earlier that I hate you. I don't know if she heard me, but if she did, I think she'd want to know all of those things.

Your Uncle Hugo and Scott Shamwell left the hospital twenty-two minutes ago, after I promised them I would go home and sleep after I drop Donna Hays off at her motel. She can stay only two more days before she has to go home.

"Victor has to go out of town on work and Kyle can't be alone," she said. "Well, he probably can, but I'm not ready for that. Our house isn't ready for that."

Donna and I talked in the Cadillac DTS as I drove to her motel.

"How's Kyle?" I asked.

"Enormous. Sweet. Strong. He misses you."

"I miss him, too."

"When this all calms down, you and Sheila and your daughter can come out and visit."

"I'd like to. Will this all calm down?"

"It has to," she said. "Sheila will be all right. She's strong."

The scent of your mother is in our bed. It's comforting.

Tomorrow, you and I are supposed to meet. I resisted and told the NICU nurse that I didn't want to see you until your mother was ready. He said you need to hear my voice and feel my touch. It's important, he said. It's vital to your development.

So we meet tomorrow.

I wonder how that will go.

Goodnight, kid.

AUGUST

MY GIRL*

*—this is the name of a No. 1 hit by the musical group
The Temptations in 1965. It's a very happy song. It's also the title
of a 1991 movie starring Macaulay Culkin and Anna Chlumsky.
It's a very sad movie. I prefer the song.*

It's August 1st. I came home last night to sleep, and didn't. I stayed up all night reading about premature babies (preemies, a word I dislike) and what they go through as they try to gain strength after leaving the womb early. It was fascinating reading, or would have been if I hadn't been vacillating (great word) between being excited about being your daddy, being crestfallen (another good word that I wish I didn't know) about your mother and being overwhelmed by all there is to know about taking care of you.

Right now, your immune and nervous systems aren't fully developed, and you're so small (three pounds and thirteen ounces at birth), so the people at St. Vincent Healthcare want to keep you for a couple of weeks and put some weight on you.

What I've read online says that I can spend this time establishing physical contact with you and talking to you, so we can bond.

Soon, I hope, your mother will join us, so we can all bond together. That's how it should be.

At the NICU, they wouldn't let Donna Hays come in with me. My baby—that's you—is still in a delicate state, they said, so they want to limit her (your) exposure to the outside world. But I'm your daddy, they said, so I could see you for a little bit.

They brought me into a small room and asked me to sit down and wait. Donna Hays suggested that I bring your mother's pillowcase with me, since it has her scent on it. I held the pillowcase in my fingers, and I lifted it to my nose and breathed in your mother. She loves Dove soap and lilac shampoo, and those clean smells spread out in my head and made me think of times she lay in bed and faced me, her head on her pillows. She would tell me about her day, or we'd finish a conversation we'd started at dinner, or she'd just tell me she loved me, and that was my signal to lean in and kiss her eight times on the lips.

The door opened. I stood up fast and clutched the pillowcase with one hand and rubbed my eyes with a finger from the other.

A man in hospital scrubs (a kind of clothing) wheeled in a deep plastic container with small holes on the sides.

"This is your daughter," he said.

"OK."

"Come on," he said, "get closer. Look at her."

I stepped forward and looked through the clear plastic. Your eyes were closed. Thin wisps of blonde hair covered your head. Your legs were curled up under you, and one of your tiny hands—I couldn't believe how tiny—made the tiniest, most perfect fist ever. Better than your Uncle Hugo's.

You're the second-most-beautiful thing I've ever seen.

"You can talk to her," he said. "Let her hear your voice. You can reach through these holes and touch her fingers and her toes, if you want to. You can't hold her yet. Soon, though."

"This is my daughter?"

He put a hand on my shoulder. "This is your daughter. I'll give you some time."

He left, and I sat down and pulled the chair up close. Your lips opened and I could see your little tongue.

"I'm your daddy," I said. "My name is Edward Stanton. But you can't call me that. I called my father 'Father.' You may call me that if you wish. Or maybe something else. We'll see."

We'll see.

You scrunched up your face. I reached in and took your left big toe between my fingers and I massaged it, and you gave a little kick. But I held on. You're little and tiny and beautiful and perfect.

I'm not going to let go.

Dear Mother,

Dr. Bryan Thomsen came to the hospital and saw me today and told me that you'd called him. He said you're very sorry about what happened to Sheila and that you hoped he might help you and I come to an understanding. You should know that Dr. Bryan Thomsen has good boundaries and said he won't intercede. He did tell me, however, that he believes you to be sincere in your desire to reconcile with me.

I shall be equally sincere and say I hope we find a way to do that. It would make me happy.

But you must understand that these are the facts of my life now. I have a wife who's facing an uncertain challenge—in fact, I am writing to you while I wait to be able to see her—and I have a daughter who will need all of the attention I can give her. These are the two most important people in my life. But that's not all. I have friends who are steadfast with me, at least one of whom does not meet your approval. That's not for you to say. Scott Shamwell is my friend, and you cannot compel me to choose you or him. That's overstepping your bounds.

And, Mother, I have a brother. And that's another place where you cannot force me to choose him or you. That, too, is overstepping your bounds.

I want you to know that I'm trying to understand how painful the memories associated with Hugo are to you. Dr. Bryan Thomsen has been very helpful in putting that into perspective. I don't condone what Father did, and I'm not unsympathetic to the ways his actions must have hurt you. But Hugo Hunter did nothing to you or to Father, and he's been nothing but a good friend and a good brother to me. He's helped carry me during this time. And I think, in the years ahead, I will have to help carry him.

This is my life. If you accept me, you must accept all of that.

This is not a negotiation.

I love you,

Edward

P.S. Dr. Bryan Thomsen told me that you said you would release *the funds Father gave me as a gesture of reconciliation. While I appreciate that you see this as a significant overture, I've come to view this money as a hindrance to our being able to understand each other. We've done little but fight about it, in one way or another, since he died.*

My business is doing well. We have a comfortable home. Thinking about money while so much is uncertain with Sheila makes me feel sick to my stomach.

Put it in a trust for your granddaughter. Maybe she can grow up and do better with it than you and I have. By the time she's grown up, maybe millions of dollars won't even buy a carton of eggs.

AUGUST 2ND

My bitchin' iPhone started ringing, and I looked at the digital clock on your mother's end table and saw that it was 6:17 a.m., and I prepared to stomp a mudhole into someone's ass, as Scott Shamwell would say.

I answered. "Yeah?"

"Some mouth," your mother's voice came back at me. "You owe me kisses."

It took me four minutes and three left turns to get to the hospital, kid. I didn't even care.

The nurses helped your mother from her bed into a wheelchair, and I draped a blanket over her lap and feet so she would stay warm. One of the nurses accompanied us as I wheeled your mother down the hallway.

"I don't want to be in this thing," your mother complained. "I need to be walking."

"Not yet," the nurse said.

"When?"

"Soon," she said.

"You're back and ornery as ever," I said. Your mother craned her neck and looked up at me and said, "You got that right."

And then she reached her right arm—the weakened one—across her chest and touched my hand on her shoulder.

The nurses at the NICU brought you in and then lifted you out of the plastic box. One of them came to your mother and opened her gown. The other nurse brought you over and set you in the cradle of her left arm.

"Let her rest against your chest," one nurse said.

"I know how to do it," your mother said.

You wriggled against your mother's skin, and your mother began to weep.

"She's perfect," she said.

"Yes," I said.

"Have you held her yet?"

"Not yet."

"You have to."

The first nurse asked me to sit down and asked me to unbutton the front of my shirt, and she oh so carefully took you from your mother and asked me to hold you against my chest. They said the skin-to-skin contact would help us bond even more, and that my body heat would keep you warm.

I don't like my chest being touched—I don't even like it when your mother does it—but I have to tell you something, kid. You felt great. You're warm and cuddly, and I could feel your heart beating against mine. I began to cry because you're so beautiful, and your mother leaned her head over and set it on my shoulder.

"What are you going to name her?" the other nurse asked.

"We have some ideas," I said. "Don't we?"

Your mother smiled. "Yes."

I kept you for only a minute or so; I must confess I wasn't timing it. Your mother held you again, and then the nurses said you had to go back to the NICU but that we could do it again, and longer, tomorrow. They said you're putting on weight and gaining strength and that it won't be too long till you get to come home with us.

The nurse put you back in the plastic box, and I reached through and nudged your hand with my index finger. You tried to grab hold—you don't yet have big enough hands to grip my big fingers—and then you turned your head and your eyes opened for just a whisper of a second, and your mother and I gasped.

They are the same blue as your mother's, the color of a high-mountain lake.

Your mother wept. I think I know why. I held her shoulder while she let her emotions come out.

As I'm writing this to you, hours later, I'm weeping, too. I think it's partly because of the blue eyes. It's partly because of your mother and how much seeing them affected her.

But mostly, I think it's because there's no reason to write to you anymore. I started this because your mother suggested I do it to get my thoughts out while we were waiting for you to arrive.

We're not waiting anymore. You're here. We've all met now, and soon you and your mother will be coming home with me.

Tonight, I thumbed through all these pages I've written, and all those pages your mother wrote, too. It's hard to believe this all started with me calling you a poppyseed. But that's what happened. I was there. Your mother was, too.

And so were you.

SEPTEMBER

.

THE SHAPE OF THINGS

I guess I have more to tell you after all.

Your mother came home on August 6th. Scott Shamwell and your Uncle Hugo helped me relocate our bed to the first-floor living room so she didn't have to climb the stairs for a while. I think we underestimated your mother. Within three days, she was slowly walking up and down the stairs several times a day, so the next weekend Scott Shamwell, your Uncle Hugo and I put the bed back where it belongs.

Your mother moves slowly—there's been significant loss of strength on her right side—but she's surely making progress. Her physical therapist gave her exercises to do, and she attacks those with gusto. It's been a month now, and she's well on her way back to where she was before the strokes. The best part is that she should have no lasting cognitive impairment, the doctor said. That means you'll grow up knowing your mother as I found her.

I'm so grateful.

We went up to the hospital and saw you every day until August 18th, when you at last came home with us and we began settling into life as a family here on Avenue B.

Most days, I take you and your mother to Mark and Lainie Westerly's house before I go to work at the shop. Lainie and your mother do exercises and go shopping and sit and talk, and that frees me up to earn money and do work. Lainie drives you both home in the early afternoon, and when quitting time comes I get there just as fast as I can, within the rules of the road and polite society. The best part of the day is seeing you both again.

Sometimes, you come to the shop with me, but not often. It's loud in there sometimes, and you need your sleep. And sometimes Scott Shamwell says something like "frog-faced fuckmonger," and neither your mother nor I think those should be your first words.

I do have to tell you about one funny thing, though: One time, Scott Shamwell and I had just had lunch at a restaurant in the Heights, and we were trying to get your bassinet out the door and into the Cadillac. An older man and woman stared at us, and Scott Shamwell pushed his sunglasses down his nose and said, "What's the matter? Haven't you ever seen two gay guys and a baby before?" The older couple hustled into the restaurant, and we at last got you into the car.

Once Scott Shamwell and I were seated, I said, "We're not gay, Scott Shamwell."

"How do you know?" he asked.

"Well, I'm not gay."

"Whatever you say, dude."

I drove away. At a stoplight, I said, "Are you having fun with me, Scott Shamwell?"

"Yeah."

"OK."

He's pretty funny sometimes. And oh, how he loves you. He makes faces at you and you stare, stare, stare at him. But that's OK. That's what most women do when they see Scott Shamwell.

I'm pretty funny sometimes, too.

While we were waiting for you to be strong enough to come home, your grandmother wrote me a letter and she said nice things about your mother, after being so mean before, and she said she badly wants to meet you. But she also said I need to understand her pain about Uncle Hugo and respect her wishes, and I think that last part is asking too much of me. I don't know what to do, so until I have more clarity I won't do anything. Too many other things are going on where I'm certain of my duties. It starts and ends with you and your mother. I have a brother. We have friends. We all have people who love us, and that's enough for now. And your mother and I are working things out. She doesn't boss me around so much anymore, and if she does, she's quick to apologize. And I don't hold everything in until it comes out sideways (this is an idiom). We talk. We cry. We marvel at you. And then we cry again.

Your mother still gets tired easily and needs a lot of sleep. Sometimes, after dinner, she goes to bed, but you and I stay up and watch *Dragnet* on the TV, and then I read you as many books as I can until I'm too tired. We've even read your Uncle Hugo's book, but I think *One Fish, Two Fish, Red Fish, Blue Fish* is more your speed.

You're usually asleep by the time I run out of steam (there is no actual steam). I try to catch my own sleep while you're down, because if you're awake, I'm awake and your mother is awake. Don't get us wrong, sweet girl, it's a privilege to be your parents. But once in a while, you really could let us sleep in.

You don't cry much the rest of the time, though, and I thank you for that. But when you get riled up about something? Goodness. You've got a set of lungs.

Not so long from now, it will snow here in Billings. That's not so much a prediction as an educated prognostication based on years of tracking the weather patterns. There are a lot of firsts coming. Your first Thanksgiving. Your first Christmas. Somewhere in there, it will be a year since you were conceived. I think about that sometimes, how much things have changed in the brief time we've known you and known about you, but in other ways, I can only feel time moving faster than I want it to.

I've been thinking a lot about time and how I've wished I could control it, the same way I've always tried to control what happens in my life. Neither of those things, I'm afraid, can be done. The time you have is like spooled thread. It comes off, little bit by little bit, until there's nothing left. Your life is unspooled.

There's so much I want before that happens. I want to be here as long as I can be, with you and your mother, and I want to teach you as much as I know, for as long as you'll let me.

I wonder sometimes how you and I will be together, and how you and your mother will get along. Right now, you need us for everything, but the so-called circle of life is partly about pulling away from dependence and moving toward independence. One day, we'll have to let you go where you want to go. If we do our part correctly, we'll want that for you, just as much as you'll want it. I think this is the part my mother, your grandmother, doesn't understand.

In the meantime, it's you and us, and we have to figure this out together. Whether we get along or fight, whether we like the same things or are completely different, whether you stay in Billings or go somewhere else someday, we're going to make sure you know one thing every moment of your life, Ruby Maureen:

We love you without hesitation or condition.

That's a fact.

ACKNOWLEDGMENTS

He's a funny guy, this Edward Stanton. He and I got acquainted in 2008, during a feverish November when I wrote the story that became *600 Hours of Edward*. I figured then that he'd said what he needed to say.

A few years later, he spoke to me again. *Edward Adrift* came out. We again parted ways. And, as before, I figured that was that.

Well, you can see what my figuring amounted to.

So, whom do I thank for his reappearance? First, always, are the fans of the stories, who have been so wonderful to me and to these books. The notes, the tweets, the friendships we've struck online and in person—all of these things mean the world to me. Thank you.

Seeing a book from the keyboard to the shelf, in a bookstore or online, begins as a solitary endeavor that slowly gains allies and co-conspirators. I'll try to get to all of them here.

Thanks to Lake Union Publishing, my home base, for opening the wider world to the Edward stories. I've gone it alone on this one for a variety of reasons, but I expect we'll be back in cahoots sooner or later.

I'm indebted to Jim Thomsen for his editorial excellence and abiding friendship. We entered this crazy racket at about the same time, with a lot of the same dreams, and it's been fun to watch the rises and falls and manic fits of productivity together. I wouldn't write a book without your involvement in some form.

Thanks to the booksellers, especially the independent ones on my home turf of Montana. Ariana, Andrea, Marc, Gary, Barbara, Garth, Debbie, Gustavo, Lorrie, and your wonderful staffs: I love all y'all (as we say in Texas).

I'm blessed as a writer, a worker and a human being by my friendships with Scott McMillion and Bob Kimpton, two guys who feed me work that keeps me going and fellowship that fills my cup.

I'm grounded by family, the ones I grew up in and the one I've added along the way. To the Lancasters, the Clineses, and the Lorellos, and all the various offshoots: thank you for sustaining me and welcoming me.

And, finally, there's Elisa. I found my heart when I found you, my love. Every day, I'm thankful. Every day, our story grows.

ABOUT THE AUTHOR

Craig Lancaster is the bestselling author of such novels as *600 Hours of Edward* and *Edward Adrift*, and a frequent contributor to magazines and newspapers as a writer and an editor.

600 Hours of Edward, his debut, was a Montana Honor Book and the 2010 High Plains Book Award winner for best first book. His work has also been honored by the Utah Book Awards (the novel *The Summer Son*) and with an Independent Publisher Book Awards gold medal (the short-story collection *The Art of Departure*), among other citations.

Lancaster lives in Billings, Montana, with his fiancée, Elisa Lorello, also a bestselling novelist.

CONNECT WITH CRAIG LANCASTER

On the Web: www.craig-lancaster.com
Twitter: @AuthorLancaster
Facebook: www.facebook.com/authorcraiglancaster

Made in the USA
San Bernardino, CA
16 June 2017